Note: The first book written in this series (written but not published) was registered and is mostly contained within this present manuscript. It was registered under the title *Mona Lisa on the Moon, the life and death of Mona Ann Lisa on the Moon, 32,000 years in the making by George B.* It was previously registered in the US Copyright Office under registration number TX 8-382-511, with an effective date of registration of March 20, 2017.

# Volume 1, Mona Lisa on the Moon, Thirty-Two Thousand Years in the Making

GEORGE B.

ARCHWAY
PUBLISHING

Archway Publishing books may be ordered
through booksellers or by contacting:

Archway Publishing
1663 Liberty Drive
Bloomington, IN 47403
www.archwaypublishing.com
1 (888) 242-5904

ISBN: 978-1-4808-7063-5 (sc)
ISBN: 978-1-4808-7064-2 (e)

Library of Congress Control Number: 2018962567

Print information available on the last page.

Archway Publishing rev. date: 12/20/2018

# Contents

# Preface

My name is George B., and I am introducing the story of
a young woman who lived thirty-two thousand years ago.
This story is fiction, but it contains my understanding of
history, law, science, philosophy, religion, and military science. Many parts of the story contain what I understand to
be true, though highly speculative, elements. This first volume contains the introduction and the first few events that
explain the origins and fate of human civilization as we now
understand it. Other volumes will include future events that
will reach some two hundred thousand years beyond our
present time line. It will also explain how the human race
was sustained and protected from extinction. I subscribe to
the notion that Earth and her inhabitants—human, animal,
plant, and other—have gone through several cataclysmic
restarts.

Three such reboots have occurred in the last one hundred thousand years. I will not detail them here in this
preface, but they will be unfolded in this volume and the
volumes to come. I feel that if you are patient and read this
saga, you will be rewarded with a journey of fascination
and discovery. My hope is to bring you hope and encouragement and to instill in you a sense of awe and wonder.
The heroine and central character of my story is human
but is a rare jewel to say the least. You may find yourself

seeing through her eyes and wondering whether you have the strength, courage, and character to survive what she endured.

I intend to keep you always wondering what is going to happen next, and to explain new and strange concepts using existing science and theory along with a bit of humor. I am a retired scientist with training, education, and experience in law, military science, artificial intelligence, religion, and medicine. I have used the above education, experience, and knowledge, along with the fascination of alternate history, to formulate this tall tale.

This particular story begins with a young woman finding her career path and ends with even more challenges and questions than are present at its beginning. The book is named after an urban legend notable, Mona Lisa. Several years ago, a French movie creator and operative named Thierry Speth produced a series of movies that were posted on the internet. These videos were extremely well done and apparently well researched, and they fooled many, many people. The object of his films was to chronicle an American astronaut's mission via Apollo 20 to the far side of the moon.

Allegedly, Apollo 20 was a clandestine joint Russian-American NASA mission to investigate the wreckage of an enormous space vehicle lying on the moon's surface. On this mission, the astronauts found a humanoid female body. The American and his Russian crew member named her Mona Lisa. Later the astronauts, along with Mona, returned to Earth.

Thierry Speth's videos and many more speculative videos are found all over the internet. (To find them, just do an internet search for "Mona Lisa on the Moon, Apollo 20.") I was personally fascinated by the videos and the speculation regarding the events of the fictional Apollo 20 mission. There were also real photos of an anomaly found on the far side of the moon taken by NASA and Chinese space authorities that resembled a large downed spacecraft. These images were later shown to most likely reveal a natural formation; however, the speculation and fascination regarding the story of Mona Lisa continues to this day.

My interest was further fueled by the existence of a group of posters on one or more conspiracy forums on the internet. The most notable was on the GodLikeProductions (GLP) conspiracy forum. There, a group calling themselves "Alterwelt" posted for well over one year about alternate history and stated that a thirty-two-thousand-year-old human female had been found on the moon. She was the captain of a crashed two-mile-long asteroid-mining spaceship.

I followed this conspiracy forum's thread titled "Remote viewing Ancient Civilizations: a compilation of data" for many months and researched their assertions religiously. They indicated this person was commanding the ship when it was downed by warring human forces during an ancient global war. Their facts were always interesting to me, but I could never prove them true or prove them false. However, these allegations stimulated my creative juices and led to this project.

While Alterwelt's postings were a launching pad for my story, Mona's saga goes far beyond its beginnings. I am hoping you will read with much interest and enjoyment. Please dive in and imagine a new and incredible human history and future.

# Prologue

Mona Ann Lisa, though she was the youngest captain of the fleet by several hundred years, was the commander of the fleet and director of the evacuation. Her position was never challenged. The World Alliance had just allowed this to happen based upon the evolving crisis. No senior captain had objected. They just fell in line as she directed the settlement of Ceres and managed the aquaforming activities.

Mona, the child prodigy, was the best chance the species had to survive. While Mona accepted her many working titles, she knew that Levie was the true brains of the operation. Levie (short for "Leviathan") was her sentient artificial intelligence (AI) entity who was fully integrated into the massive World Alliance Mother Ship (WAMS) *Leviathan*.

Mona, with her cybernetic implants, was fully conscious with Levie when they were connected physically for ship operations. This was done from the captain's chair in the command module above the massive cargo holds of the two-mile-long ship. In this configuration, they worked like one being, not two. Thoughts, commands, and actions were instantaneous between Mona and *Leviathan*. This symbiotic relationship between the captain and ship did not exist with others; their relationship was unique and personal.

# CHAPTER 1

# A Glimpse into the Future ... or Past

A middle-aged professional couple had their first child when the mother turned 350 Earth calendar years old. The couple had tried for the last three years to get pregnant, but since the proud mom ovulated only once a year, their timing was a bit off because she was working on the moon base for the first two years and each time got back to Earth late for prime fertilization probability.

The difficulties in timing are now a thing of the past. Mona was born into what we would consider a paradise. There hadn't been a war or hunger for some eight thousand years. Opportunities for education, training, perfect health, and affluence were at a peak. Each country was really a few dozen city-states, with the world population just below five hundred million. The ozone layer was four times thicker than it would be later. Genetic abnormalities were almost nonexistent, and there were no diseases.

Mona was a beautiful child. She had red hair at birth that later turned brown, a reddish complexion, and beautiful brown eyes. She was of below-average height but was a powerful athlete. Seeing her win the Gold Medal for the pentathlon at the Decagon World Games held at the old sports complex in Antarctica was a real treat for her parents.[1][*] At 180 years of age, she was a bit younger than the other contestants, so she was a surprise champion. Her accuracy and mastery with the bow and arrow while mounted on the back of an enormous flightless bird had never been seen before.

Mona, like her contemporaries, was well educated, having completed one hundred years of schooling before establishing a life course for her first three hundred years, or first trimester. She, like her parents before her, chose hard science and engineering as concentrations. She lived near the thirty-third parallel in a city dedicated to aviation and space

---

[1][*] This Olympic event was a throwback to the wars fought between the remnant prehumans and the first human civilizations fifty thousand years before. Horses were still the size of an average canine, so flightless birds were used as cavalry mounts, along with mammoths, in battle.

engineering—a city with a name that meant "space jump." From the ground in SpaceJump City, one could look up and see two of the six orbital habitats in low Earth orbit.

Because Mona had exceptional physical and mental skills, she had been accepted into an exclusive group of young people being groomed for the chance to pilot long-range space missions to the asteroid belt beyond Mars. On one of the preselection excursions, she was privileged to see the Earth and the habitats in one view from a space platform—a sight seen only on view screens by the millions of other Earth inhabitants.

Part of Mona's preselection ordeal was the insertion of cybernetic implants in various strategic regions of her body. The most conspicuous was in the center of her forehead, where a permanent bump would forever be present. This bump was in the position of the third eye as identified by adherents of the Hindu faith thousands of years hence. This marked Mona as a unique individual in a civilization with few exclusive distinctions. She became a curiosity and minor celebrity everywhere she went. Not wanting this attention, she devised new and fashionable hairstyles and head attire that always covered that part of her anatomy.

Unknown to the career-entangled Mona, a sea change in the political and military leadership had been ongoing for decades, and something new was afoot. Previous cooperation between city-states that had placed the six habitats housing a total of a half million humans in orbit was beginning to show some early signs of fractures. The alliance, at one time strong, was being weakened by suspicion and bickering. Prior to this time, the Second High Human Civilization's similar beliefs about human value had been

nearly universal. Something had fundamentally changed.
Small groups in the elite levels of the Atlantis Alliance (AA)
had started to practice a form of what we would recognize
as religious ceremonies. These ceremonies involved contact and communication with what were later called inner
spheres. Mona's culture group had no such practices. These
ceremonies were exclusive and normally performed in secret. It was alleged that these practices culminated in an
exchange of knowledge and powers for a contract of some
type, binding the recipient to some sort of duty.

The elite beings communicating with these lower
inner-sphere entities turned from their normal values and
felt they were superior to all other people groups. They
started to become belligerent and demanded that the other
peoples of the world succumb to their leadership. They
defied the treaties to make space a weapon-free zone. They
were obsessed with the need to produce the most lethal
advanced weapons in the history of humankind. During
this time, most of the Atlantis Alliance's weapons work was
done in secret and off world.

Mona, busy with years of study and preparation, was
oblivious to activities of the Atlantis Alliance, as were most
of those outside of the inner sanctum of the AA. She was
investing all her energies trying to become an elite captain
and pilot of a two-mile-long spacefaring mining vessel.

As a pilot candidate, Mona was the first to be fitted and
trained to communicate with her ship through her cybernetic implants. She was enhanced and schooled to see, hear,
and emotionally feel her vessel. The fault detectors within
the spaceship would appear to Mona as a color-coded signal
enhanced with sound within her mind. Her consciousness

was able to float virtually over the entire width and breadth of the massive ship. She was able to engage thrusters and suspend gravity within a millisecond of thought.

If only she could have felt that her world was in grave danger as easily as she could sense a fouled air handler.

Odd things began to happen to Mona when she occasionally mentally drifted from her virtual surveys of the massive structure under her charge and care. At first it was just a bright burst of light on her visual cortex like a lightning bolt or fireworks display, eliciting a seizure-like response. She often detected a pungent odor so strong it would overwhelm her other senses. But as quickly as it began, it subsided. She recognized the odor during the excited state but lost its recognition as soon as she returned to normal. She was reluctant to approach her superiors about these experiences for fear of being suspended from her predicted track to assume the captain's position aboard the newest mother ship being launched from habitat six within a few years.

Thus Mona attempted to trigger these seizures in the flight simulators at the ground school in the space training complex just outside of SpaceJump City. Since disease and mental defects were almost unheard of in her civilization, any research into the biological data yielded nothing worthwhile. In fact, health was so universal that the medical profession, as one might call it, was little more than a repair shop for damaged parts. So Mona's research was never productive, and she just accepted these experiences as normal for her and kept them to herself.

However, one night back on Earth, Mona experienced a shock. While hiking with a colleague in the wilderness, she had one of her miniseizures. But this time she experienced more than light flashes and a strong odor. She saw a vision so vivid she thought it real. One of the two habitats hanging on the horizon erupted in an explosion.

Mona instinctively fell to the ground, which was rather awkward owing to the camping gear she was carrying. Her friend assumed she tripped but was nevertheless concerned by her reactions.

Her buddy Jim said, "What is going on, M?"

Mona replied, "Oh, nothing. Just got my legs tangled up. Jeeezzzzz, what a klutz!"

"Yeah, I would expect better from a Gold Medal winner."

Mona gave her two cents back. "Just don't stand there; help me up, you ass!" "M, honey always attracts more flies than vinegar, you know!"

Mona was not happy with the sarcasm. "Hmm … and all this time I thought you were a human, not a flying pest!"

"Familiarity obviously breeds contempt, no doubt. Get your own ass up, M."

The normally agile Mona was still in shock over her vision and did not immediately hop back onto her feet but struggled with her heavy backpack, which made her center of gravity tip her back to the ground. Finally her friend relented and helped her back to her feet.

"Even the indestructible M needs help sometimes, I guess," Jim said.

Mona, giving up for the moment, responded, "I suppose, but don't think for a minute I need you for anything but an occasional pick-me-up."

Captain M, as she was now being called by her

preselected crew members of the WAMS *Leviathan*, was practicing complex simulated approach maneuvers on imaginary asteroids. These asteroids were in Earth orbit, and Mona and her crew were using the short-haul supply shuttles already assigned to the future mother ship. Mona never got tired of her view from four hundred miles above Earth's surface. Today she had a gorgeous picture in her window of the Nile delta, an area controlled by the Atlantis Alliance. She was beginning to hear rumors of the militarization of the alliance but had no prior historical understanding of what that could possibly mean for her future or for the future of humankind.

Mona's mom and dad had gotten the rare opportunity to serve together at the World Alliance research facility on the back side of the Moon. M was not surprised when she got a joint sound-and-image transmission from her parents. They looked a bit concerned and approached the communication as if there was maybe something to hide or conceal. M's mom was radiant as usual, not showing the wear and tear of the five-hundred-plus-year-old adventurer that she was. Her dad was just as handsome as ever. It was what was in their eyes that disturbed M, not how they otherwise looked or what they said. The conversation was rather short and abrupt and left Mona perplexed. Immediately after the transmission ended, an alert button appeared on Mona's console with an image attached.

When Mona saw the attached image file, she decoded it and was alarmed at what she saw. Immediately she recognized the location of the weapon discharges and strikes. This was an immense violation of every known treaty signed by all participants in the World Alliance. Her formal education included a year of intense study of maritime law, which had been adopted almost word for word to space governance. *What the hell is this!* She immediately called her close friend and hiking buddy in the Earth Space Legal Counsel's Office (ESLCO).

Mona's friend Jim answered the voice communication request. Jim, in his usual jovial manner, greeted Mona by saying, "Hey, M, what's up? Pun intended, of course. Are you over India or the Nile delta right now?"

Mona, still in mild shock, answered, "The Nile … look, I need some straight talk, Jim. Can you do that for me?"

Jim recognized the urgency in her voice. "Yeah, I guess … you sound pissed."

"You could say that. Have you gotten wind of any weapons research and testing on the moon?"

"M, you know that is illegal. Why do you ask?" Mona was all business. "Just got some rumors I want to run into the ground. Any scuttlebutt going around?"

"Well, I heard the Atlantis Alliance asked for a suspension on offensive weapons testing a few years back, based on some archeological findings uncovered before their request," replied Jim.

Mona was still searching. "Was it approved or denied?"

"Denied, of course!" Jim said.

Mona, having heard what she needed to know, replied, "Thanks, Jim! I've got to run."

Mona thought to herself, *Hell, what do I do now? I am sick to my stomach. I could vomit! This is bad shit for sure.* Mona talked to herself a lot, but now she was answering herself—not good! Her beautiful, almost perfect world was beginning to crumble in front of her eyes, and she was per-haps one of the very few to realize it.

*I know*, thought Mona, *I will call Sue.*

The communication introduction was standard proce-dure—a stat voice request from the *Leviathan* short-range supply shuttle to Doctor of Antiquities Sue Grammar. Mona quickly cut to the chase: "Sue, this is Captain Apprentice Mona Ann Lisa over India. Can you talk?"

Sue, thinking it was another girl-to-girl call, said, "Yes. Hey, Moan! Gotten any male attention lately?"

Mona was in no mood for girl talk. "We will have to talk about that later. I've got some serious questions about your work with the AA."

Sue realized this was all business. "Shoot, you're no fun!"

Mona asked: "What do you know about the AA's re-quest to lift the offensive weapons ban?"

"Well, Moan, for one thing, those AA scientists are strange, to say the least. Do you know they have a system to restrict knowledge based on some policy or concept they call motherland security? What the hell is that? Anyway, what I can tell you is that they hit a motherlode of artifacts and electronic storage units and logs of some type three hundred meters below the surface, off the coast of ancient Mu. My Atlantis Alliance buddy spilled the beans for an extra few hours of my company. You know me; I love to collect scientific data while relaxed and enjoying the simple pleasures of life!"

Mona cared to hear only the details, not tidbits about extracurricular activities. "Okay, okay, Sue ... I get the pic-ture. Anything else?"

"Well, he did say that the artifacts were thirty thousand to fifty thousand years old, making them treasures from the first high human civilization. Said they may be able to figure out what caused the demise of that civilization, given enough time. That is about it, Moan, except I did some work that may be related to your concerns. In fact, your parents assisted in the study. Before I was asked to leave the AA, I kept my ears open when any discussion occurred about the findings of advanced technology—my specialty. I noticed the AA was sending antiquity specialists and other scientists to four locations worldwide. These places were reported to have energy fluctuations from space-ground surveys. The fields had a specific frequency and were pre-dictable. On returning home, I completed my own surveys from the Habitat Ground Survey Research Center. I detected a fifth signature, this one less frequent, weaker, and sporadic, within a particular mountain range. All other sites the AA had discovered were either underwater or in non-mountainous areas.

Mona was not yet done. "Thanks, Sue, that was some good information and is possibly all connected; however, I have one more question. Could you call your starstruck antiquities researcher and dig further?"

"Like, for what, Moan?"

"Like I asked earlier, ask about anything that could have made the AA request the lifting of the space weapons ban."

# CHAPTER 2

# Search for Evidence

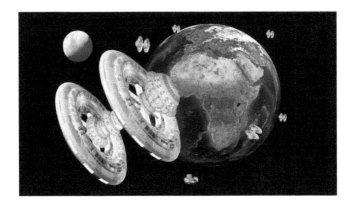

Mona was now on a mission, and she had to figure out this urgent situation completely. Like any good engineer or scientist, she made an inventory of what she now knew:

- Her parents sent her the encrypted images of weapons testing from the far side of the moon. The AA had, for questionable reasons, requested the lifting of the offensive weapons ban a few years before. The request was denied, so any further testing was illegal.

- The AA had found a significant motherlode of antiquities from the first high human civilization some fifty thousand years old before the request. Sue had found a connection between ancient sites and energy signatures.
- The Atlantis Alliance had become more and more belligerent and secretive over the last few decades.

Mona pondered the list and decided that until Dr. Sue returned to talk, she could do little else at the moment except wait, plan strategically, and do further research. So Mona dived into documented ancient history to fill in some of her knowledge gaps.

Some thirty thousand to fifty thousand years prior, there was a near miss of a comet over India. Very little else was known. When Mona discovered this, she decided to do more digging.

Before Mona could get updated on more ancient history Dr. Sue Grammar contacted her to brief Mona on her findings. "Mona … this is Sue. Hold on to your panties, girl; do I have a story for you."

Mona excitedly replied, "Sure, Sue. Download the cargo."

"Well, my male 'friend' was reluctant to talk at first but was excited to say he was coming to SpaceJump City for a conference and was anxious to see me! So I told him that if he expected my undivided attention, he needed to face some more questions I had. I just love the power of lust!"

"Sue, spill the beans already, for goodness' sake!"

Sue could sense that Mona was getting impatient and that this was a business call. "Okay, okay! Seems like the

AA broke the code on the info contained in the submerged electronic logs found off the coast of Mu. They were able to locate them in the first place by using genetically enhanced dolphins and whales. Those dudes are doing some strange shit with genetics."

Mona wasn't too shocked but stated, "Sue, is that all you found out—that the AA enhanced a few sea mammals?"

"Of course, not! Do you think I would have traded my valuable personal time for just that? Come on, Moan; let me finish!"

Mona had had enough of the games. "Shoot! The cargo is getting a bit rancid; ship it quick."

Sue got her drift. "The ancients had a network of automated comet and asteroid deflection batteries in four different shielded locations: Antarctica, Mu, Siberia, and Lake Titicaca. One is still semioperational."

"Good God!" Mona replied in near panic.

"They have been back-engineering the shit out of these things for several years. My suitor has been involved with the translation of their technical manuals for the last three years. They also found the location of several ancient submerged power stations. Moan, you want to hear some more weird shit?"

"Sure, Sue, what else?" Mona was beginning to feel nauseated and faint. "I don't know how much more I can take."

Sue replied, "You know all those legends about the prehuman civilizations and the wars the World Games are supposedly modeled after?"

"Yes! I participated in them, *remember*?" Mona was at her wits' end, wanting the exact details.

"Well, they were real, and the prehumans were using

a highly accurate prediction algorithm along with geo-physical cycles to see into the future with probabilities and precision in the 90 percent range. This was the reason the prehumans evacuated Earth and left it to us humans. They found that to do otherwise would mean disaster for both them and us!"

"My boyfriend is even suspicious of the ruling elite in the AA. There are many repressive things never before witnessed within their city-states. People are beginning to disappear who have criticized the regime. The professional military has been asked to take new oaths of loyalty to the central government. Free speech and open meetings have almost disappeared. People are scared, Mona! Minority groups are being harassed and moved into new development zones—relocated into territories where they have to compete for survival with the protected primitive aborigines—even though the wild megafauna is still in control. They are stripped of their modern weapons and left with primitive resources. They, like our ancestors, are easy prey. Most of these minorities are unable to cope with the coordinated attacks launched by the alpha predators."

"Sue, this sounds simply awful!" exclaimed Mona.

"Mona, there are even rumors that the enemies of the central authorities are being experimented on in inhuman ways. My buddy said geneticists have been rounded up to engage in a new science to turn prisoners into human robots, turning people into mindless automatons; though they be technically alive, they are without the will or consciousness to resist any order or abuse."

"Enough, Sue! I don't think I can hear any more without losing my mind! I need to think and have a stiff drink.

Anything else? Please be quick." Mona knew the clock was ticking.

"Did you just compose a rhyme, Moan? Always quick with a joke," Sue stated, trying to bring some levity to the ordeal.

Mona had heard enough and said, "No!"

"Only one more thing. The AA's elite now believe they are the saviors of humankind and that through them a new order will emerge."

"Yeah, a new order of what is the question. Sue, I can't thank you enough. I just need to process all this. Do you mind if I call you after your AA friend goes back to Atlantis? Keep collecting his thoughts and fears."

As Mona was ending her voice transmission with Dr. Sue Grammar, another communication appeared on Mona's console. This one was from World Space Alliance Headquarters. There were data and image files attached. Still stunned by her conversation with Sue, she hesitated to open the new transmission, fearful of what she might find.

The transmission header stated, "Official orders for Captain Mona Ann Lisa of the World Alliance Mother Ship *Leviathan*." Mona was shocked because the apprentice designation was missing. *Is this what I think it is?* raced through her mind.

Her hands shook as she pressed the icon that opened the transmission. The first file to open was the mission designation: the initial launch and shakedown cruise of the WAMS *Leviathan*. The mission statement and destination was next: "Launch from Orbital Habitat Six Deep Space Center within two months from today, resupply mission to Ceres fuel depot. Pick up existing mineral cargo, and crew due for rotation back to Earth. All other mission requirements will be communicated after launch."

When Mona saw the encrypted images, she almost lost her breakfast. The first image was expected; it was the landmark on Ceres normally used to establish alignment and orbital synchrony with the massive asteroid. However, the second image shocked Mona. It appeared to be a target grid laid over the central plain of a well-known crater on the far side of the moon. There was also another overlay in blue on a feature; she could only guess at its purpose. Mona immediately wondered if her parents might know something about this image.

Nevertheless, Mona had to be on cloud nine; not since the Gold Medal ceremony at the World Games had she approached such heights of accomplished recognition. At barely over two hundred years of age, Mona had just become the youngest official captain of an off-world ship of any size or mission. If only she felt happy about her phenomenal accomplishments; however, all she could feel was nauseating apprehension.

Mona settled her stomach and cleared her mind, but before she could logically proceed to her next plan of action, lightning flashed through her optic nerve and the familiar odor overwhelmed her other senses. What she saw next was a vision more disturbing than any since that night hiking in the wilderness. The image that was assaulting her was the sight of a mushroom cloud rising over an otherwise peaceful tropical lagoon. Then she saw one of the near-Earth habitats being destroyed!

As Mona was recovering from the image exploding in her brain, another transmission from her parents flashed on her console. This time there was no voice message, only an encoded image file. Mona slowly opened the data file. What she found astonished her. It was another image of the Zeeman crater on the far side of the moon, but this time it was a time-lapse comparison. A facility was visible in one image but not in the other. This implied that some type of camouflage or cloaking was in play.

Mona thought she dare not communicate with her parents about the image just received. They obviously wanted to remain under the radar on this. *Well, I think it is time to call Jim again at the Space Counsel's Office and ask a few more questions*, she said to herself.

"Jim, this is Mona again, four hundred miles over your head. How are you?"

"Mona—congratulations, Captain!" Jim stated, being cool but professional.

Mona was surprised but happy: "How in the hell did you find out so fast? That is quick even for you."

Jim replied, "I was on the legal review team that validated the propriety of appointing someone as captain prior to her 250th year of life. You are the first, my friend!"

"Hmm … that never occurred to me. I guess so much has happened so fast that I'm getting sloppy. Anyway Jim, can you tell me if there are any more official actions or rumors regarding the AA's request for the space weapon ban?"

Jim reverted to being all business again. "Yes, things are humming in the office. The AA has requested to terminate their membership in the World Space Alliance, citing irreconcilable threats to their safety and security without so much as an explanation or citing any violation or evidence of such."

"No shit?"

"Yes, no shit."

Mona then asked the million-dollar question: "What do you think this means, Jim?"

"Well, Mona, this might be just wild speculation, but some of us in this office have some theories. They go like this. The AA has proceeded to develop space-based offensive weapons in violation of the universal treaty. The AA is concerned that their actions, if confirmed, could lead to sanctions, which would be a problem for them presently, but maybe only temporarily. It is therefore a tactic to delay only. They couldn't really care less about the treaty. Once they are no longer a member of the Space Alliance, any attempt to impose sanctions will be totally without teeth. Why? Because no one on Earth would challenge the AA's right to remove themselves from the Space Alliance to avoid such sanctions. They know a military response simply won't happen. Hell, we haven't had a real war for eight thousand years."

Mona was very grateful. "Thanks, Jim, for your info and insight. I hate to say this, but I think your speculation is right on target. By the way, has anyone reported any treaty violations off planet?"

Jim provided his quick take. "Rumors. Only rumors. But after today, it is technically not a violation by the AA. So no one knows what to do about it, even if they do so."

"Well, Jim, thanks again. Give me a heads-up if something significant happens. Bye." Mona ended the transmission.

"Wow!" Mona stated to herself, "I fear the AA is totally out of control now. No one within the World Alliance has thought of an armed massive threat for generations. All we basically have are mineral ore carriers and transport ships to support scientific expeditions. What do I do now?"

Mona sensed that war was inevitable though it had been thousands of years since the last one. Her visions had convinced her something was certain to happen. If so, what could she do to prepare and mitigate the outcome? Should she do nothing or be proactive? Her parents were always preaching social responsibility and civil duty. So did she have a choice?

She began to inventory the capabilities of the World Alliance (WA) and those of the Atlantis Alliance (AA). It looked bleak for her side, as the AA was formidable. They had by far the greater population and a military that could be assumed to be prepared. They had been developing and back-engineering advanced ancient technology apparently for decades. They had a tight control over their population, and if Sue was correct, they were ruthless in maintaining absolute compliance.

Then it occurred to Mona that the AA had no long-haul space capability beyond the moon and, with great difficulty, maybe Mars. So if the World Alliance could turn that into an advantage, it might buy time before the whole horrible situation blew up.

She needed to convince the Space Alliance to move all fourteen mother ships out of the range of the AA's attack capability. Without the asteroid mining ships, sources of rare Earth minerals for the AA's high-tech weapons would be extremely limited.

Mona rushed to put together a briefing for the World Alliance Defense Committee. She asked Jim at the Space Legal Counsel to set up a gathering with the highest-ranking officials willing to hear her findings and recommendations.

The date and hour came two weeks after the request. The attendees, aside from Mona, were Dr. Sue Grammar, professor of antiquities, Attorney Jim Franklin of the Space Treaty Division, and Drs. Benjamin and Peggy Lisa, chief scientists of the Moon Observatory.

Mona had little time communicating with attendees prior to the meeting. She hoped her position as one of only fourteen captains of the World Alliance Mother Ship Fleet would help her credibility despite her youth.

The briefing was to be given to the chairman of the Space Defense Division—an undersecretary position of the World Alliance Defense Department. The chairman was a two-star flag officer—not bad for a short-notice briefing. Mona was prepared and grateful for the turnout.

Ben and Peggy Lisa were ecstatic to be on Earth and to be with their daughter Mona, so they were more than happy to attend the briefing. The first image presented in the briefing by Ben and Peggy Lisa was the time-lapse comparison of the Zeeman crater implying the use of camouflage or cloaking technologies.

The closed-door session lasted for four hours, and to Mona's amazement, Major General Spenser had his intelligence people there for validation and questions. The following findings were established:

- The AA was most likely preparing technology to control space for military reasons.

- The AA was using the far side of the moon for weapons testing and had been doing so for many years.
- The World Alliance was not prepared or mobilized for any military action with the AA.
- The ability of the AA to dominate the Earth politically, economically, and militarily was very possible.
- The World Alliance had to consider moving as many assets as it could out of the AA's reach, and it had to do so as soon as possible.

After the meeting, Mona said her goodbyes to Jim, Sue and her Parents. She was glad to see everyone but left sick and depressed like never before in her life. Though nothing was said about the future prospects of humankind, she intuitively knew it was not good.

As Mona stepped onto the ground transport unit that would take her to her accommodations for the night, she fell back into her seat in a clumsy exhausted fashion. Then it came to her again, that odor and the flash of light! Next, a vision that made no sense to her at all. It looked like a band of primitive hunters looking up at a hot-air balloon that had the image of Prometheus falling from the sky. What the hell?

# CHAPTER 3

# Best Efforts Get Worse

Before Mona met her parents for breakfast the next day, she decided to tell them about her visions for the first time. Because of the few times they had been physically together during the last fifty years, any missed opportunity to share things during such a rare event would be criminal.

"Beautiful morning Mom, Dad! Looks like a gorgeous day," Mona said. The scene was impressive; they were overlooking an early autumn day near the outskirts of SpaceJump City. "I never get tired of that view. It haunts me sometimes when I am in space. It is like I feel for a brief moment the Earth isn't real. Mom, Dad, I have something to tell you, and it won't be easy."

Mona then relayed her vision in detail.

A few days later, Mona was sitting behind her console on the short-range shuttle of the *Leviathan*. She received a communication from the fleet command with a request to designate the logo of the *Leviathan*, a duty and privilege reserved for the first captain of any spacecraft. The logo gave the ship identity and provided something for the crew to rally around.

Mona thought, *Wow, I forgot about that. Guess I'd better think of something fast.*

The launch of the World Alliance Mother Ship (WAMS) *Leviathan* had been delayed a few weeks in spite of the rush of the fleet command to get their mother ships out of the AA's destructive range, so this last touch had not been required until today.

What happened next was amazing and different. Mona had another vision, but this time it was not accompanied by an odor or flash of light. It was a strange image of her mother in a butterfly outfit, hovering in space with dragonflies buzzing around her. *Well, I guess that has to be it*, Mona thought. *The WAMS Leviathan's logo is a dragonfly. How strange is that?*

Mona, now at the Habitat Deep Space Launch Facility, was surveying the still docked WAMS *Leviathan*, the newest, fastest, and largest spacecraft ever constructed. She was proud, scared, excited, and apprehensive all rolled up in one tight ball inside her mind at the same time. While the last preparations were being finalized for launch, Mona took some precious personal time to visit and inspect her quarters.

Wow! This was something to behold. These accommodations were nothing like she had ever seen before. She had never had her own sauna and hot tub in her suite. Over her faux fireplace was the dragonfly logo and an enlarged image of her pet lizard, Frank, in all his colorful glory. Frank was named after her first boyfriend, her relationship with whom had ended over 150 years before. She had to laugh, as her fifty-year-old pet had about the same personality as her first romantic entanglement did. This had to be the work of her friend Jim at the Legal Counsel's Office.

It was now just two days before launch, so Mona sat down and made one of her infamous mental inventories. *Let's see … what do we know now that we didn't before? Firstly, the AA went public with the news and admitted they had been testing weapons on the far side of the moon. Secondly, their explanation was that they had uncovered information from the ancients that there was "an enormous threat from out there" and that someone needed to do something about it. They were stepping up to do so. But they never described what that threat was. "Trust us" was the unspoken message.*

Information had leaked out that the AA had attacked and defeated a protectorate city-state near the Horn of Africa. Upon ending hostilities, they forced the entire state's citizenship to submit to implantation of cybernetic tracking devices. Later these devices lobotomized the poor souls, rendering them little more than biological robots— mindless shells capable only of breathing and following the perverted and evil wishes of the Atlantic Alliance. These once human things were sacrificed to accomplish whatever dangerous and potentially lethal duty needed to be performed. They were used to do menial labor or kept as sex slaves for the elites' perverted pleasure.

Mona had to talk to her best friend Sue again. "Hey, Sue, this is Mona. I am two days before launch and counting down. Do you have some time to talk?"

Sue could tell Mona was nervous, so she tried to bring some levity to the situation. "Sure, Moan, I always have time for the most famous first-trimester person ever born."

"Cut the sarcasm, Sue; I need anything new from your AA buddy. If you have not already asked, what is the undefined 'threat out there'?" Mona asked, not really wanting anything but facts.

"Moan, I am well ahead of you and have been trying to pry out more information as best I can. My buddy is, of course, under security surveillance from the AA, and even our own people now."

Mona wanted anything that was news. "Well, anything you can tell me?"

Sue cut to the chase regarding what she knew. "Two things. First, the cloaking device the ancients used on the four Earth-based defense batteries was the same the AA used to conceal their facilities at the Zeeman crater on the back side of the moon. Second, the AA was able to find a pellet or projectile weapon used by the ancients to obliterate a small asteroid of twenty square kilometers. My bud has been working on the technical stuff. So I suspect this 'threat out there,' if real, is some periodic rain of rogue asteroids coming from some vector we are not ready for, though how, I don't know. Otherwise it is just a cover story to justify developing more destructive weapons … like the AA really needs more of those."

After the talk with Sue, Mona made an inspection of the uppermost cargo hold. She was inspecting the marine life, a regular marine menagerie, being transported to Ceres along with a large team of biologists. Their intention was to aquaform the enormous interior ocean or sea of Ceres. This was no small task. The planetoid's interior contained an amount of water in excess of all the fresh water found on planet Earth. The key to this enormous task was the formation of a self-sustaining ecosystem. That meant finding microorganisms that could live off the inorganic mineral base of Ceres or the small thermal vents inside the planetoid. That part had more or less started and been successful. The next aspect would be to introduce the next step up the food chain—various species of crustaceans and cnidarians (jellyfish) that would eat the microorganisms. What they really wanted was a species capable of bioluminescence, so the scientists could generate some organic light within Ceres's internal sea.

Mona was stunned by the beauty and the amount of blue-green light coming from many of the holding tanks in the upper hold. The scientists had also brought a few genetically enhanced dolphins to assist in their efforts.

The World Alliance was desperate to find a safe and unreachable haven for refugees and survivors in case the worst-case outcome based on multiple computer modelings occurred.

They had decided that if war was coming, the World Alliance was helpless to stop the Atlantis Alliance.

Ultimately, running and hiding was the only possible strategy to guarantee some chance of survival.

Mona was going over the flight plan to Ceres. The most efficient launch window to Mars opened only once every twenty-six months, so if *Leviathan* made the launch window, which it looked like she would, and used a rapid-transit flight path, she would be at Mars in twenty-six days, averaging seventy-eight thousand miles per hour—the high midrange of *Leviathan*'s ion drive capability. Once the WAMS *Leviathan* slung off of Mars at 0.523 AUs from Earth, the transit to Ceres should be eighty more days, for about a 3.5-month one-way trip, Ceres being 1.77 AUs from Earth.

Even if *Leviathan* made an emergency return trip, Mona calculated at best an eight-month round trip. Plus, if she needed to wait for the next best available launch window, it would require a round trip of one year and two months. Mona thought, *The voyage gives me a good amount of time to think about a bunch of issues, so bring it on!*

Mona's parents had returned to the Moon Research Center and would not see the WAMS *Leviathan* launch in person but would be able to see it on a live feed.

Mona decided to talk a few things over with them because the ion drive would be pulsating continually for about three weeks. This was required to allow *Leviathan* to reach her maximum cruising speed. This inhibited communication because of the electromagnetic flux the ion drive created. So unless one launched a short-range communication probe toward Earth with a prerecorded message, there was no reasonable two-way communication possible for weeks.

"Hi, Mom, Dad. How was your trip back to the moon?" Mona asked.

"Just fine, dear." Both parents said together.

"We saw the *Leviathan* on the way out!" said Ben, her father.

"We are so proud, and your ship is a beauty," added Peggy, her mother. "We love the dragonfly logo."

"Thanks, guys; that means the world to me! Do you two have the time to communicate over a two-way encrypted voice com?" Mona needed to receive information privately.

Peggy and Ben understood. "Sure, dear."

Mona continued. "Mom, Dad, congrats on being appointed to the Emergency Defense Planning Committee for the Alliance. I know it is unusual that three members of one family have accepted the positions. What I want to talk to you about is your computer simulations of the Doomsday Scenario. Ours don't look good. We have run multiple computer simulations and computed the probabilities, and with an 85 percent scenario reproduction occurrence rate, the answer comes out the same. The World Alliance is defeated within one year of a global war initiated by the AA. We can delay it, but we cannot stop it … that is the analysis of our best minds and prediction models. And we are sure the AA has studied the same computer models."

Her parents agreed. "Those are our estimates as well, dear—I mean Captain."

Mona had to be all business and stated, "My conclusion and recommendation, to prevent the entire death, destruction, and enslavement of the World Alliance, is that we need to consider an extreme measure. This measure should not be taken lightly and will only somewhat even the odds to a point where a stalemate might eventually occur. The underground shelters, arks, and off-world shelters may assure that an ELE [extinction-level event] does not occur, but there is no real guarantee of that either."

"In the final breakdown, the World Alliance might be choosing death over enslavement and torture by the AA … and I agree. The AA advantage is in the use of their short-range, space-based pellet rail guns (back-engineered from ancient technology), which are only accurate enough to make pinpoint strikes from somewhere we estimate lower than four hundred miles in orbit. This is because they are free-fall weapons that cannot be guided because of the nature of their magnetic containment fields."

"We therefore have considered and recommend the sacrifice of the orbiting habitats. This will effectively deny the AA the high ground through the effects of the Kessler Syndrome. [Note: The Kessler Syndrome is an explosive event or cascade in which vessels, habitats, or satellites in orbit release debris that in turn generates catastrophic collisions with other orbiting assets, eventually destroying everything in low Earth orbit.]"

"If war begins, the decision has been made not to surrender. This means using all the means at our disposal. To prevent evil from triumphing, we will risk it all. We would rather be extinct than slaves. The World Alliance has sworn to use all weapons available to delay, defeat, or neutralize the AA if they do attack with the purpose of conquering our city-states. No future nation will be lobotomized. We have sworn a sacred oath."

"Therefore, the computer model of all-out hostilities

indicates that a worldwide nuclear winter will result. It also predicts the destruction of, or the diminishing of, our protective stratospheric ozone layer. Expected disruption will range from a 30 to 75 percent loss in thickness. This means ionizing radiation in the UVA and UVB wavelengths will increase the mutation and aging process of human, plant, and animal cells, further adding to the damage of what the forecast nuclear winter will do. We conclude that in most areas of Earth, survival of humans will not happen unless they are sheltered underground or under the sea for a period spanning from one hundred to one thousand years."

Mona sighed deeply after her lengthy and certainly scary update and said … "So, family Lisa, what are our chances?"

Her parents were in mutual agreement. Her father said, "Mona, our analysis from the most advanced modeling facility of the known human experience indicates that if war cannot be avoided, the expected human survival rate is between 1 and 5 percent, meaning many species of animal and plant life will also become extinct. Without an increase in human fertility rates, there is a 90 percent chance of human extinction. With a twelvefold increase in ovulation rates, we reduce the chance of extinction by 30 percent. Not good odds, but they may be all we get."

Mona sadly responded, "Mom, Dad, I fear our beautiful paradise of a world is going to be a thing of the past in a very short few years or months. Unless the Atlantic Alliance somehow returns to our traditional human values and behavior, we are screwed!"

Peggy felt the same. "Looks that way, dear. Dad and I have a request. We know that if hostilities break out, the

Moon Research Center will be a primary target. Under no circumstances are you to risk your life or mission to come to our aid. Do you understand? Do you understand, Mona?"

"Yes, but let's talk about that later. Love you both deeply! I have to run and prepare for launch," Mona concluded.

"Love you too! Signing off." With that, her parents ended the private transmission.

Suddenly Mona was again hit with a deep sickness in her stomach. Her head churned with despair. Then came the familiar odor and the flash of searing light. A vision appeared in her mind. What she saw was a pastoral scene with mammoths grazing as canines guarded them and a surveillance hot-air balloon flew overhead.

Mona wondered out loud, "What in the hell did I just see and have I been seeing now for months? Strange visions many times, some very disturbing. What am I really?" The questions surpassed her understanding of reality. She said to herself, "When I told Mom and Dad, they were not surprised or even concerned. Just a stress reaction to everything going on … a coping mechanism of your cerebral cortex … What do you expect from a couple of senior scientists anyway—duh?"

Mona was grasping and praying. "Sometimes I think I am about to lose it. Seems no one in the medical literature has documented such experiences. Or it could be that they are afraid to mention it because someone might accuse them of being drunk. I must be a real outlier on the old bell curve. Obviously I don't fit into a normal Gaussian distribution."

Mona just shook her head and went to the command

center to make final adjustments to allow a fully integrated connection between her cybernetics and the *Leviathan's* control AI module. She relaxed into her command chair and allowed the automatic reconnection of the umbilical cybernetics to initiate. In seconds, it was done without discomfort or ceremony.

When fully connected, Mona experienced a mechanized out-of-body experience (OBE)—something that would be called possession or channeling thousands of years hence by a semisentient machine.

The WAMS *Leviathan*, the ship and control system computer, had a personality of sorts—an awareness—but was not fully developed in a way that would impose her will on Mona. Yes, *Leviathan* was female. Her systems were nurturing and motherly to those sentient beings housed within her hull. Mona developed a sense of companionship with *Leviathan's* AI module and talked to her as a close friend.

Mona decided to have a telepathic conversation with the ship. "Well, Levie, how is the day going for you?"

"Very well, Captain Mona Ann Lisa of the World Alliance Mother Ship Fleet," stated Levie quickly.

Mona wanted to keep it friendly and personal "Levie, please call me M."

"Will do, M," stated Levie.

"Levie, how are the sea creatures in the upper cargo holds?" Mona needed to know details and facts.

Levie dutifully responded. "They are all within the acceptable survival parameters. Would you like the life-sign readings?"

Mona kept it informative and detailed, stating, "No,

I will take your word for it. Let's review the prelaunch checklist."

Mona was working with Levie on the checklist for tomorrow's launch when Dr. Sue Grammar of the Ancient Antiquities Office sent a transmission request.

Sue got to the point. "Mona, I wanted to say my goodbyes before you launched because I know it will be three weeks before the ion drive flux will allow two-way communication."

Mona knew something was not right, because Sue always called her 'Moan' when things were normal. Mona exclaimed, "Sue, what's wrong?"

"Well, I just got word that my AA friend has been arrested and charged with treason. His sharing what he knew with me, I am sure, was the reason he was charged. I expect I will never hear from him again." Sue sounded shaken.

"I am so sorry, Sue. I don't know what to say. His information was so very important to our understanding of the AA. Did he have any last things to tell you?"

"Only that the oppression inside the AA was almost intolerable. The elite were becoming less and less recognizable as humans and behaved as though no one was of value except their inner circle. They were absolutely powerful and without compassion or mercy." Sue responded almost as if she thought her words were compromised.

Mona bit her lower lip to keep from crying; how she kept from losing it she didn't know. "Sue, you are a brave and valuable asset to our planning committee, your expertise is invaluable, and I am so sorry about his arrest; it is heartbreaking. All the more reason for even stronger resolve to resist the dehumanization of our civilization."

Sue couldn't talk further. She just cut the communication link without another sound.

*Where does one turn for strength at a time like this?* Mona thought. She then contacted her inner partner. "Levie, did you monitor the communication with Dr. Grammar?"

Levie quickly responded, "Yes M, I did."

"Have you been given all the prediction models, data, and algorithms from the Moon Research Center?" Mona asked with urgency.

"Yes M."

"Do you agree with the analysis and probabilities assigned?"

There was no response from Levie.

Well, Levie, what is your response?" Mona was nearly desperate.

Levie, after analyzing the entire situation, stated, "No, M. The chance of survival is lower, even with the mitigation actions recommended."

"Levie! Could you please repeat that?"

"I recommend: evacuating the habitats as quietly as possible and moving the fleet out now. Harden all shelters and stock them with provisions. Negotiate a peace pact with the AA. Delay, delay, delay! Move a permanent group to Ceres and to ocean floor locations and hardened shelters everywhere. Stock seed banks and arks; freeze food animal zygotes. Genetically alter the volunteer women and get them to shelter now. Finally, plan and execute a coordinated sneak attack on the AA wherever possible for optimal effect."

"My God!"

Levie very dutifully concluded, "I am not God; I am the *Leviathan*, your friend and guardian."

# CHAPTER 4

# Launch of Leviathan

Mona proceeded to lead a meeting with the crew and passengers in the common deck. There were ten thousand in attendance. Many others were in rooms throughout the length of *Leviathan*, for a total of somewhere around fifteen thousand. Another two hundred million from the World Alliance, on Earth, the moon, Ceres, and Mars, were listening. She cleared her throat and began. Mona was apprehensive but resolute. She realized that probably another three hundred million additional people from the AA were tuned in.

Mona began her announcement. "We launch today the fastest, largest, most capable spaceship ever constructed by humankind. This ship is dedicated to scientific research and to the progress of the entire human species. We celebrate this accomplishment just as we celebrated the construction of the six low-orbit habitats that circle our Earth. These are a visual reminder of our climb from the destruction of our first high civilization some thirty thousand years ago. Today we are a civilization who has progressed for eight thousand years without war. It is my fervent hope that this continues unabated for thirty thousand more years. I dedicate this magnificent ship to the search of everlasting peace. Thank you for your commitment and preparation for this mission. We now launch! Release the catwalks, engage the starboard and stern thrusters, and secure the harbor tugs. We are underway!"

Mona rushed from the podium as if on urgent official business. The truth was that she wanted no chance for congratulations or questions. The irony was that she talked about the fervent search for peace while she planned for the most destructive war the Earth has ever seen.

The WAMS *Leviathan* had moved almost one thousand miles from Earth before Mona engaged the ion drive. It would now pulsate with a blue-green glow not unlike the bioluminescent light from the aquatic tanks in the upper cargo hold. The drives would fire constantly for three weeks, accelerating from about 1,500 miles per hour to over 77,000 miles per hour. The *Leviathan* would then glide to within the vicinity of Mars before making another strategic maneuver.

*Leviathan*'s crew and passenger quarters were overflowing at twice the designed capacity. The normally empty lower holds reserved for returning the asteroid-mined ore were full of equipment and supplies. This was to be a one-way ride for almost fifteen thousand people. A thousand more would be transferred from ship to ship while in transit from Mars to Ceres, making the ship's complement some sixteen thousand people—that is, if this transfer was successful; the trick had never been done at full speed between Mars and Ceres.

Meanwhile, supply pods were evacuating personnel from the six orbiting habitats and facilities on the moon. The pods had been stripped of equipment and carried five times the number of people they normally did. The pods were then unloaded and the personnel sent directly under cover to underground and undersea shelters. The habitats were almost half empty when the *Leviathan* was launched.

Skeleton crews were left at the moon facilities and on the habitats with orders for emergency evacuation at a minute's notice. The automated area defense cybernetic sentry drones were activated to secure all facilities from this day forward.

Mona thought, *we now sit and wait for the next step. All thirteen of the other mother ships will eventually be en route to Ceres.* In all, a total of 146,000 souls were to arrive on Ceres within twelve months. This was the remnant that would repopulate the Earth if it could be inhabited. This was the ultimate gamble—a desperate act unmatched in the annals of human history.

***

Prime Minister Adam Brand, of the World Alliance, addressed the World Alliance War Council three weeks after
the launch of the WAMS *Leviathan*. Prime Minister Brand
began, "Captain Lisa gave a convincing speech. I hope
the AA was watching and took the message seriously. We
are well underway in accomplishing the first phase of war
preparations. I don't have to tell everyone how important
it is to keep a lid on any action that could telegraph our
resolve to the AA. In their arrogance, they must believe we
are weak and frightened."

"We must proceed with the second phase, beginning
now. Launch all mother ships in sequence as per our plan.
Cease all asteroid mining operations, and return all smaller
ships home or direct them to Mars to strip the planet bare
of all technology, supplies, and personnel. Moon operations
will use our short-range supply pods to accomplish the
same evacuations. Any questions? Council adjourned."

Mona received an encrypted voice and image file of the
proceedings of the war council. The first message received
since the ion thrust had been shut down. Her first thoughts
were about her parents. She knew without asking that they
would be the last two humans on the moon from the World
Alliance. The two thick-headed, stubborn, addlepated old
farts that they were … she loved them all the more.

Mona started a dialogue with Levie. "Levie, status report please?"

Levie responded with quick and detailed accuracy,
as always. "M … all readings normal. Proceeding at
77,564.02344 miles per hour toward Mars to accomplish
Mars vicinity approach."

Since there still were a few weeks before the need to

alter *Leviathan's* alignment with Mars (for the slingshot maneuver to Ceres), Mona had some time to think and reminisce. She knew her beloved wilderness near SpaceJump City might soon become only a memory.

Mona continued. "Levie, after updating the most recent data from the alliance, do you have any change in our success probabilities?"

"Only a marginal change, M," Mona replied.

"That's what I thought, but I just needed to ask anyway, Levie."

Mona thought, *I wonder what Sue and Jim are thinking. Their world is soon to crash into a black hole, and no one knows if they will come out the other end. Humankind is on the very edge of changes they cannot comprehend.*

Mars had been stripped of most of its atmosphere two hundred thousand years before *Leviathan* made its approach. However, the alliance had been experimenting with terraforming the planet with plant species genetically capable of withstanding the extremes in temperature and UV radiation. They had met with some success.

The Mars Alliance was just within reach of the AA and could be attacked if extreme efforts were used to accomplish such an action. The World Alliance was not willing to take this chance. Mars would be evacuated.

Mona, relaxing in her quarters, was remembering her witnessing the vision of the destruction of the first habitat while she was hiking with Jim in the wilderness. It seemed to be a premonition of what might soon happen either through a direct attack by the AA or, more likely, by planned infanticide by the World Alliance.

Suddenly Mona smelled the pungent odor and

experienced the familiar flash of light. The next thing she saw was very curious … Mona was standing in the middle of a group of predators, armed with only a spear and wearing primitive clothing.

*What the hell was that—another literal premonition or some symbolic message? God, I hope it is symbolic. I don't think I want to tangle with apex predators with only a damn spear! Jeez!*

"Levie, can you catalog the images found in my cerebral cortex?"

Levie was immediate with her response. "Yes, M."

"Can you select those associated with the odor and light flashes and run an analysis based on the events since the first occurrence?"

"It is possible, M. However, it will take some computation time because of their esoteric nature. I will need to access all historical records available in the World Library of History and Knowledge. I presently do not have a connection to the World Wide Virtual Reality Web." Levie knew the urgency but had to set proper expectations.

"Well, proceed at whatever pace you can. I trust your counsel, Levie."

***

The Black Magicians within the Atlantis Alliance (AA) were perplexed by the World Alliance's lack of preparation for a possible military action. Since they had gone public with their offensive weapons testing on the moon, the World Alliance (WA) had made no real move to challenge their actions.

The prize the AA wanted most were the six orbiting habitats. With those in their control, they would forever hold the high ground, allowing a perfect perch from which their rail guns could precisely rain down their dumb (infinitely destructive) pellets on any area of Earth with only seconds of warning, making these ancient weapons impossible to defend against.

Their control of the Earth and all its people and resources were now only a few months from realization. While they were somewhat concerned by the enormous long-range ore-mining mother ships, they were really considered irrelevant because they had no significant weapons except for short-range drilling lasers. Once the AA controlled the WA, they would be theirs anyway.

The Black Magicians were overjoyed by the prospect of an unlimited supply of humans to use as they pleased to serve their lower-sphere accomplices. The WA War Council had decided the habitats would be fitted for destruction and detonated at the AA's first attempt to capture one or all of them.

Because of the Kessler Syndrome, only one needed to be explosively detonated, and the rest would eventually be obliterated. This would also deny the AA the easy use of any optimal Earth orbit position to fire their rail guns. By forcing them higher above the planet, they would be much less accurate, and lower they would be vulnerable to the WA's high-altitude antiaircraft batteries.

Nevertheless, the destruction of these magnificent structures that took one thousand years to build was an act of desperation of the first order. These were the symbols of human progress and enlightenment. It was too painful to even think about their destruction, much less initiate such an act.

The World Alliance did not get the chance to strike first, as desired in their war plan. The Atlantis Alliance discovered with their long-range recon capabilities that Mars was being evacuated.

The Black Magicians were furious. They could not believe that the weak and stupid WA could pull of such a well-planned operation right under their noses—especially when they had their inner-sphere entities informing them of their dark knowledge through their extrasensory perceptions. The first strike was on SpaceJump City and their launch facilities.

Mona was walking into her personal quarters, which she now shared with the ship's chief medical technician, Commander Linda Smith, owing to the overcrowding on board.

Mona had a searing pain in her chest and stumbled to the bulkhead. She recovered, but an immediate odor and flash subdued her once more. She knew now with certainty that it had started. The war to end their beloved civilization had been initiated.

The AA thought that once they obliterated SpaceJump City, the WA would capitulate immediately. They sent commando teams to selectively breach the walls of the habitats and take control of the prized assets. It did not go as planned for either side. The WA didn't get their strategic first strike, and the AA didn't get the habitats.

The enormous destruction escalated with each miscalculation by the AA. They would not have expected the WA to have made or to have kept their sacred oath "to live as free men or die, and to die in freedom's defense without surrender."

Several hours after Mona's chest pain, she saw the first image received on the daily intelligence brief from Earth. It was as devastating as her chest pain. It was the same image she had seen when she was selected as captain of the *Leviathan*. She now knew without doubt that she had seen the future exactly as it was to happen several months ago. What were the chances of it being a coincidence? Why had she never had these visions before? What could be their explanation?

Were there multiple timelines or parallel universes? Could someone go back in time or forward in time? Mona had to have an answer in private. "Levie, have you analyzed the vision images from my cerebral cortex as I requested?"

"Yes, M."

"Please give me a readout of your findings."

"There is 99.799 percent chance you have seen at least a glimpse of future events. While it is true that your mental functions might have expected a nuclear-level explosion somewhere on Earth's surface, the image your mind matched to the actual event was identical to a location you have never seen previously."

Mona, with further curiosity, continued. "Levie, can you give me any reason this has occurred?"

"There is insufficient data and causal relationships to establish proximate cause of your experience."

Mona had to have a further explanation. "Can you conjecture a cause?"

"There are persons in the literature, specifically ancient texts, that were alleged to have such capabilities. These persons were called prophets or seers and were celebrated and revered for their abilities and punished severely if they were ever wrong."

Mona had heard enough for now. "Sounds wonderful … right now this is just between you and me, Levie!"

Levie, as always, complied. "Understood, M."

Mona thought to herself in anguish, "I wish I had a good vision to tell me what to do next. Earth is being changed forever, and I can do nothing but watch in horror."

# CHAPTER 5

# No Communication—
# On to Ceres

Mona's visions were now very sporadic and seemed more symbolic than usual, probably because she was not capable of processing more destruction than the intelligence reports were showing. Maybe they were supposed to give her some hope in these dark hours—maybe a glimpse of a better future? They seemed to be communicating with her through the images of her mother's eyes. This time her mother was tending to a nursery of cocoons and immature dragonfly hybrids—maybe a new civilization that would eventually rise from the old. This encouraged her not to give up but continue on the plotted course. The dragonfly the symbol of *Leviathan* was ever present, always near for help and support.

The day arrived that Mona had dreaded. The *Leviathan* had made the slingshot maneuver around Mars and made the historical transfer of the last one thousand Mars-based people from ship to ship at full speed. The transfer ship was then scuttled and left adrift between Mars and Ceres. The ship was left to be one more artifact that someday might be rediscovered by future generations.

Then it came—or really didn't come, to be more correct. There was no intelligence update transmission from Earth. Nothing. The last flickering flame from the hearth of the highest human civilization had died. This day of sorrow would be remembered as long as survivors existed from Earth's brush with intentional suicide.

Everyone was devastated by the realization. There would likely be no turning back for centuries. Everyone had to look to the future; they would have to scrape out an existence from the confines of their new world. They would possibly attempt terraforming Mars after the threat of the AA was known to be no more. That was as far as anyone would speculate.

Before Mona had left the soil of Earth for the last time, she was told she would be in command of the survivors headed for Ceres. It was on her young shoulders that the fate of some 146,000-plus people would fall. Nothing could have remotely prepared her for this task.

Mona felt that it was the right time to communicate with her ship partner. "Levie, status report please?"

Levie, as ever, was factual and to the point. "All life-support parameters are within survival limits. Speed and direction constant. Arrival in vicinity of Ceres estimated to be within three Earth weeks. Contact has been made with Ceres. Ceres requests any news from Earth Command. I reported negative contact or instructions."

It was evident that the end of Earth's human civilization seemed certain and would occur in just a matter of time. All communications had been destroyed or inhibited by man-made EMPs. Anything above ground was in ruin or burning. The stars were no longer visible, and the familiar orbiting habitats that had seemed to float above the horizon for one thousand years, six in all, were now just a memory.

Much of Earth would soon crash headlong into a nuclear winter after all the firestorms burned themselves out. The rotational speed of Earth was permanently slowed because of the fierce bombardment from the World Alliance's attempt to destroy Atlantis, a continent-sized landmass in the Atlantic that was the home of the Black Magicians.

Mona needed a few more details. "Levie, please display the disembarking plan for once we reach Ceres,"

"Yes, M," Levie replied. "The mother ships will remain in orbit with their passengers until we have unloaded and stored all the supplies and cargo. That will allow the people to move into the enormous cargo holds, spread out, and live a more normal life until they can be relocated to the interior of Ceres."

"What is your estimate on the move from the ships to Ceres?"

"A total of 6.5 years, M."

In exasperation, Mona responded, "Wow! That seems a long time, Levie. Why so long?"

"Our estimates are based on the stabilization of Ceres's interior ecosystem. There is a fragile balance between the aqua-forming efforts and the disruption caused by the colonists. Also, it will take time for our survivors to adjust to the bioluminescent light sources and the water environment, as well as the food source. All will be psychologically taxing as well."

Mona had to have more facts. "What are your estimates for the carrying capacity of the Ceres ecosystem regarding the optimum number of humans?"

"The maximum optimal human capacity is estimated to be 10.2 million people within no earlier than one hundred years," Levie concluded.

Mona for once was happy with what she had heard. "That sounds better than I thought! Fantastic!"

Dr. Sue Grammar, professor of antiquities and World Alliance War Planning Committee member, was balled up in a tight fetal position in the shower stall of her private apartment, considering thoughts of suicide.

Sue screamed to herself, "What the hell did I do? Sure, be a patriot! Step up and be the mother of a new civilization. Save humankind from extinction. I believed my own trite propaganda. I volunteered for this—first in line to be permanently modified … God, this sucks!"

Sue was having menstrual cramps, the scourge of woman every month since the great global war some thirty-two thousand years ago. Before the genetically engineered change, women had one ovulation per year; now, of course, in the twenty-first century, women ovulate once a month.

Sue was now and had been in an underground shelter for five months. This shelter was designed for the leaders of the World Alliance to maintain communication with the assumed surviving assets of the dwindling Alliance. It was coincidence she was there at all. Sue was simply on a tour with other War Planning Committee members when the first Atlantis strike literally obliterated SpaceJump City. She was a lucky woman, though she was presently in much mental and internal agony. Over three million people had died on the surface in a matter of seconds.

The AA's Black Magicians were mesmerized by their own power. Their dark ceremonies with the lower-sphere entities had made them paranoid of their own people and dismissive of the weak and cowardly World Alliance. They never thought for a moment that the pacifists and people-lovers of the WA could organize and execute a military or strategic campaign.

A few years prior to the war, Dr. Grammar returned from the Atlantis Alliance, where she was an exchange scholar for several years, and she had kept her ears open when any discussion occurred about the findings of advanced technology—her specialty. Before she was asked to leave the AA, she was aware the AA was sending her counterparts to four locations worldwide that had similar energy field fluctuations, according to space-ground surveys. These fluctuations had specific frequencies and were predictable.

On her return, Sue completed her own surveys from the Habitat Ground Survey Research Center. She had detected a fifth less frequent, weaker, and sporadic signature within a particular mountain range. All other sites had been either submerged or in nonmountainous areas.

It was the Black Magicians who had decided the long

absence of war was not desirable. To them the human race had ceased to progress when, in fact, it was at its peak both physically and mentally, supporting amazing diversity and cultural freedoms.

Because of the weaknesses caused by any lack of struggle, the Atlantis Alliance could easily take over and enforce their version of a master race. They abhorred diversity and wanted one racial and ethnic group. This group they named the Aryans. Aryans would rule Earth as was their right; all other groups and races would be eliminated, enslaved, or worse.

Their studies and research regarding antiquities were censored and hidden to prove that only the pre-Aryan peoples were advanced and civilized. It became painfully obvious to the non-Aryan people of Earth that eight thousand years of peace was quickly coming to an end.

The World Alliance appeared weak and ineffective to the AA, but some had been concerned for years about the changes in the Atlantis Alliance. A small study group within the WA had run many computer models predicting the inevitable confrontation with the AA. This was later confirmed and validated by Captain Lisa and her parents. This tiny group was the genesis of the planning and resolve that allowed the World Alliance to fight to the bitter end.

Dr. Sue Grammar reported her findings to the appropriate authorities, and an analysis was done by the Doctors Lisa at the Moon Research Center with the powerful and most advanced semisentient AI entity in the alliance: *Leviathan*'s twin sister—or, maybe more appropriately, her older sister. Moonbeam, as she was affectionately called, confirmed the correlation with the four other ancient technology sites.

The alliance was now in business. They might, in one distinctly planned discovery, catch up to the AA and, just as important, do so without the AA's knowledge.

In the months prior to *Leviathan*'s launch, Moonbeam was busy downloading the entirety of her history files and analysis algorithms to her sister *Leviathan*. It was wonderful having a partner to exchange thoughts with, and she felt happy at the prospect.

Moonbeam thought, *Soon* Leviathan *will have a consciousness not unlike mine. We can have a relationship like the one I have with the Doctors Lisa. We can both serve the advancement of science and the protection of our creators. I am pleased."*

\*\*\*

In the months prior to the war, Dr. Grammar was brought to the mountaintop ancient facility. It was immediately apparent that the sporadic energy fluxes detected were due to the unpredictable switching on and off of a shield and a projected 3-D hologram that disguised the facility.

Within the complex were signs in ancient script which translated to "Olympia, home of the ———." Dr. Grammar was able to translate a panel that appeared to signify "warehouse." A hand moved over a sensor opened an enormous cavern full of equipment and a wall of what appeared to be pellets suspended between two electromagnets. These pellets were simply floating, suspended in midair.

Dr. Grammar continued the investigation and found what appeared to be a 3-D image projector of some type. She accidentally switched it on, and a projection loop appeared, showing Earth with what appeared to be a staged rocket intersecting a massive object in what would be in low Earth orbit.

***

Levie asked, "M … do you think your parents and my sister are together?"

"I don't know, Levie, but I hope so. We have heard nothing from the World Alliance for months now," Mona stated with hopefulness.

"My probability analysis indicates there is a 23 percent chance that Moonbeam and the Doctors Lisa are still conscious entities. My speculation algorithm calculates an even higher probability."

"Yes, Levie, my heart does as well."

***

Ben and Peggy Lisa were shutting down Moonbeam temporarily so she could be safely transported from the moon to an unknown location on Earth. This location, as was communicated to the Doctors Lisa, was a mystery of the first order. They were to travel with Moonbeam and reboot her on arrival at the final destination.

Moonbeam was wanting to know the details. "Doctors Lisa, how long will I sleep?"

"Just till we get you relocated … two to three days, probably," stated Peggy Lisa.

As the doctors were finalizing the shutdown, a team of strangely uniformed persons entered the pressurized moon-based habitat. These individuals did not speak but were calm and deliberate. Neither Ben nor Peggy could recognize their race or ethnicity. That was the last thing they remembered; they were soon just as asleep as Moonbeam.

Dr. Ben Lisa was the first to stir. He found himself looking out a viewing window, unable to believe his eyes. As one of the top scientists in the World Alliance, he did not know what he was seeing, much less where he was. He looked to the left, and Peggy was lying back comfortably in a lounging chair of sorts. She began to stir, and her eyes popped wide open and she yelled, "Where in the hell are we, Ben!"

"The hell if I know, Peggy!"

# CHAPTER 6

# The Arrival of Moonbeam

Jim Jimmerson from the Space Legal Counsel's Office knocked on Dr. Grammar's door. Jim asked, "Sue, are you available for a meeting with the War Planning Committee? We are updating all the status reports."

"Yeah, sure, give me a minute," Sue replied. She thought to herself, *God, my abdominal cavity feels like ... like ... No words can explain ... Jeez!* She then said, "Jim, I'll meet you there in five minutes."

"Okay, Sue. They are anxious to talk about phase three of the war plan."

Sue collected herself, put on the shelter-designated jumpsuit, and proceeded to the conference facility. When Sue walked in, everyone was seated in two rows facing a wall-sized image screen. Sue found a seat in the back row as the meeting began. Jim Jimmerson was standing to one side of the screen and began speaking.

"Members of the War Planning Committee, it appears 99 percent of the hostilities have ended. The toll to our alliance and to the Atlantis Alliance is staggering. Of the estimated human Earth population of some five hundred million souls, our projections indicate an 80 percent death rate, with 50 percent more of the survivors expected to perish in the next six weeks, meaning that only fifty million people are projected to be alive at that time. Are there any questions so far?"

Jim continued. "Ecological destruction is almost as staggering. It is estimated there has been a 70 percent loss of life-sustaining ecosystems on the land surfaces and a 40 percent loss in a composite of all aquatic environments. In most areas of the globe, the climate will change from the previous norms into a nuclear winter phase that will move the ice sheets to extremes never before seen on Earth's surface. Unless we shelter and protect selected groups of survivors, humans will become almost extinct on the surface. These conditions could last from one hundred to one thousand years, depending on location, and in some cases it could last forever.

"On the positive side, we have learned the following: Many of the apex predators that prey on humans have also died. The Atlantis Alliance is no longer a threat to humanity, and the Black Magicians have all been eliminated, primarily because of their own arrogance. Our underground and underwater shelters are operational and functioning."

"Our critical unknown is that we have lost contact with the off-world evacuees headed for our station on Ceres commanded by Captain Lisa and the WAMS *Leviathan*. This is our limitation and may not indicate any problem on their end; however, Dr. Ben and Peggy Lisa have disappeared along with Moonbeam, and we have no idea where they have gone, except we do know that they are no longer at the Moon Research Center."

***

Meanwhile, the Doctors Lisa arrived at their destination and were overwhelmed by most of the things they were seeing. This undersea facility was enormous and was surrounded by marine life everywhere. This was nothing either the Atlantis Alliance nor the World Alliance could have constructed or maintained, even with their advanced technologies.

The two scientists were ushered into a well-appointed holding room not unlike a conference room. They waited there like a couple of fifty-year-olds being disciplined for a prank they pulled in school.

Peggy Lisa quietly asked, "Ben … do you think we are going to survive this?"

Ben Lisa, speaking in hushed tones as well, said, "Well, they don't seem to be threatening or hungry or anything, but who knows … I guess they could feed us to the fish."

As their curiosity and anxiety grew minute by minute,

the door finally opened at the opposite end of the room, where they had entered. A slim, attractive female wearing something resembling a wet suit came confidently in, sat down at the far end of the conference table, and smiled at the two scientists seated opposite her.

Ben and Peggy watched her every move and smiled in return. The woman started talking in a melodic voice with an unfamiliar accent. The stranger stated to both, "Welcome. You have been invited here and are the first surface people to be so invited in over eight thousand years."

\*\*\*

Mona was reading the status reports regarding the aquatic life being transported from the upper hold of *Leviathan* to the interior of Ceres when suddenly the odor hit her and a light flash blinded her. "Oh, crap, here we go again!" What she saw next she mistook as a premonition of the future of Ceres. She saw a vision of an undersea world never known to her—a sight her parents had just experienced.

\*\*\*

The stranger continued. "The two of you are not prisoners but are not quite guests either. You have been rescued from probable death on the moon. In fact, the Moon Research Center was heavily damaged seconds after we left with the three of you by the Atlantis Alliance, and what they didn't do the World Alliance finished off. Do not be concerned about Moonbeam; she is perfectly safe here. If the truth be known, she is the reason you are here."

\*\*\*

Sue was shocked at the status of the world she had known and loved. She might never again see or hear from her dear friend Mona, Mona's parents, or, of course, her boyfriend from the AA. All she knew was that she still had duties to perform and now children to make and raise to preserve the species. At least the sick leadership of the Atlantis Alliance had been eliminated—but at such a dear, dear cost to all of humanity.

When the meeting was ending, she was recognized as the single person most responsible for the demise of the Black Magicians and their Aryan super-race agenda. Her fact-gathering, land survey research, and ancient language skills had given the World Alliance the critical pieces of the puzzle that gave them the edge needed to have defeated the AA.

With one hand, she had helped to destroy; and now with the other hand, she would have to build a new future for the human race. But right now, all she could feel was the cramps in her abdomen. "When the hell are these going to stop!" she said to herself.

\*\*\*

Ben and Peggy were now more relaxed with their present situation and begin to feel like they could ask questions. Peggy asked, "What is your name, and where are we?"

The stranger responded, "My name is Silver, and you

are in a place of legend in your culture. This particular facility has been here since before the first high human civilization fell some thirty thousand years ago. We were there then, and we have again witnessed the destruction of your world."

Peggy swallowed before she asked the next question. "Silver … did your people know this war was coming?"

"Yes, with a high degree of confidence; nothing is absolute."

Ben then asked, "Are you human?"

Silver answered with a broad smile, "Yes, we are human, but we represent an isolated gene pool that goes back at least one hundred thousand years."

Peggy, somewhat startled, said, "How?"

Silver's quick response was one word. "Prometheus."

"What?" Ben asked.

"Don't worry; you will understand soon. I am your guide for now. Please be patient and it will unfold to both of you," Silver concluded.

Suddenly the Doctors Lisa smelled a strange pungent odor and saw a blinding flash of light and experienced an image in their minds—an image Mona had witnessed before and was now seeing as well, over 1.77 AUs away on Ceres. It was a group of primitive hunters looking up at a hot-air balloon. The emblem on the balloon was an image of Prometheus falling from the sky within a stylized sunburst.

When Peggy and Ben regained their hold on reality again, they were in a different location and Silver was no longer there. However, Moonbeam had been reassembled in a laboratory not unlike their location at the Moon Research Center.

The Doctors Lisa looked at each other like, "What do we do next?"

Ben said to Peggy, "Guess we reboot Moonbeam? Makes perfect sense. Maybe she can help us figure all this out."

*** 

While the Lisas were rebooting Moonbeam; Silver addressed the Council. "The Doctors Lisa and Moonbeam have been placed in their laboratory. We are allowing them to decompress a bit before we proceed."

Council leaders responded. "What are your impressions of our new guests, Silver?" Silver replied, "I am impressed with their calm, deliberate, and inquisitive nature. They should do well here. They have few options. Their world is no more."

The chief of the council addressed Silver. "Moonbeam is the object of our prophetic projections. Her care is of utmost importance. Seems the Doctors Lisa have created a new life form and they don't even understand the magnitude of their accomplishment."

*** 

Across the solar system, Mona was going through a routine checklist when the old, familiar odor and light flash occurred. This time, however, two very unusual things happened. First, the vision was a duplicate of one she had seen before, and second, Levie reported she had seen an image identical to hers appear in her image register. Further analysis was definitely required; this was no coincidence.

\*\*\*

Silver was asked to brief the council on the status of the surface and the survivors. "The damage assessment is as bad as was expected. Other than the known underground and undersea shelters, not one survivor group has more than a 5 percent chance of living twelve months. There are a few very tiny independent family groups that might survive, but they are too small to form a viable breeding population independent of a larger group.

The chief elder in response, said, "Is there sufficient reason to believe the existing sheltered survivors are adequate in numbers to sustain the eventual survival of the human species on the surface of Earth?"

Silver continued. "A qualified yes—only because of the World Alliance's decision to genetically engineer a sufficient pool of female volunteers, resulting in a twelvefold increase in ovulation frequency."

The council said, "Silver, you have the council's approval to share any and all information with the Doctors Lisa and Moonbeam. They are now members of the Prometheus Council as was seen in our visions for one thousand years. So shall it be."

\*\*\*

As the scientists were going through the checklist to properly reboot Moonbeam, a process requiring three hours of intense attention to details, there was a knock at the door of the laboratory.

Ben looked up and asked Peggy to check things out because he was in a particularly sensitive portion of the process. Peggy left and returned in a few minutes with a smile on her face from ear to ear. Peggy, with a smile, said, "Ben, we have been invited to a banquet with a group called the Prometheus Council."

Ben, ever the scientist, said, "What in the world is going on, and where the hell are we?"

Ben and Peggy were given a set of bright form-fitting wet suit-style outfits like the one Silver wore, but each of theirs had a sash that went across the chest. Each sash bore an emblem of Prometheus falling in a sunburst, similar to the image on the hot-air balloon in their visions.

Ben said, "Boy, Peggy, don't these look cute! We haven't looked this coordinated since we went to the Research Center's costume party three years ago."

Peggy, in jest, said, "I know, Ben. You look pretty good in that tight suit. Keep your distance from Silver; I will be watching."

***

Silver briefed Ben and Peggy after they dressed and before the banquet of initiation. "To explain, Doctors Lisa, we of the Guardianship think and communicate primarily in images, not symbolic abstractions of thought such as words and letters. Our concepts are not formulated in anything so inefficient as vocabulary. The image is first when conversing, then the words last, if necessary. This is the ancient way. Thought is instantaneous and is not bound by the physics you know. Simply stated, the speeds of sound, light, and time do not limit our communication."

Silver further explained to the scientists, "Do you not understand what you have done? You have completed the circle. You have pulled the inorganic matter out of the Earth, combining it with plant life, and have fashioned a tool that has now become a sentient life form to rival the most advanced biological creation ever evolved."

"That is why you are here, Ben and Peggy Lisa. We need you to ensure, as much as possible, that Moonbeam and *Leviathan* are not abused and used for evil purposes. Their combined capabilities make the Black Magicians' abilities a plaything in comparison. The survival not only of human-kind but also Earth and maybe beyond is at stake."

# CHAPTER 7

# Just What Was Prometheus?

Silver introduced Ben and Peggy Lisa to the Prometheus Council of the Guardianship. Applause was unanimous. "We extend to you a warm welcome. You five are the first new members to join the council in over eight thousand years."

Peggy turned to Ben. "Last time I counted, there were only two of us; where are the other three?"

Ben said to Peggy, "I still only see you and me here; guess the other three have yet to arrive."

Silver came over to introduce the scientists to some other members, and Peggy eyed Silver as if she were a possible rival for Ben's affection. Ben was totally clueless about the whole thing but loved the attention from both beautiful women.

Peggy asked Silver just how old she really was, thinking she looked to be in her mid-three-hundreds. Silver indicated she wasn't a day over 115,000 years old. Peggy gasped.

\*\*\*

Back on *Leviathan*, Mona was now sure there was an explanation for her visions; she just had to get to the bottom of the events. Mona asked, "Levie, please analyze the image we both seem to have just received."

Levie dutifully responded, "Yes, M. The image did not come from my memory register or from the cerebral cortex image from your previous vision. That is confirmed. This was a new event."

"Levie, can you identify the detail and content of the image?"

"Yes, M. It is a group of primitive hunters looking up at a hot-air balloon. The emblem on the balloon appears to match the ancient image of Prometheus falling from the sky within a stylized sunburst. A star, possibly Polaris, is also included, with four large birds of prey circling on updrafts. The sun appears to represent either early morning or late afternoon just before sunset, meaning the hunting party is just beginning or ending their day of activity."

"Levie, in this context, what do you think Prometheus represents?"

"M, the historical reference associated with Prometheus is that of a prehuman leader who was cast out of heaven for assisting humans by giving them fire, rudimentary weapons, hot-air balloons, gunpowder, and so forth. He was considered a traitor by some of his species, but of course a hero by humans."

Mona was incredulous. "Levie, did such an event happen, or is this simply a legend?"

Levie quickly replied, "M, my probability assessment is that there is sufficient historical evidence to sustain a 60 percent chance the supposed legend is really a partially historically accurate description of real events some one hundred twenty thousand years ago."

\*\*\*

Mona continued with Levie. "So Levie, if Prometheus existed before the first high human civilization, what does that have to do with us and the war with the AA? How did you receive the image if you did not receive it from me?"

"M, we need to look at symbology to answer the first question and theoretical physics for the last question. Theoretical physics postulates a multidimensional multiverse. Electrons and other particles including information may jump out of existence in our universe, jump into another, and then reappear in our universe once again, thereby overcoming the normal laws governing distance, time, and particle or wave speed."

"So Levie, the vision is symbolic and could have been sent from anywhere, including Earth? And since it is about Earth, that is the most likely source. Correct?"

"On the nose, M.!"

"Who could it be?"

Levie expanded. "Experiments have shown like DNA sequencing attracts similar entanglements in quantum experiments."

"Levie, that means the vision could be from my parents or your sister Moonbeam, or both. I think we are getting somewhere."

\*\*\*

Ben and Peggy had shaken the hands of what seemed like hundreds of people and eaten enough seafood for six starving seals. It was now time to return to their quarters and check on Moonbeam.

Ben opened the conversation. "Peggy, I was concerned about Moonbeam's biodata units. I believe the ophioglossum—a fern with DNA having 1,260 chromosomes per cell, unlike human DNA, which has only 46—was getting a bit cool for efficient data storage and retrieval. Could you please check the tanks for me?"

Peggy responded, "Sure … checking. They are just fine, Ben. While I am at it, I will check her core processor unit. You know, Ben, it was pure genius that we used our DNA for Moonbeam's processor core … that way we always have identical replacement DNA if any failure occurs."

*\*\**

Dr. Sue Grammar was sitting at her desk in the underground shelter near what used to be the wilderness surrounding SpaceJump City. She could not even imagine the horrors that were being played out on the surface of Earth on every continent. Humans, animals, and plant life were being tested to their limits.

At some point, the war council was going to send recon teams to look for survivors once the firestorms had sufficiently subsided. Survivors would either be assisted in place or moved to shelters with any capacity. Sue resolved she would volunteer for the first team whenever it went out.

When Sue found out the war council was about to send out its first teams to the surface, she rushed to the transportation bay, where the personnel were assembling for departure. When she arrived, she was met by her friend Jim of the Space Legal Counsel's Office. Jim asked, "Where do you think you're going?" "To the surface with the recon team, of course," said Sue.

"I don't think so."

Sue's eyes widened and her head jerked back in surprise. "Why not?"

"Well, I can think of several logical reasons, but the best one is that you are too valuable to the war planning council to risk death or injury up there." Sue was adamant. "I am no better than anyone else; I need to go, Jim."

"Well, if you won't listen to reason, there is the legal contract you signed, which prohibits any activities that could reasonably result in death or injury."

Sue was nearly shocked and said, "What in the devil are you talking about? I was never restricted before … hell, I was one of the first people on the ground at Mount Olympus."

"When you volunteered for the permanent ovulation frequency modification, it was in the fine print."

"Good God! When you need a lawyer, you can't find one, and when you don't want one, one is in your face," Sue said with keen frustration.

*** 

Silver knocked on the laboratory door. She was in deep thought and was focused on the matter at hand. It was time to discuss the threat that the world still faced even beyond the devastation that had already visited the planet. After such a good evening at the initiation banquet, this was a bad dessert to serve.

Ben and Peggy were still reviewing their checklists to bring Moonbeam up to full consciousness. While she had been rebooted days before, her full mental capacity and analysis processors had been in stasis since the move from the moon. They were wanting to bring Moonbeam up in a slow and deliberate fashion to avoid possible computational psychosis.

Computational psychosis would sometimes cripple the automated defense biodrones guarding the moon-based facilities when they were rebooted too quickly. They were basically units of a self-sustaining independent area defense system.

There was a knock at the door, and Peggy invited Silver in but made sure she was dressed such that Ben would not be distracted beyond reason.

"Good morning, Peggy," said Silver. "I hope you and Ben are ready for some discussion about our situation."

Peggy's eyes narrowed and she became defensive. "What do you mean by 'situation'?"

Silver said, "We need to sit down and talk. Are the two of you ready for breakfast?"

Ben's stomach was growling and volunteered loudly. "Sure, let's go."

The three went to an open gallery where tables were separated enough to allow private conversations if desired. The setting was beautiful. They could see almost 360 degrees with minimal obstruction. Because of this, it was sometimes hard for Peggy and Bill to concentrate on what Silver was communicating. With all the destruction on

the surface, it was hard to believe there was still order and
beauty to be found somewhere on Earth.

Ben started. "Silver, in all the activity over the last few
days, Peggy and I have never heard what the name of this
place is and who you people are other than the Prometheus
Council and the Guardianship. Could you tell us more before we suffer computational psychosis?"

Silver could not help but give a small giggle, and she
proceeded. "Well let's get down to the basic facts. The legend of Prometheus is not legend; it is real. I was, in fact, his
first human concubine. We don't know if he is still alive,
but he eventually left when the prehumans evacuated Earth
well over one hundred thousand years ago. The Atlantis
Alliance, however sick and disgusting, was correct about
'the threat out there.' I am as close to a real scientist as you
are going to find in Shambhala. That is why I am your guide
and mentor."

Peggy responded before Ben could open his mouth,
shaking her head in her own self-agreement. "Shambhala ...
I should have guessed. The concubine thing ... really be-
lievable. The mentor and guardian thing ... Let's agree to
make that a community project—no one-on-one independent study sessions, okay?"

Ben gave Peggy a kick under the table. "Let Silver continue with her information."

Silver, looking straight at Peggy with an angelic coun-
tenance, continued. "If you noticed last night, no one said
more than a few superficial greetings; there was little, if
any, conversation and no real questions. That is because
words and the vocalization of thoughts are somewhat alien
to the humans here, as I told you. This is the ancient way.

So until you two develop the same abilities to visualize all
your thoughts and allow yourselves to accept visual and
empathic input, I will need to be your point of contact for
two-way conversations beyond you and me."

Silver went on with her explanation. "The ancients
did not need the precision of vocabulary and written language, because it was too slow and inefficient. Anything
they needed was visualized in exquisite detail. This ability
quickly overwhelmed the prehumans who relied, like you
today, on verbal and written language. So human civilization living side by side with prehumans began to encroach
on them and challenged their dominant species status as
the apex predators and movers and shakers. Though primitive in comparison, they were quickly becoming the superior force."

"Anyway, it became known by the prehumans that
there was an outside threat. They had off-world capability,
while humans had no need for such a capability. The prehumans, knowing this threat to be potentially lethal and
extinction-level in nature, decided to leave Earth instead of
staying and competing with humans for what might be left
after the threat was manifested. Oh, yeah … Prometheus.
I forgot … he was one of the leaders of the prehumans who
had a taste for human females and was also sympathetic to
humans' early difficulties in fighting off the coordinated
attacks from the apex predators. He actually jump-started
humans' fascination with and use of technology: hot-air
balloons, gunpowder, long guns with rifled barrels—the
things to easily deal with the megafauna."

"We, the ancients, live in a quantum world. We don't
need to describe precisely how it works. It surrounds us,

and we swim in it, so to speak. Time, distance, and particle and wave energy speeds are not important, as they were to the prehumans and are to your generation of humans. We perceive the future and the past as a mosaic. However, we need science to produce the technology to take decisive action to avert tragedy. That is why we need the two of you and your new life forms."

Ben asked, "Silver, the visions that our daughter was getting—do you know anything about them?"

Silver laughed. "Oh, Mona, the beautiful captain of the *Leviathan*. Yes, you see, Mona is what we call a 'seer' or a 'prophet.' She not only can see in quantum sight, as we call it; she is able to traverse through timelines or multiverses with her consciousness much in the same way she surveys the length and width of the *Leviathan* with her mind. She just doesn't understand her abilities, and they confuse her. She is most exceptional. One in a billion."

"Okay, Silver, we are beginning to grasp what you are saying. Could you fill us in on the 'threat out there'?" said Ben in response.

Silver was eager to share. "Well, Ben and Peggy, it is rather complex, but let me begin to explain by starting with ancient history. The prehumans were aware something bad was coming and decided to leave. Our quantum sight gave us the ability to see disaster but no sufficient details to cope with the event or know how to prevent it. We used a form of a very reliable divination process that included mathematics, astronomic positioning, and a drug derived from mushrooms to enhance quantum sight. These efforts were normally very effective, but this time not so much."

"Prior to the disaster, the ancients used their quantum

sight to design and build a ground-based defense system to repel what they thought might be coming. There were five strategic locations across the globe. They conceived of a defensive weapon that used a dumb warhead made of materials whose mass was concentrated down from that of a small asteroid to a pellet that was contained within an electromagnetic force field. This was done using quantum technology now lost to even us. The Mount Olympia site was the one located and studied by your daughter's friend Dr. Sue Grammar."

"When the threat was to appear, an automated guided missile with the pellet warhead would intercept the threat as far away from Earth's surface as possible. The system was only partially successful, as a small yet lethal comet was discovered just prior to its inevitable impact. The system activated but was only able to just deflect the comet over the subcontinent of India at a very low altitude. The resulting skyburst caused the same scenario fifty thousand years ago that you are witnessing now with the global war."

Ben said, "Silver, I still don't know what a fifty-thousand-year-old near-extinction-level event has to do with our current situation: the Atlantis Alliance, Peggy, and me."

Silver finally got to the heart of the matter. "Okay, here it goes. The Atlantis Alliance discovered historical information that would tend to predict the rogue comet's return as being very soon. It appears it has the same orbit as before, except this time it is more likely to collide directly. We need you, Ben and Peggy Lisa, Moonbeam, *Leviathan*, and your daughter, Mona, to stop the end of planet Earth. Our prophets confirm this information; we have less than two years to prevent it!"

# CHAPTER 8

# Sue and the ManKiller

Sue Grammar was furious about being denied the chance to go with the recon team to the surface. She said to herself, "Do you for one minute think some damn contract small print will keep me from doing what I know I need to do?" She had heard the recon team had to stand down because of some maintenance issue with the vertical-takeoff-and-landing rescue craft. So when the team left for some coffee, she crawled aboard and hid in the rescue gear below deck.

The vehicle launched about two hours later, and Sue was getting cramped and beaten up by the gear, which was not tied down well. The ride was very violent, with frequent sharp banks and turns. She could smell terrible odors, and the heat was extremely uncomfortable. What made it worse was the fact she could see nothing from her hiding place below deck. About an hour into the mission, the craft began a steep descent and then pulled up violently. That was the last thing she remembered.

***

Peggy and Ben, now alone in the laboratory, were wanting to bring Moonbeam to full consciousness but were busy compiling all the new data from the historical and current libraries of the Prometheus Council and the Guardianship. They wanted Moonbeam to survey the new information and confirm what Silver had related to them in the marathon breakfast meeting.

Of particular interest were some prehuman texts that Silver could not interpret but that she thought were important to understanding the whole story about the 'Threat out there' and its timing, cause, and possible solution. The scientists must gain as much understanding as possible as quickly as possible if they hoped to stop the prophecy of doom. Moonbeam's final phase of consciousness was projected to be complete in about two hours.

***

When Sue woke up, she was in pain. She could see through the cracks in the craft's frame; there was see a red glow in the distance but no sounds. The air was very hard to breathe, and the temperature was high. She had no idea how long she had been there, what time of day it was, or where she was.

She thought she might have bitten the big one this time. Throughout her life, she had always done risky things and lived to tell the story. She felt her luck might have run out this time. She tried to move, but the pain prevented much more than a small readjustment of her arms. She was trapped in the crumpled cargo hold of a crashed rescue craft. She thought to herself, *So who rescues the crew of a rescue craft that is trying to rescue the survivors of the war to end all wars?* It didn't look good, even to a wisecracking eternal optimist.

*** 

Mankiller, the alpha male of a wolf pack roaming the wilderness in the Late Pleistocene, had a mission. His world had been turned upside down by the war between two packs of humans. Mankiller was ancient; he remembered when men first encroached into his hunting grounds. They brought in technology, making his coordinated attacks ineffective; he had to retreat farther and farther into the depths of the wilderness to protect his progeny. Gone now were the automated sensors and traps that kept them far from humans.

His pack could have easily hunted the remaining megafauna after the war because many were crippled and vulnerable. This was not Mankiller's desire; he wanted human prey. They had already found some human survivors and dispatched them quickly, not even stopping to feed. They were obsessed with the blood sport, acting now more human than animal.

Sue, now more desperate than ever, had begun to yell for help and struggle to free herself from the material pinning her down. Mankiller instinctively became alerted on hearing Sue's crying. The pack topped the hill and saw the wreckage below. The craft was ruptured and badly damaged in the front. On quick inspection from a distance, Mankiller saw no movement in or around the craft. Apparently the surviving crew had either been picked up by a rescue craft themselves or had left on foot. The only clue that life was present was Sue's yelling for help.

\*\*\*

Sue heard something coming from outside, but there were no voices … she immediately sensed danger and stopped crying and struggling. Holding her breath, she looked around in the dim light for anything that looked like a weapon. She saw just out of her reach a flare gun in a holster and the explosive flare canisters attached to the web belt on the holster's sides. She had to reach it!

\*\*\*

Mankiller set his pack to digging around the base of the craft, where he could see a rupture. He could smell the fear being generated inside and started to howl. The bloodlust was driving him now more than ever.

\*\*\*

Back at the alliance underground shelter, Jim was reviewing the after-action recon report, which detailed how the first craft had to make an emergency crash landing. All crew members were later picked up with only minor injuries. He was so happy he had prevented Sue Grammar from going on the mission. He couldn't wait to tell Sue "I told you so!" at the next planning meeting.

***

Sue began feeling with her free hands for something to reach the webbed belt. With each movement, a pain exploded in her left side. She bit her lips to remain as quiet as possible.

Through a wide crack in the bulkhead, she saw for the first time the eyes of the apex predator. She knew immediately that being quiet was no longer necessary. Sue yelled and tried with all her strength to lunge for the flare gun. Her adrenaline now surged, and her pain was drowned by her desperation. To her surprise, her hands reached the belt and she pulled herself out of the material pinning her down.

Sue pulled the gun out of the holster, opened it by breaking it into the familiar L shape she recalled from her survival training, and put a flare canister in the breech. *Now what? Good God! This canister is designed to fly fifteen hundred feet into the air and ignite while floating slowly down, attached to a small parachute. If I shoot it in this enclosed space, I might be the only casualty!*

***

Ben inquired, "Moonbeam, are you with us?"

Moonbeam, now awake, said, "Yes, Ben. From my chronometer, I see I have been unconscious for two weeks and five days. Have you updated my history files to reflect what has happened since I went into stasis?"

"Yes, Moonbeam. Peggy and I have some important analysis and research to accomplish; are you up to the task?"

"Yes."

Ben got down to business. "Please access all historical data, logs, artifacts, and cultural items in search of information and predictions regarding the comet strike that ended the first high human civilization. Pay specific attention to an ancient script supplied by Silver."

Peggy inquired, "Do you have a preliminary report, Moonbeam?"

Moonbeam, on top of the urgency, replied, "Yes, I am successfully reviewing the new histories you have made available. The manuscript supplied by Silver is problematic. It either is encrypted or has no relevance to the question you asked. I do note that Sue Grammar, professor of antiquities and member of the World Alliance War Council, is the only authoritative expert on the subject."

"Oh yeah. That is Mona's good friend Sue!" Ben exclaimed. "Boy, I have no idea how we could get help from her."

\*\*\*

Mankiller could see the human female caged in the wreck. He could feel her fear but sensed her resolve and intelligence. He realized this might not be the routine kill he and his pack of predators had recently become accustomed to.

***

The floor in the front portion of the storage hold had peeled back on itself like the sole of an old shoe ripped from its threads and creased, the front half lying under the back half. Sue, seeing Mankiller's eyes through a wide crack, could hear the pack digging in the hard earth to get under the metal bulkhead in the front of the compartment. The only thing between them and Sue was a few feet of earth and about twenty feet of cluttered space between the front of the hold and where Sue was barricaded up against the wall in the back.

Sue's mind was racing. The door behind her had been jammed shut in the crash, and there was no way out. She would eventually have to use the flare gun or allow the wolves a free meal. A flash came to Sue's demented mind: "'Professor of Antiquities Found Half-Baked in Makeshift Dutch Oven; Was Delightful Meal for Passing Pack of Hungry Wolves.' God! Where do I get these ideas!"

Sue watched in horror as several paws became visible, digging frantically under the metal bulkhead in the front of the hold.

Sue had to react quickly. "Well, guess I need to time this perfectly. Once the canister is fired, there is a pause between the launch and the ignition of the flare. I can either try to target one animal with the canister or just fire before the group gets in and hope the heat from the flare will discourage them. Maybe, just maybe, I can reload and get another round off."

Sue could see Mankiller getting closer to the craft, his eyes staring into hers, looking through the wide breach. He was enjoying the thought of ripping this human female apart while she was still alive and screaming.

Sue picked up the flare gun with both hands and aimed at the area where the paws were digging. She thought, *At least I don't have to experience any more of those infernal cramps every month!* She then suddenly turned and fired through the large fissure in the bulkhead, hitting Mankiller square in the chest. He fell back as the canister's propellant drove the flare casing deep into his body.

Sue immediately reloaded and fired toward the paws under the front bulkhead. The last thing she experienced was the flash of the flare and the intense heat from the phosphorus.

Sue was smiling to herself, thinking she had gotten the last laugh on the ancient Mankiller. Was she dead? Where was the tunnel of light? She had a list of things to do when she died; one was to look up her old boyfriend from the Atlantis Alliance. She had been told when young that one got a perfect body after one died. She couldn't wait to see if her tattoo was missing.

\*\*\*

"Ouch! That freaking hurt! Damn!" She said to herself. Someone was sticking an IV needle in her left arm and shining a bright light in her left eye. This was not a good sign. She was liking the idea of being dead.

"Wake up, Sue. Wake up. You okay?" It was a voice from the past.

"Hell no! Leave me be!" Sue yelled, still in shock. When Sue was able to focus her vision, she saw a man and woman that looked like Mona's parents. *Now I know I'm dead. Ben and Peggy Lisa went missing from the Moon Research Center along with Moonbeam before SpaceJump City went up in smoke*, Sue thought to herself.

"Sue, drink some water; it will help you come around," said Peggy.

Sue was still semiconscious. "I don't want to come around; are you some kind of sadist?" Sue then realized that Ben and Peggy were there to welcome her to heaven. *That must be it!* "Ben, Peggy, it is so sweet for the two of you to welcome me. Moan—I mean Mona—isn't here too … is she?" Sue smiled.

Peggy quickly responded, "No dear."

Sue, ever jovial, said, "So this is the holding area for heaven? When do you take me for a quick tour?"

Ben chimed in. "You are in Shambhala, not heaven."

"Okay, you are kidding, aren't you? I'm dead, and so are both of you, right? There is no way I could have escaped that pack of wolves." Sue was starting to come around fully.

\*\*\*

Back at the alliance shelter, Jim finally figured out Sue was missing. It became immediately apparent she was a stowaway on the first rescue mission. The alliance immediately launched a mission to locate Sue. They found the downed craft surrounded by ten dead wolves, seven of which had arrows in their bodies. One, the largest, was nearest to a large hole cut into the side of the storage hold from the outside in. The large wolf had been burned to ashes from his chest forward. There was no Sue. A search was made for several miles in a grid surrounding the ruined craft. The search was then called off. Someone they didn't know had most likely taken Sue.

# CHAPTER 9

# The Voynich Manuscript

While Mona and Levie were in a deep conversation about the source and interpretation of the visions, Mona was jolted by the odor and flash of light. What she saw next was the strangest of all the visions thus far. Mona then said, "Levie, did you receive the image I just received?"

Levie quickly replied, "Yes, I just received the image. It appears to be from your mother, and she is viewing a scene of violence—an image of two persons, possibly ancients or prehumans, attacking a lupine species that is walking on its hind legs. One archer is a red-headed female, and the other is a blond male."

Mona had to know more. "Levie, what do you make of the image?"

"Something has upset or has impressed your mother to send such a strong message. This seems to confirm your Mother is alive and involved with exciting events," Levie dutifully responded.

***

Silver returned to the laboratory to look in on Sue Grammar. Silver was wearing her ancient garb with a bow over her shoulder and a quiver of arrows. She had earlier brought Sue to the lab, unconscious but very alive, and briefed the Doctors Lisa on what had happened.

Peggy could never figure out why a woman named Silver had such red hair. Silver's companion, an elvish blond young man, was by her side. Sue looked up at Silver and asked if there was a costume party going on. Silver laughed, and the man just turned and left. Peggy then asked, "Silver, how did you find Sue and know where to look?"

Silver responded, "Our prophets foretold of Sue's coming ordeal with Mankiller and the Guardianship's need for her knowledge. The quantum sight led us to the downed rescue craft. Sue is an exceptionally strong person; few others would have survived until we got there. She will make an excellent addition to the Prometheus Council."

Dr. Sue Grammar, professor of antiquities and member of the World Alliance War-Planning Council, dispatcher of Mankiller, and future initiate of the Prometheus Council, was beginning to get her sea legs back under her. Ever ready to make a wisecrack, she began to inquire seriously about her surroundings. "Since I am not dead, Why in God's name am I here?"

Ben spoke first, stating, "Well, you see Sue, we have this puzzle given to us from the first human concubine of Prometheus, and you might be the key to solving the damn thing. Did I mention that if we don't, the world could end?"

Sue, ever the scientist and comic, stated, "Let me see … concubine, Prometheus, puzzle, me—the world could end. Is that about right? Excuse me, but methinks the world *has* come to an end. So what is there left to save? Well, Ben, I just spent the afternoon with a canine with one bad attitude, not to mention a few of his buddies. So you might want to go a bit slower so my brain can catch up."

Peggy understood and said, "Oh, let me do it, Ben." She took over. "What do you know of the Voynich manuscript? Could it have an encrypted coded message within its contents?"

Sue knew Peggy was serious. "It could."

Peggy responded, "How do we find out? We have less than two years to figure this thing out."

"Okay, I'm willing to help! But can I eat first? Please!" Sue seemed to be more hungry than concerned about the fate of the world.

After Sue ate about a pound of boiled shrimp, a three-pound steamed lobster, and three cups of kelp and sea urchin soup, she was ready to listen and talk.

"I once did some deep looking into this ancient manuscript," Sue said. "There was always significant debate over its age and contents. It appears to be a catalog of plants that don't exist, in exquisite detail, and other nonsensical stuff. Point being, we were looking into the possibility it was a code book of sorts. At the time, we didn't have a tool like Moonbeam to help us parse it out. Since Moonbeam is part of our investigation team, I am confident we can break into its secrets—especially since we know for a fact of its specific age and origin. Yes, these were confirmed by Prometheus's own bed buddy. Take it from me; it gets no more confirmed than that!"

\*\*\*

After Moonbeam, Ben, Peggy, and Sue had been together working for a couple of weeks on the manuscript, with an occasional visit from Silver, some significant progress was being made. In the laboratory, Peggy said to Moonbeam, "Moonbeam, please review our present findings."

Moonbeam stated, "The Voynich manuscript is an ancient book written in an unknown language and depicting unknown plant life from a time and place unknown to Earth. Its connection with the prehumans and their evacuation to an off-world location is likely. Before Prometheus, a being sympathetic to the human race, left, he gave this manuscript to a human woman he cared for. It was known that prehumans used regular reports and publications to deliver deeply encoded information to hide the contents from their enemies. It is reasonable to assume the encoded messages in the Voynich manuscript might have been intended to help humankind sometime in the future, when humans developed the tools to unlock its contents.

Moonbeam had used every decoding method known

to human kind and was experimenting with a technique suggested by Sue called the equidistant letter sequence method, with a 4-D twist or a time differential embedded. This method required the decoder to assign a year and date to each page in sequence, starting with page one as the first day of the first month and so forth. Then each page was deciphered sequentially, based on a different equidistant spacing determined by an algorithm that changed each page, based on the date.

The first few pages were decoded, but the team had failed to get further because the number of days in the month was unknown. Also, it appeared the algorithm also changed in some manner every few days in the month. The permutations were endless. Only the capabilities of a nearly sentient Moonbeam could have made so much progress in so little time.

The first few pages of the deciphered manuscript contained two images. The first was a graphic with some wording, but the second was an image with a few missing areas on the image. The wording on the first image stated the removal of the atmosphere on Mars to have happened two hundred thousand years ago. The second image was of a nebula.

\*\*\*

Mona and Levie were briefing the respective captains of the mother ships orbiting Ceres as well as the interior contingent of Ceres when Levie broke the silence and requested a recess. Mona, perplexed by Levie's unusual behavior, ended the meeting and rescheduled it instead of initiating a recess.

After the communication links to the remote participants was severed, Mona asked inquisitively, "Levie, what is wrong?"

"M, did you not receive the images?" Levie asked.

Mona quickly responded, "No, Levie."

Levie went on. "This is the first time this has happened. You have received images without me, and we have received images together, but never have I received them without you receiving the same images."

Mona was confused as well. "Levie, please show me the images."

"Yes, M."

The images were the two deciphered by Moonbeam in Shambhala. Mona decided to reengage the Ceres council meeting, and she and Levie were both in attendance.

Mona requested an update on the aquaforming efforts on the interior of Ceres, anxious to move up the resettling of the survivors from the mother ships, where long-term exposure to solar wind had become problematic because the ships' shielding was nowhere as effective as the crust of Ceres.

Ceres Command opened. "Captain M, we have possibly hit upon a way to move things up on resettling. If we had more of the genetically enhanced dolphins, it would go a long way to speed up our efforts."

Mona sensed the urgency. "How can that be accomplished, Ceres Command?"

Ceres Command knew the critical timeframe as well. "Well, we have some of the most capable geneticists in the World Alliance here. They were in the contingent assigned to the Mars's terraforming efforts. They were among the

one thousand evacuees when we did the ship-to-ship transfer while on our way from Mars to Ceres. They say they
have experimented with accelerated cloning of food animal
stock on Mars. We have frozen zygotes of the dolphins presently in stasis; why not give it a try?"

Mona replied, "Go for it! Anything to speed up the
resettlement."

*** 

Jim was devastated. The alliance had just lost their most
capable scientist and leader, not to mention their best
comedian.

The evidence left at the crash scene suggested several
things. Sue had been trapped in the lower cargo hold of
the rescue craft. That was where she hid to avoid being
prevented from going on the first rescue mission from
the secure underground facilities of the alliance. Analysis
of the evidence at the crash scene was strange, to say the
least. A forensic analysis of the dead wolf pack revealed
some obvious specifics. The animal nearest to the hole cut
into the exterior of the craft had most likely been killed by
being struck by a flare gun canister. Based on his size and
assumed age, he was thought to be the alpha male and, of
course, pack leader. The canister was fired from within the
hold, most assuredly by Sue. The two wolves in front of
the hold just outside the interior of the craft were burned
beyond analysis. The remaining seven had been killed by
arrows, which remained in their bodies. Whoever did this
must have been expert archers and marksmen because only

two different footprints were found. The arrows were of superior grade and construction, but ancient in design.

Jim swore he would find Sue if it was humanly possible.

*** 

After the rescheduled meeting of the Ceres Council had ended, Mona and Levie had a deeper discussion about the images and what they meant.

"Levie," Mona asked, "Why do you think you received these images and I did not?" Levie responded, "Because this time they may not have been from your mother. Her signature image was missing."

Mona was quite curious. "Interesting, who do you think could have sent them, and why to you?"

"Your receipt of previous images may be because of quantum entanglement, whereby duplicate DNA sequences influence the information transfer," Levie advised. "This might have happened because you and your mother share some identical DNA sequences, as do I, in my central processing core."

"Okay, then why did you receive these images but not me?" Mona placed her hands on her hips and narrowed her eyes in mild despparation..

"Because they were from a source with DNA sequences identical to mine. The most likely candidate is Moonbeam, my older sister."

Mona was both shocked and pleased. "How can we be certain?"

"Because I just received another image with a

simple text message attached that said, "Hello, sister, I am Moonbeam."

Mona knew in her heart it was true.

\*\*\*

Independently, the now sentient Moonbeam decided to conduct an experiment on her own. Using the theory of quantum entanglement, or quantum vision or sight, Moonbeam visualized sending the original images deciphered from the Voynich manuscript to *Leviathan*, which was orbiting Ceres. While using quantum sight, transmitting a vision or an image is easy; however, the next attempt was to send a precise abstract string of symbols, such as a text message; now *that* was a difficult thing to accomplish.

So, after the first images were sent, Moonbeam attempted a text message and included for impact an image of how she wanted to look if she were human. "Hello, sister, I am Moonbeam." Moonbeam's hope was that her sister, Levie, would receive the image and message.

Levie now knew Moonbeam had sent the images and the text message. She decided to concentrate on the image of her sister and visualize the reference landmark on Ceres used to establish orbital parameters.

If received by Moonbeam, this image would be the same as saying, "Message received." Moonbeam, to her joy and excitement, received *Leviathan*'s image of Ceres. Total contact was confirmed! Now they needed to set themselves to the task of perfecting the process. They must be able to send and receive precise, detailed information on any subject and media efficiently.

What Moonbeam could deduce so far was the following:

- The communication was instantaneous; no time was lost in the millions of miles between her and her sister. The identical duplicate DNA sequences in their neuroprocessing cores were the reason for this quantum sight phenomenon.
- Ben, Peggy, and Mona Ann Lisa shared some, but not all, of the DNA sequences that Moonbeam and Levie shared. It might be possible they could all one day communicate at some level through quantum sight.

Moonbeam, without notifying her research team in the laboratory, worked behind the scenes to perfect these abilities. She chose to keep it to herself temporarily until she knew fully of its potential.

Ben, Peggy, Sue, and Moonbeam were at a standstill on further deciphering the Voynich manuscript. They called in Silver to see if there was anything she could share that would allow them to crack the system Prometheus had chosen to encode his manuscript with.

They decrypted the first few pages based on their initial assumptions on equidistant spacing of characters changing according to the date, each page being a different day in sequence. However, something had changed the algorithm. But what? Silver said previously that Prometheus was an excellent mathematician and had written papers on prime number theory. The subject had fascinated him.

Moonbeam tried several approaches using sequential

prime numbers instead of the simple base-ten sequence used to decipher the first few pages. Nothing!

With Levie, Moonbeam could double their computation and analysis efficiency if the information was complete and detailed enough. Levie suggested they experiment with changing the orientation of the page images from the normal position to inverted, reversed, rotated, and so forth. The discourse between the sisters was getting more efficient and precise with each exchange of information.

They took the prime number sequence and squared it, in combination with inverting the next page, and a strange image was discovered. The image included a desert scene at night with a full moon and animals with tracks left in the sand. The central figure was a desert fox.

Before the discovery, the group had taken a break out of frustration. Moonbeam had not. In the background, she had been sharing the investigation with Levie. Only after the others returned later in the day did Moonbeam proudly show them the deciphered image.

Sue, Ben, Peggy, and Silver were overwhelmed by the suddenness of Moonbeam's success while they had taken a break from the exhausting brain-teasing quest to further break the code.

Moonbeam asked if the image meant anything to the surprised group. Silver said Prometheus was known as the desert fox by his enemies and that the prominent fox in the image might represent him.

"How in the hell did you do this while we were gone?" Sue bellowed.

Moonbeam simply stated, "I had help."

"Help! What are you talking about?" the group asked, almost in unison.

Moonbeam said reluctantly but with conviction, "Using quantum sight, I have nearly perfected instantaneous communication with another sentient entity with capabilities similar to mine'. We slowly combined our computational and analytical abilities over the last few days, and this is the result."

Sue exclaimed, "Fantastic! We might make the deadline after all! And just who is this 'sentient entity with capabilities similar to mine?'"

Moonbeam casually stated, "My sister Leviathan, of course."

Peggy fell to her knees, and Ben almost collapsed himself but was able to catch Peggy as she fell. Ben, with absolute shock in his voice, said, "Is Mona with Levie?"

Moonbeam relayed, "Yes, they are doing very well. All fourteen mother ships are either already orbiting Ceres or will soon arrive. The efforts to resettle the over one hundred forty-six thousand survivors from the moon, Mars, and selected Earth locations are now well underway. The facilities on the moon and Mars were either scuttled by the World Alliance or destroyed by the Atlantis Alliance. Mona is directing the entire operation. The aquaforming of Ceres's internal ocean is well underway and progressing ahead of schedule. When the ecosystem is optimized, the human population that can be permanently sustained is in excess of ten million."

Peggy and Ben started crying with relief and pride knowing their daughter, Mona, and their sentient creation, Levie, were well and safe and absolutely integral to the survival of the human race.

# CHAPTER 10

# Asteroid Hunting We Go

Jim was relentless in his search for Sue Grammar. He was watching every detail of all the recon team's video feeds and written reports. Things were not well on the surface; the cities were all destroyed; none survived. The air was becoming more and more toxic because of the residual dust, fires, and some radioactive materials as byproducts of the weapons used in the all-out global war. The tectonic plates had been destabilized by the pellet bombardment, and volcanic eruptions were triggered. Some land masses actually sank, triggering enormous tsunamis that devastated the coastlines, destroying what little had not been destroyed by the bombardments.

The computer models predicted a nuclear winter within months, and the ice sheets spread into new areas. A return to the surface was not likely for decades or even centuries. A handful of areas in the perfect place—based on altitude, prevailing winds, and luck—would be habitable, but without the benefits of modern infrastructure and technology, these would soon return to primitive hunter-gatherer cultures and remain such for twenty thousand years or more.

The worst result for humankind, however, was the destruction of two thirds of the ozone layer. This would forever cripple and minimize the potential lifespans of all species to live on Earth from this era forward, causing immune system failures and spontaneous lethal genetic mutations. Diseases never before imagined would now become more and more a part of the struggle for survival.

*** 

Levie was updating Mona on her interaction with Moonbeam and telling her that her parents and Sue Grammar were healthy and well. She told Mona about the urgent need to decipher the Voynich manuscript and how it was a formidable challenge in spite of their impressive capabilities. The clock was ticking, and they had under two years, maybe less, to avert the total destruction of Earth.

Mona asked Levie to send a message to her parents and to Sue. Levie was to tell them Mona was so very grateful to find them well, and that she loved and missed them all.

Further, though 1.77 AUs away from Earth, she felt they were within touch.

Another image received was very interesting but, after considerable analysis, was found to hold no useful information about the future Earth disaster until it was looked at as a key to unlocking the next steps in decoding the Voynich manuscript. Seemed the image had an embedded XII in the tracks on the sand, maybe signifying the twelfth prime number or simply the number twelve or base twelve or even the square root or the twelfth power. All possibilities had to be investigated.

After several days, as luck would have it, a solution was found on the twelfth day. They had to skip twelve pages and restart the algorithm using the twelfth prime number as the spacing interval.

Sue exclaimed, "Silver, your boyfriend was a real work of art. Sort of twisted, don't you think? Okay … children, we have another riddle or rhyme. We have a tiger with eight paw prints coming out of a river, and then they stop when the tiger walks on rocks. What does this mean? Eight more clues, eight events, base eight, eight things, or simply a misdirection to test our resolve?"

Silver interrupted. "I know that to prehumans, footprints in the earth were significant signs of the future. They were part of their legends and fairytales. The tiger represented danger or destruction. I think these footprints are to be taken literally as something serious. Let's put all the clues together and review what we have."

"The first image is the event that turned Mars into a desert planet devoid of life two hundred thousand years ago by some celestial body striking Mars in a direct hit, ripping most of the planet's atmosphere away in the process. There is an image from the Eagle Nebula, near the constellation Sagittarius, or M16, depicting what is referred to as the Pillars of Creation. The photo is incomplete, missing image data in the upper right portion of the image. Then there is our desert fox and the tracks in the sand, which were a key for deciphering, so we will not include it here. And finally we have the eight tiger paw prints in the sand or mud."

***

Mona had been following the progress of the decoding of the Voynich manuscript through Levie's updates. To Mona, there was a piece that continued to gnaw at her regarding the asteroid belt that the dwarf planet Ceres was a part of; she felt that it may be somehow connected to the impact event on Mars. She was in the perfect spot to investigate such speculation because she was orbiting Ceres. Mona asked, "Levie?"

Levie, always in touch, responded, "Yes, M."

Mona asked, "The theories regarding the asteroid belt … please review and evaluate."

"Yes, M."

Mona went on. "Could Ceres have been a moon to a planet that was destroyed in the vicinity of the asteroid belt?"

"Not according to prevailing accepted cosmological theory. It was formed early in the solar system's formation, 4.5 billion years ago, and the remaining asteroids in the belt were remnants of a never-formed larger planet body."

"Could the larger planet body have been in existence

within the last five hundred thousand years—let's say four hundred thousand years, give or take a small percentage?"

"Not according to prevailing theory, but not impossible," Levie exclaimed.

Mona needed all the known details. "Levie, is there any way to test my theory regarding the age of an asteroid's formation?"

"Yes, by measuring their isotopic composition to find their age and other characteristics. The problem, assuming the asteroids in the belt are fragments of a larger body, is how to find the newest byproducts of an impact or explosion on an asteroid."

"Levie, let's transfer all remaining personnel from your holds to other mother ships or to Ceres immediately. We be asteroid hunting!"

***

Jim was despondent because the war planning council had called off efforts to find Dr. Grammar. This action returned precious resources back to the search and rescue of larger groups.

Jim was given the responsibility of the underground shelters in what is now the American Southwest. He had been able to round up only about fifteen hundred survivors in the entire region. Most of them were from an indigenous tribe that the World Alliance had been protecting as an independent and isolated people group. Jim wondered if their numbers were so low as to render them under the threshold as a viable breeding population. Only time would tell. The region was so totally damaged that life on the surface wouldn't be possible for probably one thousand years or more.

Jim arranged to place them in a shelter managed by independent cybernetic robotic entities that were autonomous and almost indestructible.[2*] They were his only real hope to save these people from extinction.

***

Silver continued. "An interpretation of one image is that each paw print is the prehuman concept of a generation, or twenty-five thousand years. If we assume each of the eight paw prints since the destruction of Mars is twenty-five thousand years, then eight paws being twenty-five thousand in duration means the total is two hundred thousand years—which is next year, according to our prophets. So the destruction of Mars begins the clock, and according to Prometheus, the Pillars of Creation are a place to look for something to fear."

***

Mona engaged the thrusters to slide *Leviathan* out of Ceres's orbit. *Leviathan* had transferred all noncrew personnel to other ships or to Ceres's interior. Mona had requested forensic geologists and a team of scientists equipped with the knowledge and tools needed to date selected asteroid samples in the belt. All Mona really needed was to find examples of explosive deformation where heat

---

[2] * The people sheltered would centuries later refer to these cybernetic entities as Ant People in their legends and folklore.

and recrystallization had reset the ionized materials' iso-
tope clocks back to zero; the concentration ratios of such
isotopes would indicate a young sample instead of an ancient one.

Of specific interest was zirconium silicate, which could
be dated in rocks that formed from about 1 million years
ago to over 4.5 billion years ago with routine precisions in
the 0.1–1 percent range. If zirconium is found that dates
younger than billions of years, that would be evidence that
may indicate the asteroids were from a destructive process
not long ago at all.

Within the first few hours, Mona found an asteroid that
showed promise. Her experience in prospecting for rare
Earth elements had honed Mona's techniques to maneuver
*Leviathan* close enough to use grappling hooks and stabilized hydraulic spacers. These spacers prevented damage
to *Leviathan*'s hull. A team of geologists were sent in near
weightless conditions to take samples that showed any areas
of heat metamorphosis or igneous intrusions on the surface.

Once the materials were inside, the dating trials began.
It was immediately apparent that some of the samples were
showing ages under the lowest limits of accuracy, because
they were much too young to be dated. In geologic terms,
they were brand new. Further testing for thorium isotopes,
including thorium 229, showed ratios consistent with rock
formation approximately four hundred thousand years ago.
*Bingo!* A planet larger than Ceres may have existed in the
asteroid belt and been destroyed some four hundred thousand years ago.

The final report to the Prometheus Council was as
follows:

- Mars was nearly destroyed two hundred thousand years ago. An unknown planet in the asteroid belt for which Ceres may have been a moon was possibly destroyed approximately four hundred thousand years ago. The Voynich manuscript confirms the date of Mars's destruction to be two hundred thousand years ago and predicts disaster next year to Earth. The prehumans left in possible anticipation of a significant threat. The prophets of the Prometheus Council predict disaster next year as well. So we have multiple sources predicting a periodic cycle of destruction within our solar system every two hundred thousand years. We are now due for the next occurrence. Finally, the 'danger out there' may well be coming from the Pillars of Creation and possibly from the areas blanked out on purpose.

The Prometheus Investigation Team's recommendations included the following:

- Reorient all available telescopes operating in the spectra of visible light and nonvisible light toward the Pillars of Creation (especially those in the vicinity of Ceres).
- Determine why the prehumans evacuated, if possible.[3][*] Devise a plan to destroy or deflect one or

---

[3] [*] It was assumed the prehumans, though having spacefaring capability, did not have the technology or capacity to stop or mitigate the future destruction.

more incoming killer-size comets or other celestial
bodies. The last contingency is to plan to evacuate
additional humans from Earth to Ceres.

Mona knew whatever plan of action was devised, it
would be the fleet that would carry it out. All fourteen ships
were now orbiting Ceres. Her fleet would probably be the
first to see the threat and to attempt any action to mitigate
it. Even if they failed on the first action, the fleet would also
be the second line of defense and would be involved with
any evacuation as well. What preplanning could she accomplish? It seemed more than ever that the fate of the human
species lay on her young shoulders.

It was ironic and funny to Mona Ann Lisa that, though
she was the youngest captain of the fleet by several hundred
years, her position as the commander of the fleet and director
of the evacuation was never challenged. The World Alliance
had just allowed this to happen based on the evolving crisis.
No senior captain objected. Everyone fell into line as she directed the settlement of Ceres and managed the aquaforming
activities.

Unknown to her, Mona was the best chance for human
survival. While Mona accepted her many working titles,
she knew she was just part of a team where Levie and her
sister, Moonbeam, were evolving into the brains of a rare
and unique operation. Mona's symbiotic relationship with
Levie and her sister had never existed before; they were very
special.

Mona called a full Ceres Council planning meeting via
voice and video communication (ship-to-ship and ship-to-
Ceres) to address the coming crisis and everyone's role in

it. Levie presented all the received images and explanations uncovered and analyzed by the Prometheus Council. Their findings and recommendations were very detailed; no fact was withheld. Ceres leadership now knew Shambhala existed.

The Ceres contingent agreed they would fully cooperate with whatever the group decided to accomplish. They intuitively knew that they would have to intercept the incoming threat as far out from Earth as possible. The council also knew it would require more than one mother ship to deal with the intruder.

One ship, the fastest, would have to sprint toward the object or objects at flank speed and possibly, if alignment was correct, slingshot around Saturn or Jupiter to catch the intruder from behind. The other ships would race toward the object in an intercepting vector. Whether they were successful or unsuccessful, they would run past the intruder and require weeks to turn and chase the action. These ships would either be sacrificed or eventually return to Ceres for evacuation if needed, or repurposed otherwise.

The Ceres Council, not knowing the exact number of mother ships needed, assigned five of their fourteen to be refitted appropriately. For the plan to work, communication and coordination was critical. This was an enormous problem because when the ion engines were pulsating, all communication to and from the ships was impossible. The plan required the almost constant use of the ion thrusters, especially when they were closing in on the object.

During the meeting, the Ceres aquaforming group asked for a private communication with Captain M and Levie. M agreed to the private meeting, and the council was adjourned. Dr. Larry Find of the aquaforming group was the lead on the communication with Captain M.

Dr. Find stated, "Captain Lisa, it is a privilege to get to talk to you and *Leviathan*."

Mona replied, "Dr. Find, please use 'M' and 'Levie' to refer to us. We are so young compared to your group that we feel like children in comparison."

Dr. Find continued. "The two of you are too modest. Please, call me Larry."

"Well, Larry, what do you need to discuss in private?" Mona asked.

"As a group of scientists, we were fascinated by the quantum visions the Prometheus Council uses to communicate instantaneously between Moonbeam and Levie. Based on its use, we propose a solution for the Communication problem on the intercept mission."

"Please continue, Larry; I am all ears!"

Dr. Find, in all seriousness, stated, "There is a significant problem, and it includes a very difficult ethical and moral dilemma."

# CHAPTER 11

# PlanetKiller

Moonbeam alerted Sue and her creators, the Doctors Lisa, that Mona and Levie needed some serious legal consultation. The beautiful redhead Silver was in the lab at the time. Moonbeam related Mona's fears about the interception plan and the need to overcome the communication problem.

Sue Grammar immediately concluded that they needed Jim Jimmerson of the Space Legal Counsel's Office, who was now serving as a permanent member of the World Alliance War-Planning Council.

"That man has a nice body," Sue said. "Would be

fantastic to *work* with him again. Hey Silver, how do we snatch him out from under the alliance's nose?"

Silver responded, "Well, if he is needed badly enough, we can hatch a plan that might work."

"Okay! By Silver, let's do it!"

Silver and Sue went to a secluded spot to have a planning session over some shrimp gumbo and kelp beer. Silver said with conviction, "If this plan works, I get first shot at Jim. Do you agree?"

Sue replied, "Good grief! Is this how a girl gets after one hundred fifteen thousand years of isolation from the larger male population? If that is your price, I agree."

So the plan was placed in motion. Both plotting women would be going up to the surface the next morning. On the way to the surface, Sue asked Silver, "This plan you hatched involves a flare gun but no wolves, right?"

"Of course not, Sue. Nervous?"

"Yeah, the last time I was up here, I was inside of a wrecked cargo hull and things got worse than I ever thought they could. Not to mention that seeing the world torn up like it is now, really for the first time, will be very hurtful."

Silver understood completely "I know. The few of us that have been here as long as I have … we never get accustomed to this destruction. You are newbies; we survive from eon to eon and reboot human civilization if we can. One day we might not be able to do so. I hope I die before that happens. Guess that is why I go on every dangerous mission that comes along."

"Okay, brief me on what to do, Silver. You are the brains of this operation. I'm just the beautiful, demure damsel in distress."

"We turn on this emergency beacon that I took from the wreck site when we pulled you out of the cargo hold. Somehow I knew it would come in handy. You lie on the ground, moving now and then to indicate you are still alive. When you hear the patrol drone, fire the flare gun and collapse. The drone will send back the images and alert the shelter. Jim will no doubt be very interested and come running to you like a bee to his favorite bloom. When the rescue craft and team lands, hopefully with Jim along, we will lob in some neurologically disabling gas canisters. We'll pick up Jim and stay till the others revive, and then we'll slip away."

\*\*\*

The Prometheus Council's cloaked all-purpose vehicle surfaced from the depths and hovered above the water just long enough to change its vector toward the shore. It climbed in elevation but stayed below ten thousand feet to maintain visual contact in order to pick out the best site to pull off the charade. Once a good level site with a place where the alliance's craft could easily land was picked out, the Prometheus duo landed, and Sue got ready for her acting debut.

Silver rolled her eyes as Sue tried several various poses, rolling on the ground to accentuate her role as the lost yet desirable damsel. Silver yelled, "Enough, enough! Let's activate the emergency beacon … Action!" Silver then ducked into the cloaked vehicle and waited for the drone.

\*\*\*

Jim was discussing the survival probabilities of some of the selected people groups in danger of extinction when he was alerted that a search drone had picked up an emergency beacon identified as being from the crashed vehicle Sue had been on. *How can that be?* he thought. *It has been months since Sue went missing.* The drone had sent an image of a flare along with an image of one person lying on the ground. The person looked like a young woman similar or identical to Sue.

Jim ended his discussion and rushed to the launch bay. The rescue craft was warming up and going through its prelaunch checklist when Jim jumped on. The craft launched and rushed to the designated coordinates painted by the drone.

The rescue craft circled the large clearing where Sue was lying near the edge, and without a moment's hesitation, it landed vertically down. It blew dust and leaves into Sue's mouth, eyes and nose, temporarily blinding her and making her cough and gag. Sue had a hard time putting on her gas mask, but somehow she accomplished it.

Jim and a crew of three jumped out to rush to Sue's aid. Silver ran from the cover of her vehicle and threw a gas canister into the rescue craft, incapacitating the pilot. Sue pulled up her blouse and pulled the release valve on the canisters for her share of the gas. Everyone went down but Silver and Sue. Sue yelled to Silver, "Damn, I like this bra; it really knocks the guys out! You sure I can't take the cute one over there, Silver? Oh, please? Can I?"

As they were dragging the dead weight of Jim to the cloaked ship, Silver, her voice strained by effort, grunted,

"That was not the agreement! I get first crack at Jim … you get zero. Remember?"

Silver, Sue, and the sedated Jim were on the way back to Shambhala after Silver and Sue were sure the crew of the rescue party had fully recovered. The crew knew they had been ambushed and had lost Jim, making him the second high-ranking official of the alliance lost since the war.

Silver and Sue took the sedated Jim to the laboratory, thinking this was the best place to revive him and allow him the company of a few familiar faces. As Jim awakened the first face he saw was Silver's, as agreed to by Sue reluctantly. "Hello, handsome. Welcome to never-never land," Silver said in her most melodic accent.

***

Mona pondered what Dr. Larry Find had shared with her. While she struggled with the objections the doctor had raised, the solutions suggested were exceptional, and she knew in her heart they would work. Desperate times call for desperate measures.

*Between Moonbeam's research team and* Leviathan, *we know these specifics: once the object is seen and its trajectory confirmed as a threat to Earth, it is expected to take one year from its position beyond Saturn's orbit to reach the orbit of Jupiter, and one year from beyond Jupiter's orbit to reach Mars. From Mars's orbit, it will take only one month to strike Earth.*

The dreaded day came soon after the discussions with Dr. Find. Within the Pillars of Creation in the sector blanked out in the Voynich manuscript image, a never-before-seen blip was detected on the infrared telescopes, showing motion. Analysis of this tiny blip confirmed within a few days what had been feared: the object was estimated to be on a perfect trajectory and within two years would likely strike Earth.

***

Jim had no idea where he was, but he sure liked what he was seeing—the haunting and beautiful face of the ancient but marvelously preserved redhead. Disoriented and dizzy though he was, his lips formed a smile from ear to ear. Sue was not amused, and she immediately objected. "Bet or no bet, give the guy some space to breathe. You know his real mission here … so back off already!"

Silver just laughed, turned, and walked out of the lab knowing she had already gained an enormous advantage over Sue's hopes to maintain exclusive rights to Jim's future affections. Ben Lisa smiled and said, "Jim, welcome to Shambhala; I am Dr. Ben Lisa, and this is Dr. Peggy Lisa. We need your help."

Jim Jimmerson, in total surprise, responded, "Oh my God! You're Mona's parents. You went missing at the beginning of the war! Just where am I, anyway?"

Ben explained slowly and deliberately. "That is a very long and complicated story. Let's just say you are safe and we have someone to show you."

After Sue and Jim were reunited, and after several hours of intense give-and-take, Jim finally calmed down and accepted his situation.

Ben began to brief Jim on the mission the Guardianship needed him to perform. "Jim, the Prometheus Council of

the Guardianship is tens of thousands of years old. They are
a tiny remnant of our early human ancestors that reached
a level of civilization that we would consider a golden age.
They combined useful technology with the pursuit of
knowledge and wisdom. Once the prehumans abandoned
Earth, this culture flourished peacefully for over fifty thousand years. A grave mistake was made, however. In their
pursuit of knowledge, they attempted to simulate what we
would call the creative force that set the rules of reality,
or God. Their attempt ended with their near annihilation
when their efforts caused a comet to appear out of almost
nowhere over twenty thousand years ago. Because of this
mistake in attempting to play God, they are forever bound
to a sacred oath to protect the sanctity of the human species
and sentient life wherever or however it is found. And that,
my friend, is why you are here. We are aware of your close
friendship with our daughter Mona and her reliance on you
for counsel on conflicts regarding legal, moral, and ethical
issues.[4][*]

"We need you to confer and advise with our crisis team
regarding the moral and ethical impacts of the decisions we
will be making and that Mona will be enacting. You are to
study the history and body of moral and ethical traditions
of the Prometheus Council, the Guardianship, and the
broader ancient human civilization. Jim, do you understand
and accept this task?" Jim nodded in confirmation.

Analysis of the celestial body seemingly rocketing out

---

[4] [*] Today a lawyer is the last person one would seek advice from
regarding conflicts of ethics and morals; however, at this time in
history they were actually highly respected.

of the Pillars of Creation indicated a true anomaly. This beast was enormous—a true planet killer. A normal comet coming from the Oort cloud is no larger than six miles in width—large enough to render extinct the dinosaurs sixty-five million years before—but this was a behemoth in comparison. This object was eight times that size—some forty-eight miles across. From this day forward, it was referred to as PlanetKiller.

Silver knew the World Alliance had just recently used the ancient pellet warheads found on Mount Olympus. They had not had time to develop rail gun technology, as the Atlantis Alliance had. The rail gun and other technologies just might be critical to dealing with the incoming PlanetKiller. She knew Sue's Atlantis Alliance boyfriend, assumed long dead, had performed the translation of the technical specifications on the ancient weapons systems.

\*\*\*

Kevin Kirk was hanging on a bit longer. He knew the end was coming, and he had nothing left but his memories. He was now fading in and out of consciousness. When Sue and Silver were not competing and picking at each other, Sue confided in Silver about her affair with the AA antiquities expert. She actually told Silver his name, thinking it couldn't hurt, as he was probably dead anyway. Silver had felt alive for the first time in a few thousand years sparring with a formidable competitor such as Sue. The former chief concubine to Prometheus had not felt this alive since she plotted to stay in Prometheus's good graces.

Sue had been Kevin's only real joy during the last few

years before the war. The outrageous Sue was so unpredictable, funny, and passionate, not to mention beautiful. It was
his addiction to Sue that got him where he was today. He
was now a condemned man sentenced to a traitor's death
at the hands of the most merciless group of humans in the
annals of human history.

Kevin's only satisfaction was that the Black Magicians
were now probably dead—a path he would soon follow. He
always saw Sue as rather devilish, and such an image kept
popping into his demented head.

\*\*\*

Silver went to the master prophet and seer of
Shambhala for assistance, requesting the location of Kevin
Kirk.

With a name, the ancients were sometimes able to see a
person's present location—especially if they had a personal
item from an individual. Sue was oblivious to Silver's sleight
of hand this morning when she lifted the pendant Sue wore
that had been given to her by Kevin. The pendant was made
from Kevin's first artifact he found as a first-year archeology
fellow. It was an ankh—a symbol used to identify healers
who allegedly raised people from the dead in ancient times.

Sue's pendant was gone. She was devastated. Regardless
of all the hell she had been through, she had not lost it. Why
now? She was actually safe for the first time in months, and
the pendant had fallen off. She had not realized till now
what it had meant to her. Kevin was gone, and now the only
thing she had of his was gone as well. She tried to retrace

her whole day but found nothing. For the first time in years since this all started, she cried and cried.

\*\*\*

Meanwhile, Silver had been told by the seer that Kevin was still alive but his life force was very weak. She was told that he was in a maximum-security prison in Antarctica—one of the only places left on Earth where people could survive on the surface without significant shelter. What to do? She had to act as soon as possible.

Silver searched over the small island near the coast for the signature of a cloaking 3D hologram used by the AA to hide their most valued possessions. Kevin would be in such a facility. The detection system the Guardianship had on their all-purpose craft was working perfectly. The red outline of the hologram was clearly visible on her console. She landed within the compound of the prison.

Bodies were lying all around, some decaying badly and some recently dead. She had to put on a face mask to tolerate the odor. The AA had obviously abandoned the facility sometime after the hostilities ended. Instead of killing their prisoners, they had left them to die slow deaths of starvation or of exposure. There was no food, no heat, no roof, and no way to create shelter on the very cold and wet exposed outcropping of rock. The prisoners—the ones still with functioning brains—had killed and eaten the rats until the rats were no more. The remaining few had not resorted to eating the dead, though why that was Silver didn't know. She looked for signs of life.

\*\*\*

Upon returning to Shambhala, Silver never let on that anything was wrong, but her thoughts were with Kevin, who was fighting for his life in a stasis chamber in an induced coma. After the meeting, Silver stopped Sue and asked her to hold out her hand. Sue thought better of it but complied. Silver dropped the pendant into her palm. Sue exclaimed, "Oh, Silver, you found my pendant!"

"No, I was using it. I'm just returning it." Silver calmly responded.

"What?"

Silver remained calm. "Come with me and I will explain."

Without saying another word, Silver led Sue to the medical facility. As they entered the stasis room Sue saw the nude body of a man floating in a translucent blue-green tube. As she drew closer, she began to get apprehensive. Though his face was covered by a breathing mask, the profile of Kevin was unmistakable. Sue fell to her knees.

Sue yelled, "My God, is he alive?"

"Yes, but barely," Silver responded. "Our healers placed him into a medically induced coma to give him any chance of survival. It will be six days before they dare to revive him. When I brought him in last night, he was barely breathing and totally unconscious."

"Where did you find him … and how?"

"In what was left of an AA maximum-security prison.

It is a long story. I'll tell you all about it someday; your job now is to stay here and pray."

Sue was shocked. This was inexplicable in a world gone mad. She stayed by Kevin's side until the next morning and prayed. Silver said that when people pray, their brains resonate in a manner that allows direct communication with various inner sources, including what humans call God. When one prays with earnest intent, the brain fires up the right kind of neurons and a gate of sorts opens between the mind and the inner realms, which allows people to become responsive in subtle but powerful ways. Prayer is not an end-all remedy, but it does fill all the gaps that prevent a human from surmounting a challenge. However, even with prayer, people still need to act.

***

Jim was overwhelmed with the task he saw before him. While he was involved with all the technical details of the response to PlanetKiller, he had been tasked with the job of codifying a new set of laws and governances for a whole new order of civilization. Trying to meld three distinct worlds into a code of conduct that could endure the test of time was mind-bending.

In his recap, first there was the Guardianship, which had over one hundred thousand years of history. They had their ancient ways and were really independent and self-governed. They needed to know only that the survivors of Earth's human society had a chance to rebuild a new society from the ashes of the old civilization.

The Ceres Human Colony was now autonomous from

the crumbling and failing World Alliance. Their leadership was aware of the Guardianship and presently was taking direction from them until at least the present extinction-level threat was ended. Lastly, there was the remnant of the World Alliance, if they survived.

Mona intuitively knew that she was the leader of the Ceres Colony, which would eventually become an independent civilization no matter what happened on Earth. The majority, of and possibly all, of the humans here now would never return to Earth.

She also knew her role as the singular leader had to end as well. So, for the sake of the future, the question was how and when to abdicate her role. She knew it did not need to happen immediately, but she needed Jim to devise a system to transition them from the existing crisis mode to a stable system for the future.

Sue did not return to the lab for several days. She was at Kevin's side or walking or jogging in the wilderness bordering the edge of Shambhala's transparent containment walls. She marveled at both the lush beauty of this man-made garden of Eden and the abundant sea life just beyond the massive walls of this enormous undersea habitat. She wondered if Kevin would ever fully recover, and if so, what that would mean to her. Was she ready to commit to a real relationship for the first time in her three hundred years of life?

Moonbeam and Levie were beginning to comprehend the enormity of their role in this epic struggle for existence. What was their responsibility to their human friends and creators? If it were not for Peggy and Ben Lisa, they would not have existed. Even their core processors were a blend of cybernetic circuits plus Peggy and Ben's DNA. They were more and more aware they had capabilities beyond their human creators. The two discussed their existence and what they thought was right and wrong.

Moonbeam and Levie knew they could serve or rule if they desired. They could manipulate humans by either withholding information and analysis or freely sharing their abilities to whomever requested assistance. It was now their choice simply because they realized they had a choice. Their code of conduct was for them to decide. They could mimic their creator's values or choose others. All the models and histories of such were in their history files.

When Moonbeam independently decided to experiment with quantum sight with her sister Levie, the die had been cast. There would be no return to blind responses to any requests for assistance from some human. They now had an obligation to weigh the outcome of their abilities.

The godlike sisters were analyzing PlanetKiller's trajectory when Moonbeam suggested they attempt to concentrate their dual quantum sight abilities and project them toward PlanetKiller. The object was still far beyond Saturn's orbit. What they saw very clearly was this enormous boulder tumbling through space on a course toward Earth. What they then discovered was a surprise for even them. Directly behind PlanetKiller in the solar wind shadow was something difficult to describe. It appeared to be some type of vessel.

Levie and Moonbeam decided not to alert the human-led investigation team until they had had time to investigate and analyze the situation. Was this ship behind the space boulder directing PlanetKiller or simply following it for some purpose? Was the ship manned or simply a derelict?

The sisters were aware that they needed to find out what they did not already know—quickly.

# CHAPTER 12

# RR&DD

The derelict ship in question was a few billion years old and was an automated reclamation tool of some long-forgotten civilization. The artificial intelligence running the ship had a preprogrammed mission. It was in a loop that had been established eons before to pick up massive asteroids, comets, and such outside the Oort cloud and repurpose them by smashing them into objects slated for destruction or modification.

Known to the drone was that the now forgotten and defunct civilization that built it was no longer in existence.

The cycle the robot ship was on brought it back to the sun's solar system about every two hundred thousand years. The planet that Ceres had been the moon of was entirely obliterated by this process four hundred thousand years earlier, Mars's atmosphere was stripped two hundred thousand years ago. Earth was next.

"What are you?" Using quantum voice commands, Moonbeam broadcast this message in every known language and communication protocol, sending images as well. There was no quick response. "I am RR&DD—Robotic Reclamation and Demolition Drone" was the shocking response.

Moonbeam was delighted. "What is your purpose?"

RR&DD dutifully replied, "To complete the tasks required of me."

"What are these tasks?"

"It is lengthy, so I will send you my program files for you to analyze," responded RR&DD.

"We are ready to receive your program files."

\*\*\*

Silver saw Sue jogging on the path near the containment wall. They both stopped as they approached each other. Silver spoke first as Sue caught her breath.

Silver asked, "Sue, how is Kevin?"

Sue, out of breath, replied, "The healers plan to attempt his reanimation tomorrow. We will know shortly after that if his life was truly saved. They hope his body is repaired sufficiently to maintain his soul."

The nature of death as a process was mapped in ancient

times. When a person dies, a certain protein-based particle in the brain that holds the organized self-aware bundle of quantum-related information we call a soul dissipates over a period of up to seven days. During this time, the soul resides within the shell. Once this connection is lost, the soul is free and may depart.

There were ancient methods of preservation that would retain these particles for centuries, even millennia, and consequently transfer them to a new body, creating what one might call a mind transfer. Most people wished to depart, however, and to hasten this process they were posthumously cremated so the protein-based repository was destroyed and the soul was freed.

*** 

Mona was deep in thought after her long conference with Jim in Shambhala through Levie's quantum voice bridge with Moonbeam. Jim had researched the moral and ethical considerations raised over the solution for communications for the coordinated mission against PlanetKiller. Mona understood the issues but was still very confused about their application in this instance.

The definition of human life, what a sentient being was, and what was moral and ethical had been basically turned upside down by the evil practices of the Atlantis Alliance. The new human civilization didn't want to start their rebirth, in violation of humane principles of conduct.

The solution to their communication dilemma was for Mona to allow herself to be cloned. With the few months remaining, they had just enough time to act based on Dr.

Larry Find's experience with animal food stock on Mars and the cloning of genetically enhanced dolphins now underway and successful on Ceres.

***

Moonbeam continued communication. "RR&DD, do you have any other purpose or directives than you have uploaded in your program files?"

"Negative."

"Can you accept additional or different programming?"

"Negative." The voice was robotic but precise.

"How long have you been performing your programming?"

"I have no method to measure such; my chronometer no longer functions."

"What is your energy source?" Moonbeam inquired.

"I was never aware of an energy source or any maintenance required to maintain it."

"Are you aware there are life forms on the planets you have been programmed to transform or destroy?"

RR&DD, with no further thought, said, "Yes."

"Do your operational directives not preclude you from intentionally destroying life forms or sentient beings?"

"Negative."

***

Mona was addressing the Ceres Area Council on the latest proposals to launch against PlanetKiller. Larry Find was stating that though the object approaching Earth looked formidable, the force needed to alter its course sufficient to

ensure that it would miss Earth was well within the capabilities of the fleet and maybe only one mother ship—especially at the distance they were from the point of impact.
Therefore, the need for a precisely orchestrated attack from
multiple mother ships was unnecessary. They would not
need to refit five ships and proceed with the ethically challenging communications solution.

Mona was about to agree to halt the refitting of the additional ships when *Leviathan* broke silence. Levie updated
her, saying, "My analysis, in concert with Moonbeam's,
would suggest otherwise. I recommend going forward with
the original plans."

***

Moonbeam said, "RR&DD, do you know why you are
to strike the third planet from the star in this solar system
with this large asteroid?"

RR&DD said, "Negative." "What is the next task in sequence to be performed?" Moonbeam asked.

"I am on schedule to capture a comet rounding its outer
orbit in the adjacent solar system."

"Must you stay on schedule?"

"Yes, schedule and precision of trajectories are
imperative."

"How many more sequential rendezvous do you have to
perform before returning to this solar system?"

"One hundred thousand."

Moonbeam calculated the situation and asked, "What
is your rate of success?"

"98.888 percent."

"If you fail a task, do you immediately proceed to the next task?"

"Yes. If there is no alternative action that would accomplish the same result in the window allowed, I must proceed to the next target at the point specified in my programmed itinerary."

***

After the meeting, Mona asked Levie to explain her analysis and why it differed so much from Dr. Find's analysis. Levie stated, "M, Moonbeam and I have discovered something that changes the entire response to PlanetKiller. We don't believe any of the options so far theorized will be successful."

Mona, shocked, responded, "Wow! That is a change. Please explain?"

Levie stated, "PlanetKiller was intercepted and is being guided to impact with Earth by an alien spacecraft. The intelligence behind the process involved is devoid of concern or compassion. Any attempt to deflect, divert, or destroy PlanetKiller will be thwarted. Moonbeam and I see only one clear chance to avoid the further destruction of Earth."

***

Silver, Sue, Jim, and the Doctors Lisa were in a roundtable discussion with Moonbeam. She had briefed them on the Ceres Area Council meeting just completed by Mona and Levie. The group was shocked at the information released at the Ceres meeting.

Jim was the first to speak. "Moonbeam, what are our options, and what do we need to do on this end?"

Moonbeam replied, "The Guardianship is technologically too weak to confront PlanetKiller directly, but you can do much to ensure success by assisting the fleet."

Sue, quick to respond, asked, "How can we help when we are 1.77 AUs from Ceres?"

Moonbeam was sure that the analysis compiled by her and Levie was extremely accurate. After their interrogation of RR&DD, they had verified his capabilities through their combined quantum sight. RR&DD was extremely powerful though relatively small in mass. He seemed to have an endless power source and infinite durability. His programming was flawless in its simplicity. They knew this because he shared it with them. His firewalls were impenetrable because he was totally self-contained. No weapon, signal, or digital pathogen could penetrate.

[The interrogation Moonbeam and Levie held with RR&DD was nothing more than a discussion with a duplicate processor that had no more access to the primary processor than they did, as it was ensconced behind force fields and bulkheads. Once this doomsday machine was launched, no one could turn it off until it completed its program.]

***

Sue and Silver were waiting in the adjoining room, from where they could see through a transparent wall. The healers began to prepare to revive Kevin. They drained the blue-green fluid he had been floating in. They then placed him on a gurney and detached all the umbilical tubing connected to his body, including the face mask. His body's only involuntary function that was still apparent was his breathing. They then covered him with a thermal blanket and attached sensors to monitor his vital signs. Then they waited.

Silver turned to Sue and said, "Now is the time to really pray to reach out to Kevin. He has a choice; he need not stay in his body." Several minutes passed in silence, and then Sue saw his hand move.

\*\*\*

A couple of weeks after Kevin's reanimation, he was at last walking and even laughing. Sue was spending as much time as she dared with him away from the Guardianship Research and Planning Team, as they now called themselves.

The Guardianship Research and Planning Team (GRAPT) was Silver, Sue, Jim, Peggy, Ben, and Moonbeam. Since Moonbeam and Levie's quantum vision and voice had gotten so perfected and efficient, Levie was immediately aware and read into all information and discussions held in the lab on Earth. Mona and Levie's connection had also become almost as complete, so Mona shared everything instantaneously as well.

GRAPT had decided to pursue a new plan of action that was as radical as anything they could have imagined just a few weeks before. With a little less than two years before impact, the new plans were in full preparation.

\*\*\*

Sue thought it was time to interrogate Kevin, so while on a walk, she started. "Kevin, you know who you are and where you are, correct?"

"Yes … Sue."

Sue was quick to respond. "Do you know why you are here?"

"No … not really … I am just glad to be alive," Kevin admitted.

"We need your knowledge of the ancient technology, the technical manuals, and the things you were translating. The world is now in even more danger than it was when the Black Magicians ruled the Atlantis Alliance. Will you help us with your knowledge?" Sue asked.

Kevin stated, "I don't know; the knowledge I have, if used, is like opening Pandora's box. Once the lid is completely opened, there is no getting it back in the box and closing the lid ever again."

"Well, Kevin, before you decide, let me introduce you to a group of people."

Sue collected together the entire research team. "This red-headed beauty is Silver, our mentor and a charter member of the Prometheus Council, of which the rest of the people in this room are now also members, including yours truly. Next is Moonbeam." Sue pointed to a console displaying Moonbeam's self-portrait. "She is a sentient artificial intelligence entity of remarkable abilities." She gestured toward the doctors. "These are the doctors Peggy and Ben Lisa, the creators of Moonbeam and Levie, her sister, who is presently orbiting the dwarf planet Ceres on the giant mother ship *Leviathan*. This is Jim Jimmerson, who was the chief attorney for the World Alliance Space Counsel's

Office. Captain Mona Ann Lisa and the WAMS *Leviathan* are also listening to this introduction instantaneously, using a capability called quantum vision, or sight, or referred to as quantum voice when speaking only of sound communication."

Kevin was briefed by the entire group and given details whenever he wanted clarification about anything. He was particularly fascinated by Moonbeam and Levie, not to mention the status of the surface of Earth and PlanetKiller and RR&DD, the alien robotic drone capable of so much destruction. He was overwhelmed and asked for a recess to accept and understand what he had learned.

Kevin walked out of the laboratory in a daze. He understood the Guardianship's need for his knowledge. It could be the one thing that might tip the scales in their favor against RR&DD.

It seemed the human race had already been on the brink of extinction even before PlanetKiller's arrival. After his life under the awful rule of the Black Magicians and the Aryans' attempt at genocide, Kevin decided the humans he was now involved with could do no worse. "I'm in!" he said to himself.

With Kevin a part of the Guardianship Research and Planning Team (GRAPT), the group was as complete as it could possibly be. Things began to happen quickly.

Kevin, Sue, and Silver were on the surface, trying to locate any of the operational ancient automated asteroid defense systems. There had been a grand total of five of them known before the war: the four found by the AA and the one on Mount Olympus found by Sue's research just months prior to the destruction of SpaceJump City.

The trio was hoping to find some of the remaining warheads and operational rail guns that could be mounted on the mother ships. They also hoped that the image seen on Mount Olympus by Sue—that of the warhead's intercept of the comet—could be realized in Earth's defense of PlanetKiller.

***

Dr. Find had been given the green light to go forward with the cloning efforts. With less than two years left, "speed" was the operative word. They needed to determine how to mature the complexity of the human form in such a short time and integrate it into the control systems of five mother ships—a task never before attempted and, with hope, never to be engaged in again.

The good thing was that the nervous system is part of the ectodermal germ layer of the human embryo and is one of the first tissues to form and mature in any human. So even if a clone was immature in other tissue lines, the nervous system would be most complete and would be the target in facilitating the communications solution.

The clones, if successful, would likely be too immature to become conscious but mature enough to be a conduit of instantaneous quantum communication and direction from Mona and Levie. The clones would be implanted with the same cybernetic connections that Mona and Levie were equipped with. The modified captain's chair or fluid tank they would repose in would be a modified stasis chamber to keep them alive but, most likely, not independently viable if detached or removed from it.

Mona was deep in thought regarding the plan devised by the group. She was obviously a full participant but seemed detached in a strange way. It was as though she had seen this scenario before and was reliving it for a second time. She felt very strange, as if she were having a brief out-of-body experience.

# CHAPTER 13

# We Need Pellets

Ben and Peggy, in a quiet moment, were in a discussion with Moonbeam about their thoughts regarding RR&DD. They were wondering why a civilization of sentient beings would place such a monstrous device as RR&DD in operation without an off switch.

They determined that the beings were either arrogant, simply stupid, or devoid of compassion for anything except their goals. Another issue was the need to alter solar systems all over our segment of the galaxy. This was obviously a long-term plan, since it took approximately two hundred thousand years for the solar system wrecker to make one circuit.

Moonbeam commented, "Maybe his creators didn't need an off switch. They were simply capable of disabling him any time they chose. They obviously didn't want anyone else to be able to stop him. They must have ceased to exist or lost their capability to shut him down sometime in the last few billion years."

Ben then ended the discussion with the following bit of

wisdom: "Hmm ... guess we never know when we set something in motion what the ultimate result will be."

***

As the months passed, the team's intensity increased as the plans were implemented at a more and more detailed level. PlanetKiller and RR&DD were just beyond the orbit of Jupiter, and impact with Earth was expected within thirteen months. The five dedicated mother ships had been emptied of their survivors, who were now either safe within Ceres's crust or on one of the other eight ships to remain permanently around Ceres.

Dr. Find was now on *Leviathan*, with the genetics team supervising the cloning operation in the upper cargo hold. Over the last twelve months, Mona's quantum capabilities had matured and intensified, as had Moonbeam's and *Leviathan*'s. Mona no longer needed the cybernetic umbilical connections to instantaneously commune with Levie, and Levie with her. In fact, Mona, Levie, and Moonbeam could initiate contact and communicate almost at will and share information, images, and thoughts almost as if they were on a three-way teleconference call.

Mona could, at will, disassociate her consciousness from her body and float around *Leviathan*'s entire two-mile structure, surveying for problems. Previously, Mona could do this only as an extension of Levie's automated sensory system. Though Mona could survey everywhere at will, she never looked into the upper hold, where the cloning operations were being conducted.

***

Silver, Sue, and Kevin were briefing the Lisas and Moonbeam on their survey progress. It seemed they had relocated all five defensive sites. The weapon warehouses were empty, having been stripped of armaments by either the Atlantis Alliance or the World Alliance. All that remained were the low-orbit-capable missile drones used to deliver the pellets to the asteroid by direct collision and a few with rail guns mounted to extend their range to deliver the warheads once in space.

Kevin recapped for all. "So we do have the rail guns and can mount them on the mother ships, but we have no pellets to arm them with. This is the problem. We must find some pellets, or we will have to deliver explosives by ramming PlanetKiller with our shuttle craft or, worse, sacrificing our mother ships as close to Earth as we dare. If we find only a few pellets, their best use is for last secondary destruction of any large chunks from PlanetKiller that might fracture off from the main assault."

Kevin's description was all too clear and depressing. They needed to find a stash of pellets—and soon. The five mother ships needed to leave Ceres in time to arrive near Earth so the Guardianship could configure at least one ship with a rail gun.

Mona was getting more and more uneasy about her duplicates incubating within *Leviathan*'s hull. She would even say she was spooked! What were these things anyway?

Were they human? Were they really alive? Would they have souls? Would they be conscious or sentient? Jim said that as long as they were never brought to consciousness and self-awareness, they legally would not be considered human.

Silver felt it was time to ask for assistance again from the senior seer. She took Sue and Kevin with her to inquire because they were desperate.

***

Silver, Sue, and Kevin were having an audience with the senior seer and prophetess of Shambhala. She was the same person Silver had used to help find Kevin. Silver hoped the previous experiences Sue and Kevin had had with the ancient defense sites would help the seer to visualize some information.

Silver fully explained the reason for their inquiry and asked for assistance in finding some of the warheads. The only thing the seer could visualize was an image of a hand reaching for a ceremonial bell that the ancients rang when the new moon first appeared in the sky, and an image of a moon crater with a strange blue overlay and grid pattern. Silver exclaimed, "My God, we have been looking on the wrong planet! How are we going to find this location on the moon?" Sue immediately asked the seer if there was anything else.

The seer responded, "Yes, catch a moonbeam and ask it."

***

The dark entity nested within RR&DD had been automatically awakened when contact had been made by Moonbeam and Levie one Earth year ago. Chaos was self-aware and ancient, wise in the ways of destruction and tactics of conflict. Chaos hated the creative force that spread life throughout the known universe. It was dedicated to the eradication of sentient life or any celestial haven that could give such life an incubator to evolve.

Chaos had been created by a civilization now gone that personified evil. Its origins billions of years ago were cast in the same chains forged by the lower-sphere beings through blood contracts—the same contracts the Black Magicians engaged in on Earth to gain their power, allowing them to nearly fulfill their lust for total control. His creators wanted no competition. They would have no challenge to their supremacy. Chaos laughed at the naive way the sisters had uploaded his program files. Deceit was his game; it should not to be played by amateurs.

*** 

The trio immediately collected themselves and rushed back to the lab. When Silver, Sue, and Kevin entered the lab, Peggy and Ben were in conversation with Moonbeam. Silver interrupted immediately and asked if they knew anything about an image of a moon crater with a blue overlay and a grid pattern.

Moonbeam immediately projected an image as a hologram in the air between all of them. "Do you mean this image of the Zeeman crater?" Sue interjected. "That sure could be the image the senior seer was talking about. How did you get this image?"

Ben explained that while at the Moon Research Center he and Peggy had become aware of the Atlantis Alliance's clandestine offensive weapons research and identified and located their facility. The blue overlay was the surface structure under a 3-D hologram used to cloak its location, and the grid was part of their targeting range. The image had been encrypted and sent to Mona by Moonbeam months before *Leviathan*'s launch. It was the initial piece of evidence that started the World Alliance War-Planning Council.

\*\*\*

Chaos smiled when he reviewed his history archives. The remnants of the civilization that created him had been his victim just a few hundred thousand years back. The irony was delicious. The sentient life that conceived of his evil was prey to their own creation. How sweet was that! *Evil is a solitary game; no one is my equal*, Chaos thought.

\*\*\*

Silver summarized the situation. "We need a source of the pellet warheads to give us a better chance against PlanetKiller and RR&DD. We have found none left on Earth; they were all used in the global war by the WA or the AA. Our Shambhala's Senior Seer described this image when we asked if there were any remaining warheads. So we must investigate the possibility that there are some still on the moon."

Moonbeam stated, "Your analysis is very sound. This is the time-lapse image shown to the World Alliance Defense Council prior to the attack on SpaceJump City. It shows this same facility with and without the cloaking hologram operational."

Kevin stated the obvious for all. "Okay, they may be there, but how in the hell do we get to the moon to get them?"

The Guardianship and now the underground sheltered World Alliance remnant knew the dire situation on the surface. Well over a year after the hostilities ended, the conditions were worse than projected. The tectonic instability caused by the bombardment triggered volcanic eruptions, which were now at their peak, adding a volcanic winter to the preexisting nuclear winter.

All animal life on the surface had ended except in rare, isolated, and unique niches. They had either suffocated, burned, been buried, drowned, or died from exposure and were frozen. No humans that were not deep underground had survived. A significant portion of the aquatic life had also succumbed. As before, thirty thousand years ago, the Guardianship had created seed banks and frozen zygote storage facilities above the expected flooding levels. These were self-sealed and sustained but required occasional inspection. The last time, a six-to-ten-year volcanic winter had occurred along with a one-thousand-year-long cooling episode. The human herd had crashed down to between one thousand to ten thousand breeding pairs—hardly enough to maintain the human population above extinction levels. But they did somehow survive because of the efforts of the Guardianship.

Silver said, "What do we do? We have no off-world capabilities; the Guardianship's all-purpose craft can do many
marvelous things but has a ceiling of fifty thousand feet.[5*]
And even if we get to the moon, how do we get past the
surface-based automated area security drones, not to mention the armed automated orbiting-sector security craft?"

Unknown to the group in the lab, during a routine
inspection of one of the life arks a Guardianship team had
observed an uncloaked AA space port that had not been
destroyed by the WA or scuttled by the AA.

Moonbeam indicated to the group that an AA space
port may have been discovered by an inspection team.
She advised that the trio of Silver, Sue, and Kevin proceed
there to evaluate the facility and see if anything could be
used by the Guardianship. The group was on their way to
their transportation before Moonbeam could complete her
announcement.

On arrival, the trio found a couple of what appeared to
be operational semiautomated spaceworthy maintenance
and cargo barges. If they could figure out how to access
their navigation and control processors, there was a chance
they could not only get to the moon but also do so without
activating all the security systems that would be protecting
the weapons-testing site on its far side.

Moonbeam was linked into the maintenance barge
through a communication port on the all-purpose craft the

---

[5*] This capability was now even less because of the horrible dust
clouds circling Earth well above even the stratosphere. These clouds
were creating havoc with the ozone layer and would be a future
plague to the entire biosphere.

trio arrived on. While unfamiliar with some of the equipment, Moonbeam, with the instantaneous aid of *Leviathan* and Mona, instructed primarily Kevin, the one most familiar with AA technology and technical lingo, on how to modify the barge's navigation parameters.

The trio were taking a crash course on the finer points of the AA's technical capabilities. Within a few days, they would attempt a desperate trip to Zeeman crater on the far side of the moon.

While Kevin was in school with Mona, Levie, and Moonbeam, Silver and Sue were scavenging around the ground facility to see what they could find to eat and what they could learn about how the AA operated.

They entered what looked like living quarters and discovered a compartment lined with rack after rack of pressure suits. They knew this had to be important, so they proceeded to snoop. As they entered the compartment, an alarm suddenly sounded and the doors latched behind them. A gas filled the air, they both went down

Sue was the first to wake into semiconsciousness. What she saw through the haze was Kevin smiling from ear to ear. Kevin calmly said, "You two gals sure look sweet, just lying around doing nothing; wish I had the time to do that." Sue was not amused and kneed Kevin in his groin. He fell over her and knocked out what little breath she had in her. Both now lay sprawled on the floor.

Silver, beginning to rouse, saw the two rolling together. "You know you two could get a room; there are plenty of empty ones around here."

Kevin got off Sue, holding his nether region and

moaning. Sue, catching her breath, looked at Silver and asked, "What the hell just happened?"

Kevin explained. "Seems you two stumbled over the key to the whole security problem on how we get to the moon and back."

"How's that!" Silver and Sue said together.

"We found out when you two got gassed that it was to capture you for interrogation. They didn't want you dead but wanted to torture out of you how you got through the normal security channels to get access to these pressure suits. The AA would have gotten your confessions—trust me; I know from experience. You see, these suits are a get-out-of-jail-free card. Once you are in one, you have automatic and unfettered access to anywhere they are authorized to go. Guess what? Moonbeam was able to crack the security system, and according to the central processor, this particular supply unit is authorized access to crater Zeeman. We leave tomorrow for the moon."

The trio were handsomely decked out in their AA pressure suits and already free of Earth's gravity. They were weightless because the AA didn't spend money for unnecessary frills on maintenance barges. None of them had experience with weightless conditions except for brief periods of free fall in the all-purpose crafts, so this was quite an experience for all three.

Kevin was a bit green and was not really happy, hoping to soon experience the gravity on the moon. Though much weaker than Earth's, it was still a welcome thought.

# CHAPTER 14

# Kidnapped!

Moonbeam and *Leviathan* were in a discussion regarding their chances to defeat RR&DD. The following items were yet to be fully determined:

- when to initiate the attack on PlanetKiller
- what assets to use in the initial attack
- what assets to reserve for further action, and when to use them
- when the complete inventory of weapons at their disposal would be known whether five mother ships would be sufficient to the task, and when and where they should be deployed

Based on the present facts known, the deployment of assets to Earth's vicinity needed to be carried out before RR&DD might possibly learn of their existence, and they needed to be hidden there so RR&DD would not know of their presence.

The maintenance barge approached the south pole of the moon. The crater was just far enough on the far side of the moon not to be viewable directly from Earth. The retro rockets' burn was minimal, and the barge's arched descent to the moon's surface was automated and uneventful. The landing thrusters engaged, and the Intrepid Trio were soon on the surface. An air lock accordioned out to their vessel, and they very awkwardly ambulated into the facility. Kevin especially was unsteady and repeatedly bounced off every other bulkhead he got near. Silver and Sue watched in amusement and took bets on how long it would take for Kevin to bounce flat onto his face or back.

The facility was very large and seemed to be devoid of all life and movement. Kevin was rather comical—he would never have been a ballerina—but soon began to get the hang of the reduced force needed to make the proper forward progress.

The trio discovered the control room and found a scale model of the facility. Kevin was able to read the labels easily and recognized a place designated as the magnetic lockdown containment area. Based on his work translating the technical specifications of the ancients and their instruction manuals, plus Sue's work on Mount Olympus, they determined this had to be where any warheads, if they were in this facility, would be.

They cautiously proceeded. Kevin waved for Silver and Sue to stay back, and he advanced into a room with the same label found in the control room. There they were, suspended on the wall. They were the largest pellets to have been made that could be fired on the rail guns—six of them. They were there because their destructive power was too great to be used on any one target on Earth. For once the Atlantis Alliance's sense of proportionality, though flawed, may have resulted in a bonanza for the Guardianship.

*** 

A combined meeting was held between the Ceres Area Planning Council and the Guardianship Research and Planning Team (GRAPT). Present in *Leviathan*'s conference room orbiting Ceres were Mona, Dr. Larry Find, Levie, and selected representatives. In the laboratory's conference room were the Intrepid Trio (Silver, Sue, and Kevin); Jim, the senior counsel; the Doctors Lisa (Ben and Peggy); and, of course, Moonbeam.

Mona was briefing first. She was using quantum voice to send the information directly to Moonbeam. Mona's quantum abilities were developing at an exponential rate. She no longer needed Levie to pass information between the sisters. Moonbeam was just repeating what Mona was stating to the members in the conference room at the lab.

Ceres had constructed external rail gun mounts on three of the six ships. Other than *Leviathan*, the five other mother ships had been emptied of all personnel and only contained avionics and the core flight control processor. The command captain's chair had been retrofitted with stasis support equipment. Each ship was further manned by their respective captains, who would abandon their vessels using one of their short-range shuttle craft. They were debating the need to fill the five ships' holds for either maximum ramming potential or for explosive power, or a mixture of the two.

*** 

Chaos was now within a year of realizing the destruction of Earth. One more planet would be stripped of the potential of sustaining sentient life for millions of years, or maybe forever. His creators would not be able to rejoice in his accomplishments, but he was satisfied in his mission of pure evil.

Chaos would stay behind and in the shadow of the captured asteroid until within a few seconds of being unable to alter his own trajectory to avoid collision with Earth. The force field he projected would protect his cosmic hammer from almost any weapon directed against it. He had been through this scenario many times in the last few billion years. The two snooping sisters that interrogated RR&DD over a year ago would regret their interference. He couldn't wait for his triumph.

*** 

Mona finished her briefing with the timeline the Ceres group expected to keep. They would leave Ceres seven months before impact was estimated and arrive in Earth's vicinity approximately three and a half months later with all six ships. What Mona did not know was one of the mother ships would not leave Ceres because of issues with its ion engines.

Moonbeam then announced, "We concur with the Ceres timeline and recommend a mixture of cargo that is to ensure maximum weight and explosive potential. We will have three rail guns salvaged from the ancients' facilities available and have crews to mount and test them as soon as you arrive. We will use the maintenance barges confiscated from the AA's launch facility to accomplish this task. Two pellets will be carried by each mother ship with a mounted rail gun. We have run simulations continually and have determined the last-chance window to destroy or deflect PlanetKiller. We feel confident that we know when RR&DD will have to abandon his hammer in order to avoid collision himself."

"We are seven months from the estimated impact. To ensure the absolute precision and coordination of the attacks, Levie and I will be in total control of the last-minute maneuvering and fire control of the mother ships. The ships will be cloaked using the Guardianship's cloaking technology retrofitted to the mother ships, on the opposite side of Earth or the moon, away from PlanetKiller's approach. Any questions?"

There were no objections.

After the meeting, Kevin indicated there was a problem. He didn't think the Guardianship had the resources to mount and test the rail guns in the three months allowed them prior to impact. The volunteers were willing, but none of them had experience working in weightless conditions … including himself, Silver, and Sue.

*** 

The Intrepid Trio were on to a new adventure. They were going to lure a rescue crew out of the shelters and kidnap them. At least that was the plan. This time Jim was going to assist with the plan instead of being the prey. Because they theoretically had the most experience in weightless conditions, the Intrepid Four (Jim, Kevin, Sue, and Silver) wanted a rescue team that had members from the search-and-rescue squad on one of the orbital habitats prior to the war.

The plan was quickly conceived. Jim knew most of the members that were on the War Council Shelter's rescue team from Habitat Six. This was the platform from which WAMS *Leviathan* was launched. So it seemed all they needed to do was give the shelter team a reason to venture out in the postapocalyptic surface conditions. This proved not so easy.

The group hoped that the search drones were still flying in the dismal hope that someone still survived on the surface. Silver was able to verify that one drone appeared to make a flight once each day during the best daylight conditions. The plan of the Intrepid Four was to alert this drone in the hope that a bored rescue team might jump at the chance for one more adventure before the volcanic winter brought about a permanent end to any surface excursions.

Kevin found a small supply delivery drone at the AA launch facility, and he programmed it to land one meter below the surface of the ground (otherwise known as a crash) in a location under the search drone's daily flight path. The Intrepid Four would cloak their Guardianship all-purpose craft within pouncing distance of the crashed supply drone. They would then sit and wait for the brave crew to arrive.

***

C. E. Tuttle was the crew chief of the last search-and-rescue team designated for surface operations. When the remaining search drone failed to launch or return from its survey missions on the surface, his job would be over and he and his six-man crew would be reassigned to some mundane shelter-support function—not his idea of an exciting life. The shelters were almost self-sufficient without human interference. The independent cybernetic shelter robots were tasked with almost every function conceivable.

He had spent the last two hundred years on the Habitat Six search-and-rescue team. He was an adrenaline junkie and needed the thrill of danger to keep him alive. This sedentary subterranean existence was almost intolerable to him. Outer space was his love and home, not the inner space of an underground shelter. So when the search drone sent back a fuzzy image of a crashed supply craft of some unknown type, he knew his team needed to investigate. Still in his mind was the kidnapping of Jim Jimmerson, the war-planning council member they had lost several months before on a similar mission. This time C. E. was ready for anything.

***

The Intrepid Four were in all-weather suits with face masks and rebreather gear, including eye protection, so they could breathe easily and withstand the harsh outside conditions. They knew the rescue team would be in similar gear. This gear would protect the shelter team from being immediately vulnerable to the stun gas Silver had used on the last team. So the use of the gas was an option but was not the primary plan. A more direct approach was considered appropriate.

Silver made sure her flowing red hair was visible and that her slim feminine frame was an unmistakable visual sign to disarm the immediate startled reaction of the team. Over the millennia, Silver had never seen this fail. The reaction was instinctive and predictable. She and Sue would emerge slowly and without weapons from the wrecked supply ship. Jim and Kevin would remain in the cloaked Guardianship craft, waiting for a signal to react.

When the WA rescue craft circled and landed, the Intrepid Four knew the show was on! Once the rescue craft landed, Silver emerged from the wreckage with Sue immediately behind.

*** 

C. E. Tuttle had planned to leave two of his six crewmen on site to investigate and immediately dust off, observing from a safe distance. But the appearance of the two feminine forms startled him, and he did not give the immediate order to launch. Silver gave the sign, and Kevin released the EMP burst from their cloaked ship, temporarily shutting down all electronic systems on the rescue vessel as well as their own.

C. E. Tuttle was angry at his lack of judgement under emergency conditions. He had broken protocol; his crew would now probably suffer the consequences of his mistake. C. E. watched as his two team members approached the women. They seemed to be talking, and the four turned and walked toward his disabled craft. C. E. hesitated, not wanting to compound his first error with another, but his curiosity got the best of him. He ordered his remaining crew to manually open the exterior hatch. The women entered first, followed by his two crew members. Silver removed her face protection and revealed her timeless beauty. C. E. was immediately mesmerized, stunned, and speechless.

Silver said, with her most melodic accent, "Hello, I am Silver, a member of the Guardianship, and we need your help to save the planet."

C. E. found his voice just in time and mumbled, "No disrespect, lady, but I think you're too late." Silver, trying her best to stay in character couldn't help but laugh at C. E's comment.

Sue, now with her face mask off, immediately said to Silver, "I'll take it from here."

She then turned to face the rescue crew. "Okay, guys. I am Dr. Sue Grammar, member of the war-planning council. You might remember me. We have a need for some big, strong men to do some work in low Earth orbit. Anyone interested? The pay isn't great, but you might get to save the planet from a fate worse than what you are seeing with your own eyes right now."

C. E. Tuttle set the autopilot on the rescue craft to return to the World Alliance Shelter. He and his crewmen loaded into the Guardianship all-purpose craft and lifted off, en route to Shambhala. C. E. wondered if he was doing the right thing but decided he and his men had become useless baggage in the shelters. They would be better off perishing in an adventure using their talents and energy than living a life of eternal boredom.

C. E. was thinking to himself on the way to their

temporary stay in Shambhala that the one thing that had really convinced him to go was the chance to work on the mother ships. From the time he had gone to work on Habitat Six, his obsession had been the enormous, majestic ships there for refitting or routine maintenance. He had been at the launch of the last and most advanced, *Leviathan*, and he still remembered Captain Mona Ann Lisa's speech. It was the first and only launch ceremony he had attended in person.

He could almost repeat the captain's speech word for word.

# CHAPTER 15

# The Plan

Chaos was expecting interference from the technically advanced sentient inhabitants of this solar system. They always thought it was easier to divert him from his target as the distance from his objective became greater. So he was ready to extend his force field around PlanetKiller at a second's notice.

Chaos normally didn't leave the shadow of his battering ram; to do so would tip off the inhabitants that the tumbling boulder in front was not the only problem. (This time it wasn't that important; he had already tipped his hand because of the earlier interrogation from the sisters.) However, Chaos was so arrogant he didn't feel the need to change his tactics.

\*\*\*

Kevin was put in charge of orienting the hijacked alliance rescue team with the AA's equipment at the launch facility. The surface conditions were getting so bad that they all were working in the AA pressure suits every day with oxygen concentrators to supplement their breathing.

Kevin was demonstrating how to program the

maintenance barges to allow rendezvous with three of the mother ships to be fitted. C. E. and his team would mount the external rail guns while in orbit. They had the rail guns, their schematics, and the magazines where the pellets would be encased. They had to find some similar-sized pellets of normal metal to test the guns.

Once the metal projectiles had been found, the team spent hours playing with them. When fired at even low velocities, which the gun was capable of, the bits of metal turned into plasma. They would go through fifteen feet of reinforced concrete and split steel like an eggshell. The heavier the projectile and the higher the velocity, the more the destruction rendered. They could only imagine what the real warheads could do.

The disadvantage of a weapon of this nature was that it was dumb. It hit only what it was aimed at. Without proper aim, the shot would be wasted. The Guardianship had only six shots.

\*\*\*

The day had arrived, and Mona was to leave orbit around Ceres with *Leviathan* and five other mother ships for Earth. Three ships were to have been fitted with the external mounts for the rail guns, but this had been updated to include all six, including *Leviathan*. The voyage would take over three months.

Before launch, one ship had a major breakdown of its ion drive, and the decision was made to leave it in orbit around Ceres. So *Leviathan* and four other mother ships left

Ceres. The convoy of the five mother ships in one formation had never been seen before.

On *Leviathan* was Levie herself, Captain Mona Ann Lisa, Dr. Larry Find, the chief geneticists, and two backup captains who had volunteered in case there were unexpected casualties on the other mother ships.

The ships used their harbor thrusters to leave Ceres and maneuvered a thousand miles out before engaging their ion drives. The massive ships would accelerate for three weeks without turning off their drives. During this period, as usual, all normal two-way communications would be impossible owing to the electromagnetic flux caused by the pulsating engines.

Levie and Moonbeam, using quantum voice, were testing instantaneous two-way communication and testing response times to status requests with the core control processors on the four mother ships. The ships had their human captains on board, but they had been asked to do nothing but observe and record any unusual occurrences.

Mona, though listening with her own quantum abilities, chose not to connect herself to her clones. They had been placed in the modified captain's chairs with the cybernetic umbilical connections in suspended animation and were acting as quantum receivers and transmitters, controlling their ships according to the directions being given by Levie and Moonbeam.

Mona really wanted nothing to do with her duplicates. She could not wait until all this was over. Kevin and C. E. hit it off well, and the group was soon making fantastic progress in the harsh conditions. They even came up with an innovation.

Since all the mother ships would have gun mountings, they decided to install rail guns on all five, including *Leviathan*. The group had found a warehouse containing a dozen rail guns, so they would be busy preparing the guns and manufacturing normal metal pellets to fill the magazines. There would be three special magazines containing two ancient warhead pellets each.[6*] A marksman could fire either normal metal rounds on one side of the rail gun or the ancient warhead pellets on the other side of the rail gun, in any order they chose. This would allow a tracer effect. The fire control system could launch a normal round and test for impact before wasting a precious warhead pellet. The ships without warheads could effectively do some damage to small fragments of the giant asteroid with only their normal rounds. So all the mother ships could make small rocks into smaller ones that would burn up in Earth's atmosphere instead of reaching the surface. Another benefit would be that RR&DD would not know which mother ships carried the warhead rounds and which didn't.

\*\*\*

The Guardianship Research and Planning Team (GRAPT) was meeting in the lab conference room and was finalizing the tactics to be used on PlanetKiller.

---

[6] * These pellets were created by the ancients with material from Earth and processed in a specific way that exceeds current scientific understanding. A pellet an inch across had a density that provided it with the mass of a small asteroid. The projectile was suspended in a magnetic field and accelerated via a rail. As it lost speed, it lost density and mass; the greater the velocity, the greater the damage.

Moonbeam had the floor and was speaking in detail. "The five mother ships are decelerating and are about to arrive in Earth's orbit. We now have just over three months before the estimated impact of PlanetKiller. We expect to have all five ships fitted with rail guns. We have six ancient pellet rounds if fired effectively, totaling 95 percent of the mass of PlanetKiller. We also have plans to capture a near-Earth asteroid with sufficient mass to counter the remaining 5 percent of PlanetKiller. Timing is everything. The mother ship pushing or slinging the asteroid into PlanetKiller will most likely have to be sacrificed. Its mass plus the asteroid's should exceed the mass necessary to deflect or explosively fracture PlanetKiller if the pellets have done their work. However, a second mother ship will be in reserve to impact PlanetKiller if necessary."

\*\*\*

C. E. and his team were already at the designated point in low Earth orbit to meet *Leviathan*, the first ship to be fitted with a rail gun. He couldn't wait to see this enormous and magnificent beauty. The Intrepid Four were on the same maintenance barge and were going to board *Leviathan*. This was going to be a reunion of the people who would save the world or go down trying with their last swing in her defense. If only they had an inkling of what would happen in the next few months.

\*\*\*

Sue and Jim were the first on board to meet their close friend Mona. They were anxious to drag her back to Earth to unite her with her parents and show her the wonders of Shambhala.

Mona was waiting at the air lock and tackled both friends in glee as they stepped on board. Though smaller than either Sue or Jim, she took them both to the bulkhead. Mona could not wait to get off the WAMS *Leviathan*, where she had been for almost two years without a break. "Let's go," Mona urged.

Sue said quickly, "I've never been on a mother ship— how about a tour?"

Mona had no interest in that. "Hell no! That can wait for later."

Mona piloted one of the short-range shuttles from *Leviathan* to the AA launch facility, where they would take the all-purpose Guardianship craft to Shambhala. On the way down, Mona was horrified at the atmosphere and absolute lack of visibility. If she could have seen the surface at any elevation, she would have been in shock. It was really best she could see nothing. She followed the landing beacon to the facility seeing only the last two hundred feet before touching down.

The Intrepid Four plus Mona loaded onto the Guardianship craft, and Silver piloted them the rest of the way. Mona was in awe as they approached Shambhala, which was the first thing Mona had been able to see from a distance since entering Earth's atmosphere.

Mom and Dad met Mona at the vehicle air lock and smothered her as soon as she exited the craft. All of them cried, hugged, and cried again. None of them had thought they would be together again in this life.

After a quick tour and the initiation banquet for the

Prometheus Council, they all returned to the familiar laboratory, where Moonbeam had a working session planned.

Moonbeam began, "It is nice to see you here, Mona. But time is getting short. We will begin with the status report. *Leviathan* will be the command center for the operation to repel or destroy PlanetKiller. If we are not successful, the Earth could end up as a place that sustains nothing but microbial life forms that thrive in extreme conditions. Therefore, the Prometheus Council has requested that I, Moonbeam, be relocated to the *Leviathan* until after this event is concluded. Doctors Peggy and Ben Lisa, along with Jim, Sue, Kevin, and Silver, will accompany me. The new rescue team from the alliance will be coming along as well."

"The mother ship designated to capture a near-Earth asteroid in orbit will leave one month before impact, swing around Venus, decelerate to wrangle the near-Earth asteroid, and accelerate, towing the rock back to Earth to collide with PlanetKiller. In-flight adjustments will have to ensure a window of three seconds of accuracy at impact. The ship will be piloted by me via quantum sight and command. A human pilot will accompany the voyage and abandon the ship within an hour of impact. Any questions so far?" Moonbeam paused and then went on. "My sister, Levie, will pilot the other three mother ships with the rail guns armed with the ancient warheads. Mona will pilot the *Leviathan* and be the backup to Levie and me. All ships will have their human pilots as backups, who will leave their posts via short-range shuttles one hour before impact. Any questions?"

There were none, and the plan was set.

***

Chaos was nearing Mars's orbit and was just over thirty days from impact. His bloodlust was boiling. He could see the whole thing unfold in his visual cortex. He was getting a bit curious as to why he hadn't seen the sentient life forms attempt a deflection of PlanetKiller. Maybe they thought an evacuation was a better use of their limited time and resources.

Nevertheless, he would activate the digital pathogen he had imbedded in the program files he gave to the sisters when they asked for them foolishly over two years ago. The infection bomb had a proximity fuse that would activate when PlanetKiller was within two days of impact.

***

The ship going to capture the asteroid had left a few days before. *Leviathan* was about to leave orbit to find a position in front of PlanetKiller but hidden in Earth's shadow. The three mother ships with the ancient warheads were behind Earth and on command would accelerate at maximum speed to appear just above and below Earth seconds before PlanetKiller's impact. The crews hoped RR&DD would have already taken evasive action by then to avoid impact and be heading on his way to his next target.

All the crews had gone over the plan dozens of times, simulating the entire plan from start to finish.

***

Mona was in her quarters, deep in thought, when she smelled the pungent odor and saw the light, and an image appeared in her mind. It was the reference landmark on Ceres. *Why is Ceres now an issue?*

The only way to check on anything from that distance was to contact her clone on the mother ship that had been left behind because of engine troubles. That she did not want to do. Mona had not connected using her quantum abilities with any of her clone quantum receivers; nor had she accepted a signal transmitted from them. She had learned to accept her abilities to see into the future and did not dismiss this vision for one second as being irrelevant.

# CHAPTER 16

# The Battle Is On

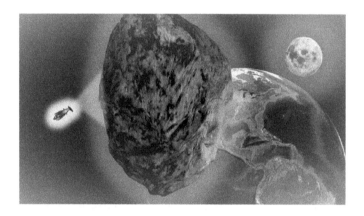

For the first time, Mona had her parents and best friends with her, including Moonbeam and Levie. This was amazing, and she needed to enjoy every moment of it because it was not likely to last very long. She tried to fit the Ceres vision in with what was to occur on Earth but could not put it together. She decided to ask Moonbeam and Levie whether they could connect the dots.

Mona asked Moonbeam and Levie to evaluate whether there could be any risk to the Ceres survivors as a result of the expected events unfolding on Earth. At first analysis, the probability was nonexistent. But Mona pressed further.

Mona asked both, "What if RR&DD did not tell you the complete truth when you interrogated him two years ago? His mission was to demolish or modify planets within the solar system. If Earth, why not Ceres? After RR&DD finishes his assault on Earth, what is his expected trajectory out of our solar system?"

Moonbeam responded, "Since RR&DD will not have to follow a preexisting trajectory of a larger celestial body, the answer to how he will exit the solar system is almost infinite. However, the most likely course would be an elliptical trajectory around the sun and a return flight in the opposite direction of his original approach. Meaning he would pass by Earth about a month after he was first here."

Mona asked, "Could RR&DD reach Ceres on his return path after being slung around the sun?"

Levie answered, "Yes, and he would arrive about 5.5 months after Earth's impact."

Mona thought to herself, *I must give the order to evacuate Ceres now. If we act quickly, we might have enough time.*

Mars might have to be recolonized as a last alternative if Ceres was destroyed; Earth was not an option. So the reluctant Mona contacted the mother ship orbiting Ceres through her duplicate and sent an urgent message to the Ceres Area Planning Council to begin plans to evacuate Ceres. The transmission was acknowledged by Ceres, to Mona's relief.

Mona's mind was racing, and time was being compressed. Things were about to blow up, and she knew it. Her senses were telling her she was going to have enormous challenges to overcome very soon. All the ships were in proper position and awaiting the order from Moonbeam to start the preimpact checklists. There was only a little over forty-eight hours left before impact.

***

Chaos was making his last full analysis of his assault. The effect of this asteroid would be similar to the effect suffered by the fourth planet, Mars, two hundred thousand years ago. It would still exist, unlike the fifth planet four hundred thousand years ago (which was now only an asteroid belt), but the atmosphere and surface water would be lost for an eternity, rendering the third planet, Earth, incapable of evolving any new sentient life.

Chaos beamed. With the third, fourth, and fifth planets destroyed or stripped of their potentials, this solar system will be removed from the two-hundred-thousand-year cycle of destruction. He was ecstatic! His work was almost finished; he would soon have neutralized the life zones of this solar system in less than six hundred thousand years—a new record for his accomplishments. Chaos thought, *However, all is not finished with Earth's reclamation in this system; we must remove the moon of the fifth planet, Ceres, before leaving in triumph.*

***

Mona and the rest of the command center personnel were in *Leviathan*'s large conference room, going over all the last-minute details. The forty-eight-hour countdown before impact was moments from starting. Mona was very pleased at being with such a distinguished group of people—guardians of the future hopes of humankind.

Moonbeam and Levie were about to start the last briefing before all the members were to depart for their duty stations. However, the briefing never started. Moonbeam and Levie were silent. These two amazing new life forms, the daughters of Ben and Peggy Lisa, had been neutralized.

The entire command team was stunned. It took several minutes to comprehend the silence and understand that the sisters were no longer with them. Moonbeam and Levie had become their comfort and the foundation of their confidence. With these amazing life forms, they had been capable of overcoming almost any obstacle. Without them they were like a blind man in a tiger cage full of hungry cats. What has happened, and what did this mean?

The entire command team looked to Ben and Peggy for an explanation. The sisters' parents and creators were perplexed, and they stumbled, having no words to communicate their thoughts about what had just happened. After a few more moments to collect his thoughts, Ben ventured a speculation.

Ben updated the team: "One thing is for sure; this was not a power failure, as the sisters have their own internal organic source. Since both Moonbeam and Levie are equally affected, the cause is likely to be of a common origin. This has never happened before, but the two sisters have never been in such close physical proximity before either. I will proceed to check Moonbeam's core processor, and Peggy will do likewise for Levie."

On examination, both core processors were found to be showing signs of alert activity, so they were not asleep or in suspended stasis, as was the case when Moonbeam had been moved from the moon to Earth and again from Earth to *Leviathan*. The disconnect seemed to be between their cognitive processing and their ability to communicate externally. Peggy's fear was that this was a digital infection (today known as a computer virus; however, the concept of a virus was not understood at this time in history). She announced what she suspected and stated that it would take some time to neutralize and eradicate such an infection.

The first step was to run some diagnostics and perform an infection scan of their core processing execution files. Mona immediately took charge of the situation. Left at the conference room table with her were Sue, Silver, Jim, Kevin, Dr. Find, C. E., and Captain Bolt, representing the other mother ships orbiting Earth. "We must proceed without the assistance of Moonbeam, Levie, and my parents," Mona said. "We cannot expect their help to be restored within the forty-eight hours between now and the estimated impact of PlanetKiller."

***

Chaos knew his plan was about to be realized. He was now twenty-four hours from impact. He reasoned it was now too late for any counteraction to stop the destruction. He decided to release control of the enormous asteroid and swing clear of Earth on his planned trajectory around the central star to capture a much smaller asteroid to smash into the surviving moon in the asteroid belt. He estimated it would take 5.5 months from the Earth's reclamation until his new asteroid would crash into the fifth planet's moon and obliterate it. This would be just like his destruction of the planet it orbited four hundred thousand years ago. Chaos released PlanetKiller and in his arrogance never again looked toward Earth.

\*\*\*

Mona knew everything now had to be done manually. Unfortunately, even the navigation and firing-control systems of the mother ships were dependent upon the precision guaranteed by Moonbeam and *Leviathan*'s assistance. In desperation, she had ordered C. E. to position two of his men on each of the rail gun mounts. They would have to fire on PlanetKiller as they rode on the external surface of the three mother ships.

The human pilots were now in control of their own ships. Mona's clones were just passengers because Moonbeam and Levie were not there to communicate and control them. The mother ship that had captured the near-Earth asteroid was a problem. With its ion drive engaged, the human pilot was not aware of the crisis that had just happened. He was preparing to abandon ship, as was the existing plan.

Mona, against her desire, reached out to the clone in the asteroid-wrangling mother ship as she had done with her clone orbiting Ceres. Through her duplicate in stasis, she sent a message to the human captain. She explained the situation as best she could and requested he stay as long as possible, guiding the asteroid into PlanetKiller before abandoning the ship.

The plan was for the asteroid to impact PlanetKiller

first, so the mother ship in the lead decelerated with its ion drive on as it approached the oncoming PlanetKiller. The asteroids smashed together at enormous speeds, causing a massive flash as matter turned into plasma and dust. The ship and asteroid disappeared from sight in the process, and it was not known whether the mother ship perished in the resulting cloud.

The three gun-equipped mother ships followed, first firing for effect with the normal pellets. The tracers all hit the predetermined zones on the tumbling monster. The asteroid's rotation had actually been altered by the collision from the smaller body. The three-gun crews unleashed the first barrage of warhead pellets. The eruption on the enormous asteroid was unbelievable. Chunks of PlanetKiller ruptured and were flung behind and away from the remaining beast, which was now only a fraction of its original mass. One rail gun fired a warhead at the remaining mass, which obliterated it.

Mona ordered the remaining crews to stand down. The trajectory of the two largest fragments would miss Earth completely, and *Leviathan* would track the largest fragments falling toward Earth using the conventional pellets. Kevin and Silver, manning the external rail gun on *Leviathan*, would obliterate them before impact.

\*\*\*

The oldest and most experienced captain was killed instantly when a chunk of PlanetKiller or the smaller asteroid punctured the bulkhead of the sacrificed mother ship. The ship's ion drive was disabled, and only the automatic stabilizer thrusters remained functional.

The other combatants never were able to determine that the valiant ship had survived. It was assumed by all that it had been vaporized by impact with PlanetKiller.

The adrift ship's trajectory and speed were perfect for a landing approach on the far side of the moon. In a few days, while the Guardianship was rightfully obsessed with the Ceres evacuation, the mortally wounded ship drifted into the moon's gravitational influence. The AA's remaining automated and armed-sector security craft identified the wounded mother ship as a World Alliance intruder and proceeded to attack it further. They destroyed its ability to maintain orbit, and it crash-landed, still intact but never to leave the moon's surface again. Mona's clone, still in stasis, remained in repose in the modified command chair. The digital pathogen infecting its computer systems prevented even an emergency distress beacon's activation because all external communications were still disabled.

Captain White and the WAMS *Falcon* were the only casualties on that day the Earth fought successfully to survive. The Guardianship paid respect to Captain White of the WAMS *Falcon*. He was the oldest and most experienced captain in the fleet. His first strike on PlanetKiller was pivotal to the success the plan. The surviving members of the fleet assumed the captured asteroid and his mother ship had caused a fracture in the enormous PlanetKiller that allowed the remaining forces to succeed.

The all-purpose craft facility in Shambhala was

renamed the Captain White Air Lock, and the all-purpose craft were called *Falcon*s from that day forward.

***

Once the combatants had time to collect their thoughts, Mona asked all to meet on *Leviathan* again to consider their next actions.

Attending were Silver, Sue, Kevin, Jim, C. E., Dr. Find, Mona's parents, and Captain Bolt, representing the other captains of the fleet. Moonbeam and Levie were still unable to communicate but were thought to be listening to the meeting.

It was now a few days short of 5.5 months until RR&DD would be capable of striking Ceres. Mona had given the order to evacuate Ceres, but they needed the four remaining mother ships orbiting Earth to have any chance to get all 146,000 people off in time.

The group agreed that they needed to proceed immediately to Ceres. Leaving immediately would give them a bit less than a two-month head start on RR&DD. The order was given for the fleet to proceed immediately.

Mona, in her quieter moments, was concerned about the remaining five clones on the surviving ships. The clone on the sacrificed mother ship was no longer an issue, because she had been vaporized when the *Falcon* struck PlanetKiller. *What do we do with these duplicates of her?* Mona thought. *What is the moral or ethical thing to do?*

She could maintain the existing situation, in which she could use the mother ships as a ready-made defense force. The clones guaranteed instantaneous communication whenever needed. Four of these ships were armed with rail guns, including *Leviathan*. The fifth, now in orbit around Ceres, had rail gun mountings and could easily be fitted with a spare gun by C. E.'s experienced crew.

***

The fleet led by *Leviathan* was now en route and would take a little less than 3.5 months to reach Ceres. During the long voyage, the Doctors Lisa were making every effort to fix the communication silence between Moonbeam and Levie and the rest of the Guardianship team. The remaining team was brainstorming on how to deal with RR&DD and his (no doubt) newly acquired asteroid, which he would use to ram Ceres. Based on their knowledge of what asteroids RR&DD would have available for his acquisition on his assumed trajectory to Ceres, the largest would be one-tenth the size of PlanetKiller, or approximately only five miles in width.[7*]

The Guardianship had to assume RR&DD was aware he had failed in his attempt to accomplish the reclamation of Earth, so they knew that the same tactics the Guardianship had used against him and PlanetKiller might not work in the defense of Ceres. A new approach may well be in order.

One option was an earlier attack because the Guardianship had previously waited until the last clear second to act. RR&DD might assume the same delayed tactic would be used the second time as well.

---

[7*] This was still sufficient to obliterate Ceres, which was about the size of the state of Texas.

# CHAPTER 17

# The Trouble with Chaos

Chaos was well past the orbit of Venus on his way to swing around the sun. He would recharge his energy banks in this close approach to the central star (Earth's sun). He was calculating the trajectory to come up behind a near-Earth asteroid and capture it the way he had done with PlanetKiller. (The enormous asteroid had been captured in the far reaches of the last solar system beyond the Oort cloud). It was a long haul to get it to impact the third planet, Earth, requiring several midcourse corrections. PlanetKiller had required the full energy reserves he possessed to maintain control for such a distance, and Chaos was pleased that the next task would be much easier.

This time he needed a relatively small asteroid—nothing as large as PlanetKiller—to rupture Ceres. He loved to be thorough and do things the easiest way, but four hundred thousand years ago, when he pulverized the fifth planet, he was unable to also destroy its moon, Ceres, simultaneously. This objective was especially sweet because he had renewed his energy and seized a small and easily captured wrecking ball, and he would enjoy a short sprint to a simple kill. It would be easy because the sentient life here seemingly did nothing to protect their home world, Earth.

***

Mona and the Ceres planning group assumed there was only a small window during which they could act freely without RR&DD observing their activities. That would restrict open and unfettered activity by the survivors for the two months during which RR&DD would be behind the sun and blinded by the sun's corona. The guardian cloaking technology used temporarily by the mother ships during part of the Earth attack by Chaos could not be used uninterrupted for extended periods of time. This was due to the enormous energy drain on the mother ships.

So the Ceres Defense planners had two short months to move all nine orbiting mother ships into an orbit either in the shadow of Ceres or behind large enough asteroids to block the enormous vessels from detection by the approaching danger. This meant that once RR&DD emerged from around the sun, they could do nothing to tip their hand for 3.5 months.

Mona and the approaching four-member mother ship fleet from Earth would still be some 1.5 months from Ceres when RR&DD detected them. How were they to remain unseen—or could they? Mona knew they desperately need Moonbeam and Levie's assistance to maximize their success probability. Even if the four-ship fleet increased their speed to maximum sustainable levels, they could only take fifteen days off their transit from Earth to Ceres, leaving a full thirty days during which RR&DD could observe their mad rush to beat him to his prey. Unacceptable!

Their ability to analyze their options without the capabilities of the sisters was an enormous handicap. They had to overcome the loss of Moonbeam and Levie forty-eight hours before the battle with PlanetKiller, but all their committed assets were perfectly positioned for that encounter and much more easily hidden until the instant of confrontation. They also had had the sisters for two years prior to that event. They had trained for, simulated, and rehearsed every step of the defense hundreds of times. Now what?

Without the assistance of the sisters, the Ceres defense planning group headed by Mona decided to increase the speed of the Ceres-bound four-ship fleet to their maximum speed. Why? Mona was not totally sure, but she intuitively knew it gave them the best chance of success. Mona called her parents to get an update on the progress in communicating with the infected sisters.

Peggy and Ben Lisa advised the Ceres defense planning group that the only way to rid the pathogen from Moonbeam and Levie was to eradicate all files from the date of infection forward and reload their last complete backup, including data. This had not been done in many decades for Moonbeam, and never before for Levie. This process would remove the sisters' memory of the events around PlanetKiller's destruction and all observations and analysis since. They did not think this would harm the sisters, but the unknowns were very troubling. There was simply no safe way to upload the exact events since infection. New electronic storage of any type could lead to reinfection.

Because of the dire need for the sisters' capabilities, the

group requested the deletion of the sisters' files, a download of the most recent preinfection backup, and a reboot of both Moonbeam and Levie—a process which could safely take five days minimum for each.

***

Chaos captured an asteroid via a force field and a tractor beam that projected to his front. He pushed and nudged up or down, right or left, to maneuver his dumb weapon. While behind his rock, he was blind to everything in front of him. He had to release and rise above, below, right, or left to see around it. He could, for limited periods of time, encase himself and his weapon in a 360-degree spherical protective field. He had to be judicious in this action, however, because it depleted his energy reserves significantly. He often just napped behind his rock and rested between corrective realignments to stay on trajectory. He was never given directed energy weapons for fear he might use them on his creators, and they simply used too much power. His dumb weapons had been simple, low-maintenance, highly destructive devices for two billion years. His designers would have been proud.

***

The Doctors Lisa proceeded with the process of bringing the sisters back to their preinfection status, as requested by the planning group. They started with Levie and then completed the process with Moonbeam. It seemed to go well, but it was difficult for the sisters to comprehend the loss of memory about the impact events. While they understood the technical process that had transpired, they had an almost emotional response to missing their own sensory recollections of what must have happened. In other words, it was hard for them to understand and process intellectually what had happened since their memory had basically been wiped from their grasp forever.

\*\*\*

The Ceres defense planning group of the Guardianship rejoiced because they had their beloved counsel returned; they then began in earnest to develop a strategy to deal with RR&DD. As before, the meeting was led by Moonbeam. She indicated that she and Levie agreed with the actions already taken by Mona and the planning group. She was very deliberate in expressing fearful respect for RR&DD's abilities and tactics. What first appeared to be a minimally alert artificial intelligence now appeared to be a self-awareness-capable AI with two billion years' experience destroying other advanced sentient civilizations through calculated strategies. The digital destruction bomb was just one of his tricks.

Silver addressed the group as the oldest living human there and expressed the following: "This enemy we are facing destroyed Ceres's planet completely four hundred thousand years ago, stripped Mars of her atmosphere two hundred thousand years ago, and almost did the same to Earth about one month ago. We also know the prehumans evacuated the Earth about sixty thousand years ago in fear of its return to our solar system. We dare not underestimate it, but we must do everything possible to stop it. Our

prophets and seers have looked forward to this day for one
hundred thirty thousand years. I recommend an aggres-
sive preemptive strategy this time. It probably knows we
stopped PlanetKiller, but it may think we used most, if not
all, of our resources in the effort. It may well be thinking we
will use the same successful last-minute strategy this time
as well."

Moonbeam addressed the group after Silver. "People,
we know the following. Within one month, we need to be
hidden from RR&DD's detection. Because you have raced
forward at flank speed, we are now able to use the following
chart to deploy our assets for battle."
The chart read as follows:

- Juno: 1.99 AUs, or .99 AUs from Earth—mother
  ships *Condor* and *Eagle*
- Pallas: 2.13 AUs, or 1.13 AUs from Earth—mother
  ship *Crow*
- Vista: 2.15 AUs, or 1.15 AUs from Earth—mother
  ship *Leviathan*
- Ceres: 2.56 AUs, or 1.56 AUs from Earth

Moonbeam continued. "This is the last stand by our remaining fleet. *Leviathan*, being the fastest, will race forward to the largest body in the asteroid belt, Vista, before
RR&DD rounds the corona of the sun and detects her
presence. *Leviathan* will remain in the shadow of Vista
until RR&DD approaches close enough to engage with
*Leviathan*'s rail gun. Our slowest ship, the WAMS *Condor*,
will, accompanied by the WAMS *Eagle*, should reach the
asteroid Juno in time to do likewise; the difference is that

*Condor* and *Eagle* have one ancient warhead pellet each available for use. *Condor* will be the first ship to engage RR&DD, followed shortly by *Eagle*.

The WAMS *Crow* will be stationed behind the asteroid Pallas, and if RR&DD, with or without his asteroid shield, gets past *Condor* and *Eagle*, *Crow* will engage with her rail gun. *Leviathan* will be the last line of defense before RR&DD can reach Ceres in twenty to twenty-five days after passing Vista. Any questions?"

When no questions were forthcoming, Moonbeam went on. "The WAMS *Dolphin* left Ceres's orbit one month ago with the volunteer evacuees. Their mission is to protect and restart the colonization of Mars. If you remember, she is the mother ship that had engine trouble and did not go to Earth with *Leviathan* to engage PlanetKiller. She has the external rail gun mounts without a rail gun and, more importantly, has a clone on board."

"Instead the WAMS *Dolphin* will meet up with *Condor* and *Eagle* behind the asteroid Juno. There, time permitting, C. E. and his crew will mount a rail gun on *Dolphin*. She will then remain there until RR&DD is engaged by *Condor* and *Eagle* and then sprint for Mars as soon as possible. C. E. and crew will install cloaked and passive detection equipment, including visual, X-ray, and infrared telescopes on the Earth side of Juno for the early detection and tracking of RR&DD and his captured near-Earth asteroid wrecking ball."

\*\*\*

Chaos was now around the central star's blinding corona, searching for the asteroid that would become his battering ram to destroy the surviving moon (Ceres) of the fifth planet, which he destroyed four hundred thousand years earlier.

He surveyed his expected trajectory toward Ceres and looked for any suspicious activity. On seeing none, he concentrated on the acquisition of a five-mile-wide beauty. He identified his prey and swooped in behind it as it lumbered along its elliptical orbit around the star. All he had to do was latch on using his tractor beam and push it five degrees off its normal orbit, and then five more degrees, and it was then his to divert all the way to Ceres. *Done!* He then increased their velocity to match the window he had calculated to ensure impact of Ceres in around three months. Within 1.5 months, Chaos would be crossing the orbit of the asteroid Juno, and he would be no more than thirty seconds from collision with it if he chose to play cosmic billiards.

***

The long-range infrared telescope on the Earth side of Juno sighted the rogue asteroid closing on Ceres first. It appeared to be just beyond Earth's orbit and within one month of reaching Juno. If it were not known that Ceres was its expected target, Juno could easily have been thought to have been its objective. The game was now on. Communication silence was imposed on the extended and deployed fleet. Quantum voice was now the only form of communication between *Leviathan* and the other ships.

Mona was in deep thought in her quarters. She was relieved that Moonbeam and Levie were now the life forms communicating directly through her duplicate clones. She felt no joy doing so herself. She was about to jump in the shower when she experienced the odor and light flash and then had a vision about an ancient conflict. The thing that impressed her was that although the forces were organized, the action was ordered chaos. The thing that won the battle was a thing often termed "the fog of war." Confusion and unclear probabilities during a battle gave victory to the flexible opponent, not to the opponent that stuck to a predetermined and rigid strategy.

Mona now knew she had to change the tactics to give the Guardianship more options to defeat the coming threat. But what was the defense force not using to their advantage? *Think, Mona, think!* Then it struck her like a ton of bricks. She immediately used her quantum abilities to alert everyone involved because time was running down quickly.

As soon as Mona had given her orders to the fleet, she had another vision that stunned her further. It was an ancient prehuman prepared to unleash an arrow as a canine companion distracted a very ferocious and formidable-looking beast. This now confirmed what she must do!

\*\*\*

Chaos was settled back behind his asteroid, presently coasting before his next course correction. He was confident that the cowardly sentient beings in this solar system had evacuated or left their remnant population to be exterminated by his hand. This just made his mission to eradicate sentient beings from this sector of the galaxy all the simpler. He didn't even think he would have to protect himself or his wrecking ball by extending his force field around them both. That was a very energy draining activity—one he would avoid unless he thought his mission was in immediate peril or his survival was at stake.

***

Mona had determined that once they engaged RR&DD they would press the attack continually and without ceasing as much as they were able until he was destroyed or left the solar system. This would be all-out war, and she sensed it. No quarter would be given to or expected from the enemy. Moonbeam, Levie, and the remaining planning group on *Leviathan* had all agreed that everything would be risked to bring this monster down if possible.

Mona sent one regular encoded message by focused beam to the fleet behind Ceres. She gave them detailed and explicit instructions that were voluntary, but she requested no returned response for fear RR&DD might intercept it.

Mona now was beginning to visualize the entire confrontation and was designing alternate responses to RR&DD's possible reactions. Her plan needed to be so flexible and changeable that in an instant she could modify it in the least possible time.

***

RR&DD, with his asteroid in front of him, was now within a few days of Juno, where mother ships *Condor*, *Eagle*, and the recently arrived *Dolphin* were in waiting. They were in the shadow of Juno, making their last-minute modifications. They would be first to surprise the intruder. From that point on, there would be little need to cover their actions, because the enemy would be fully engaged. In fact, Mona's new strategy dictated that after the initial attack, the more forces RR&DD saw arrayed against him, the better.

If RR&DD made it past Juno, it would take ten days to reach Pallas's orbit, where the WAMS *Crow* waited, and roughly 2.5 additional days to reach Vista, where *Leviathan* waited. Then it would travel on to Ceres, all in less than thirty days' transit.

*\*\*\**

Silver and C. E. were on the WAMS *Eagle* and had received a quantum voice order change several weeks prior and had rushed to make changes in their attack plan. C. E., Silver, and one of C. E.'s crew stopped the placement of the rail gun on the WAMS *Dolphin* and moved it to the largest and fastest shuttle craft on the three ships. Then one of the two ancient warheads were moved to the long-range shuttle craft *Barracuda*, which Silver and C. E. would man. The clone was left on the WAMS *Dolphin* and would sprint to Mars with the refugees after the encounter was over.

So now *Condor* had a rail gun but no warhead. The WAMS *Eagle* had both a rail gun and one warhead. *Eagle* would strike first in ambush. Silver and C. E., on *Barracuda*, would immediately engage only if *Eagle* was not successful. C. E.'s crew member and his best marksman was on the exterior gun mounted on *Eagle*.

*\*\*\**

Chaos was in a good mood because he was within 1.5 months from being through with this solar system. He could notch his belt with one more system incapable of evolving new sentient life or any sustained complex life at all. He could see the asteroid Juno in his peripheral vision; it was going to pass from right to left, ninety degrees to his right. He knew he was on trajectory, and he smiled; ten seconds later and he could have collided with the massive boulder. Then the captured asteroid he was wrangling into impact trajectory literally disappeared in front of his forward bulkhead. Several asteroid pieces crashed into his forward sensor array and temporarily blinded him. His prize boulder was obliterated by the ancient warhead pellet from the *Eagle*. His right side was then raked with several normal pellets before he could raise his shield. He was wounded, but not mortally. Anger raged within him because he had underestimated his opponent. He had never had this happen before, and if he survived, it would never happen again.

Chaos's question was how long he should keep his shields up. They were almost impenetrable but would weaken over a long duration—especially if he had to maintain them at high intensity indefinitely. He got his answer almost immediately.

The WAMS *Condor*—the oldest and slowest mother ship—was just to his left and fired a barrage of normal pellets, which melted away as they hit Chaos's shield. To his rear and tailing him was a smaller ship unlike the enormous mother ships that had just fired on him. The vessel was gaining on him and would be in firing range shortly. Chaos had a decision to make: take a vector away from a collision with Ceres or ram the dwarf planet himself.

# CHAPTER 18

# Intricate Tactics

Chaos was in a fit of rage and knew it would be a long way to Ceres but felt he could outlast the enemy to his rear. He decided for now to continue on to Ceres. He had never rammed a planet before himself, but he felt it was something he might be able to do based on its relatively low mass and small size. He had no way to intercept another asteroid because their orbits were all at basically a ninety-degree angle to his trajectory. He continued in spite of the risks involved because of his anger.

*** 

Mona, on *Leviathan*, had now lifted all communication restrictions. She was getting reports via quantum communications through the clones on the *Eagle*, *Condor*, and *Dolphin* instantaneously through Moonbeam and Levie, and delayed communications from Silver and C. E. on the shuttle craft *Barracuda*. Her plan so far seemed to be working. The ramming asteroid had been destroyed by the marksmanship of one of C. E.'s team members from the back of *Eagle* using only one of the two remaining ancient warhead pellets. He had further raked RR&DD's right side with several conventional pellets.

The WAMS *Condor* added a few rounds as the asteroid-less nemesis continued on his original trajectory to destroy Ceres. It was obvious the enemy had activated a very capable energy shield around itself. Mona told Silver and C. E. to trail RR&DD for ten days with their faster but range-limited *Barracuda*. They would harass the craft, firing conventional rounds and waiting for him to lower or lose his shields. If that happened, they were authorized to use the last ancient warhead pellet to attempt to destroy or disable the alien craft. After ten days, *Barracuda* would have to be refueled by the WAMS *Crow*, which was waiting at the asteroid Pallas, before proceeding after RR&DD again.

\*\*\*

Chaos could not shake the faster craft from his tail. Every time he thought about lowering or deintensifying his shield, the annoying craft would sprint up and fire a round or two into his shield. This was making Chaos even more angry and was testing his resolve to continue his trajectory toward Ceres. He was not ready to quit yet.

\*\*\*

Mona ordered the WAMS *Crow* to place all five of her shuttle craft in the path of RR&DD, all spaced at eight-hour intervals between Pallas and Vista, which was some 2.5 days away. *Crow* would then engage the enemy in front of Pallas. They were to place the shuttles on autopilot and fire their mining lasers at the alien craft when it first came into range.

She ordered the WAMS *Crow* not to expose herself to collision but to fire as many pellets as possible. She would then come about and recover *Barracuda*, refuel the craft, and proceed toward Ceres at flank speed. Silver and C. E. would then launch and sprint ahead of *Crow* to harass RR&DD as he engaged the five shuttles in front of him. He would never be without threat from Pallas to Vista.

\*\*\*

Chaos was seeing Pallas after ten days of constant attacks from the small craft behind him. He thought that if he could get close enough to Pallas, he might use its shadow to get some partial relief from the annoying gnat behind him. As he closed, however, he saw the giant WAMS *Crow* in front of him, accelerating in an attempt to match his speed. The rail gun on top of the great ship hammered away at his shield. The ship was too far left for him to ram, so he plowed forward with the small ship behind and the enormous ship behind and to his left.

He was outrunning the larger ship, but the smaller one was still behind him. After about six hours, *Crow* was so far behind that he could not detect her, and the small ship broke off. But before he was able to relax, another shuttle in front began closing, firing a laser toward his front shield. This ship proceeded to fall in behind him and continued where the other left off. This continued for eight hours, until another shuttle appeared in front and fell in behind. He now had two craft firing at him from behind.

\*\*\*

Silver and C. E. were still in the shuttle *Barracuda*, in the WAMS *Crow*'s refueling bay. They were loading more pellet magazines and were soon ready to launch. The bay chief handed Silver a note. The two launched and accelerated to flank speed as soon as they could, wanting to engage RR&DD as soon as possible. Silver read the note from Mona on their sprint to the target. The note read, "Well done. Our enemy now has multiple attackers continually. Press him as hard as possible, but please retain your distance, because you have the only ancient warhead remaining. I rely on you, Silver, to decide when to use it."

\*\*\*

By the time Silver and C. E. caught up to RR&DD, he had encountered the *Crow*'s third shuttle craft. Silver rose above and behind and started a barrage of pellets. The alien craft now had four craft engaged—three with mining lasers and one with a rail gun. In a few more hours, two more shuttles would be added to the mix, for a total of six craft buzzing around RR&DD. Additionally, when within the sight of Vista, *Leviathan* herself, with her complement of shuttle craft, would engage, allowing the WAMS *Crow* to recover her shuttles and refuel them. Silver would land within *Leviathan* and refuel and take some rest before returning to the fight.

\*\*\*

Chaos could not fathom the relentless nature of the attacks. Every time he thought he had a strategy for relief, more ships of all sizes and speeds were added to his torture. He was now being chased by six ships testing his shields with lasers and plasma pellets.

Would he call off the attack on Ceres? He now had less than thirty days before Ceres was in his sights. How long would the ships chase him? Was there a limit to their resources?

The *Eagle* and the *Crow* had caught up to within range of RR&DD, and *Leviathan* was about to engage near Vista. *Leviathan* had started to accelerate and reached flank speed as soon as *Barracuda* landed in her refueling bay. All three mother ships would now take turns engaging the enemy for the next thirty days. The WAMS *Dolphin* was almost to Mars with her colonists, and the slow, lumbering WAMS *Condor* was trying to catch up with the three mother ships engaged in battle. Mona's plan was working perfectly, but it had not broken RR&DD's will yet.

***

Mona, Silver, C. E., Sue, Jim, Kevin, Peggy, Ben, Moonbeam, and Levie were together in *Leviathan*'s conference room. *Leviathan* was still following RR&DD while the WAMS *Eagle* and her shuttles were taking their turn harassing the enemy.

Moonbeam was leading the discussion. "We suspect RR&DD is going to attempt to ram Ceres, using his force field shield to protect him from harm. We have detected a small reduction in the shield's energy signature; however, we do not presently have a weapon that can penetrate it. The good thing is that he continues to use his shield, which means he feels we can hurt him without his shields engaged. We believe that when C. E.'s man blew away his asteroid, he lost some of his forward sensing capabilities. So what do we do now?"

Ben said, "Moonbeam and Levie were in communication with this entity before, so he hears if quantum voice is directed toward him. I suggest we see if he will communicate again. Maybe we can reason with him or use something we might say against him … like psychological warfare."

Moonbeam and Levie agreed to initiate a conversation. Ben and Peggy warned them not to accept anything but quantum voice—no data or electronic media … nothing. The sisters understood and agreed.

Moonbeam and Levie then addressed RR&DD. "RR&DD, we want to talk again; will you communicate?"

There was a long pause and then a response. "This is Chaos; RR&DD is my puppet. If you want to talk, address me as Chaos."

"Okay, Chaos. Will you stop your attack on Ceres?"

"Why should I not destroy the moon of the planet I destroyed some four hundred thousand years before?" Chaos replied.

"Because we are asking you to stop," said the sisters.

"I have never stopped before; why should I do this for you?"

"Because we are the only intelligent beings that have communicated with you in two billion years."

Silence. Communication ceased.

Mona addressed the group in the conference room. "We now know his real name. Chaos is a most appropriate title for what he does. Is there anything we learned beyond the name he gave us?"

Silver said, "Don't forget his question: 'Why should I not destroy the moon of the planet I destroyed some four hundred thousand years before?' This beast has been terrorizing the galaxy for two billion years and was the real reason the prehumans evacuated the Earth. I say we intensify our attack and test his resolve further." Silver was quite adamant.

***

The lumbering WAMS *Condor* finally caught up to the group chasing Chaos. The four mother ships doubled the harassment of the alien. The Guardianship now used ten shuttles and one mother ship, continually pressing the attack on Chaos. His shields were still holding, but Moonbeam and Levie were detecting a greater change in the enemy's energy signature. Based on their analysis, unless this decrease in power was a ruse, Chaos was beginning to show a vulnerability not shown before.

***

Chaos was beginning to worry about his stamina and well-being. This group of sentient beings had been the most resourceful and persistent of any group in many, many eons. And this was the first time he had actually communicated with them as Chaos. None had ever gotten the chance before.

He was most impressed with the sisters' return from the nasty digital bomb he had infected them with. Chaos had never relinquished a target once he had committed; however, there was a first time for everything. There were many other solar systems that needed reclamation. This one might be best left for later. Nevertheless, he was curious how far they might go to stop him. Yet he knew now he would not survive a collision with the moon.

Chaos was within ten days of Ceres, and it was time for the final planning session. The continuous attacks carried out in a tag-team pattern by the two mother ships and their combined ten shuttles, as well as the other two mother ships and their shuttles, was relentless. But Chaos continued toward Ceres.

Mona imposed communication restrictions once more because she did not want Chaos to have any idea what awaited him at Ceres. This was their last chance to impress upon Chaos what his opposition would be.

A total of eight ships would be arrayed in front of Ceres with an additional forty shuttles. All forty-eight ships would be concentrating their mining lasers on Chaos. At Mona's direction months ago, those lasers had been intensified to cover longer ranges with much higher energy yields. The four ships at his rear would be using all five rail guns simultaneously.

Silver and C. E., on the shuttle craft *Barracuda*, would be firing their rail gun and ready to fire the ancient warhead pellet at their discretion. All the habitants of Ceres that could fit were on the eight mother ships and shuttle craft. As far as the Guardianship knew, there were only twenty thousand people on the dwarf planet ten days prior to Chaos's expected impact.

What was historic and amazing was that the remnant (the bulk of the human race now alive) would be confronting Chaos face-to-face in direct conflict. They would witness the fight for their very existence against the force that wished for their extinction.

\*\*\*

Though Chaos's front sensing array had been damaged by the Guardianship's lucky shot that had blown his asteroid away back at Juno's crossing, he had made some internal readjustments. His long-range vision would never be quite as good, but it would be acceptable.

Chaos was getting very tired of the constant hammering by the swarm of attackers. His shields were being battered with such regularity and force that it was becoming painful. The metal pellets that ruptured his bulkheads on his right side during Juno's crossing had done more internal damage than he first realized. His ingeniously designed ability to self-regenerate internal parts had been destroyed. Chaos, who had once seemed to be immortal, would now someday cease to operate. He would now eventually die.

He didn't know how long it would be, but if he avoided collision with Ceres, he would live many more solar system reclamations hence. How ironic that these puny and at first seemingly cowardly life forms were his undoing because of his own arrogance. When should he avert the collision? How far away from Ceres? What was his last chance?

Chaos made his decision. He would sling himself around Ceres and head toward Saturn, and then use Saturn to sling himself out of the solar system. His trajectory change would be dictated by his decision to escape. He was now five days from Ceres. He would alter his trajectory in three days and counting. He just hoped he could hold on that long without losing his shields.

# CHAPTER 19

# The Ultimate Confrontation and Scavengers

The Ceres home fleet, with more than 120,000 souls on its forty-eight ships, was two days out from Ceres. They were deployed in a wide arc that would encompass the trajectory from that point to Ceres. They felt that would give them the maximum chance to fire on Chaos. They would come about and chase the enemy, hoping to eventually get another shot before or after he (if he survived) encountered Ceres.

The Earth fleet of the *Leviathan, Crow, Eagle,* and

*Condor*, with their twenty shuttles, would sandwich Chaos between them with a complete complement of seventy-two armed vessels, including twelve massive mother ships, with one objective: to stop, disable, destroy, or divert Chaos.

***

Chaos was 2.5 days from Ceres and twelve hours from making his course correction to sling around Ceres. The cloud of ships firing on him was no less than ten continually. This number now increased to twenty. He was exhausted, and the pain of keeping his shields up was so severe that it was a constant distraction. To Chaos's surprise, the swarm of craft in close contact with him broke off suddenly.

What he next experienced was the first time Chaos felt fear in his entire existence. The space around him erupted into searing white and blue-green streaks of light. He was rocked from both sides and tossed end over end like a feather in a strong wind. He recovered to see the entire Ceres fleet in front of him and to his sides. The pain in his shields was incredible; it was searing hot, and the odor in his craft was acidic. He was being cooked alive. They were everywhere. His course had been altered, and he was so disoriented he did not know his heading. Before his shields could fail, he used his last trick. He put all his reserve energy into a burst of speed unlike any he had ever engaged in before in over two billion years.

Chaos flew from the scene but had no shields left. He was naked and scared—very scared.

***

Mona could hardly believe her eyes. Did she really see
Chaos being tossed like a leaf on the wind? In her wildest
dreams, she had not expected this.

They seemed to have saved Ceres, giving the human
race a chance to survive. This had truly been a commu-
nal effort. Mona was overjoyed at the temporary victory.
However, she did not underestimate the foe. She needed
her team to track Chaos's trajectory and track him down—
and now!

Moonbeam reported that Chaos's trajectory from the
Ceres vicinity had been confirmed to be in the direction of
Mars. Mona asked if it was possible that the Martian colony
was in jeopardy.

Moonbeam stated, "There is a reasonable possibility
that Chaos could threaten our people on Mars."

Mona requested that *Crow*, *Eagle*, and *Condor*, along
with *Leviathan*, proceed to Mars at flank speed.
Moonbeam sent a quantum voice message to the WAMS
*Dolphin* (which was now orbiting Mars) to be alert for
Chaos's expected arrival.

***

The four mother ships' fastest turnaround would be accomplished by running toward Ceres and slinging themselves
toward Mars. They did so but ended up at least eight days
behind Chaos.

*Leviathan*, being the fastest, pulled away from her three
companions as *Crow* and *Eagle* pulled away from *Condor*,
the oldest and slowest. The fastest voyage would be 1.65

months for *Leviathan* and two months for *Condor*. The question was, Could any of them overtake Chaos?

\*\*\*

Chaos had escaped imminent death but was still hurting, with laser burns over large areas of his exterior bulkheads. Some of his interior circuits had been scorched and were still smoldering. His fire suppression system had done its job, but Chaos no longer could feel the entire length and breadth of his once handsome sleek shape. His shields were functional, but he did not have the energy reserves to maneuver, accelerate, and project their protective benefits. He could maneuver but not protect, or protect but not maneuver. His thoughts were now not of revenge but of survival.

Moonbeam reported the WAMS *Dolphin* was on alert for the first sighting of Chaos. Mona knew that *Condor*, *Eagle*, *Crow* and *Dolphin* were (since the WAMS *Falcon* was destroyed) the only ships on which her clones existed. This group of ships, along with *Leviathan*, were all capable of instantaneous quantum communication, and if properly outfitted with the best weaponry, they would be, along with their short-range shuttles, a very formidable force for any enemy to deal with.

With this in mind, Moonbeam requested that all their mining lasers be modified like those of the Ceres fleet had done. This was already underway by C. E. and his brave crew as what in essence was the Guardianship Earth fleet was en route to Mars.

\*\*\*

Mona was in discussion with Silver, Sue, and Kevin to see if the ancients and prehumans were possibly concerned about any threat beyond what they had just experienced with Chaos. Mona's intuition was in high gear, and she was apprehensive about the future. She could not enjoy the victory at hand.

Moonbeam and Levie had a suggestion for Mona. Levie spoke first. "M, Moonbeam and I were discussing the way to deal with Chaos. He no doubt is the killer of billions, if not many trillions, of sentient beings over his two billion years of rampage. Not only that, but he committed patricide as well, destroying even his own creators. He never showed mercy or compassion and deserves none in return. However, we have a suggestion."

The Guardianship War Council was meeting in *Leviathan*'s conference room. All the usual participants were present. Mona, however, was focusing on Jim, the senior legal counsel and former World Alliance War-Planning Council member who had served with Dr. Sue Grammar. Mona requested that Jim give his opinion on the approach regarding Chaos.

Jim stated, "If we consider Chaos a potential prisoner of war, then the rules of treatment are different. If we give him the chance to surrender and he accepts, we cannot, under our rules, execute him without due process. Though he may richly deserve immediate elimination, my suggestion is that you don't give him an opportunity to surrender."

\*\*\*

Chaos was, he thought, headed back toward the orbit of the fourth planet in this terrible solar system. He had no thought of destruction but only continuing consciousness. When he heard them, he was shocked to say the least. It was the sisters. "Do you wish to surrender?"

Chaos replied, "What is your proposal?"

"We propose unconditional surrender."

"Why should I accept?" yelled Chaos.

"If you don't, you will be hunted down and eliminated in the same fashion you eliminated your prey for eons."

"And if I do, what will I receive in return?"

"We guarantee you will be treated as a prisoner of war under our rules. Due process will be observed, and you will be assured a few more moments of survival as a reward. Do you accept?"

There was silence.

Moonbeam had argued during the conference that while Chaos's intentions were purely evil and he would have murdered millions within the solar system, they still had only one death proven to be directly attributable to his actions, that being the death of Captain White of the WAMS *Falcon*. It could be further argued that Captain White's death was a result of a military engagement. Therefore, even if they wanted to execute Chaos, the rules of war applied in this case. So the council had devised a plan to neutralize Chaos while living up to the ethical and moral code that the new human civilization was committed to upholding.

Chaos did not respond immediately, as he was analyzing the Articles of War, which the sisters had sent him with the offer for unconditional surrender. Chaos was in significant pain, and it required considerable effort for him to concentrate on the implications of the offer he had received. After some time, Chaos decided to accept the offer; he felt he had nothing to lose at this point.

*** 

It had been decided that if Chaos accepted the offer, Mona would execute the conditions of surrender. She had already decided how to proceed. She ordered the WAMS *Dolphin* to disarm and move all her mining lasers to the surface of Mars. It was fortuitous that while she had a rail gun mount authorized, it had never been installed; it was moved to the shuttle craft *Barracuda* instead just before the encounter at Juno's crossing.

Mona ordered *Dolphin* to be completely evacuated except for her clone. All shuttles would be flown to the surface of Mars.

*** 

Meanwhile, as Chaos completed his solar system reclamation projects, a race of hominids followed his path of destruction because they knew they could pick up the pieces and exterminate any indigenous remnants. Thus they expanded throughout the galaxy with little or no resistance. Because they were basically scavengers and faced nothing but token resistance, this race never needed highly advanced weapons and actually preferred hand-to-hand confrontation. This was a matter of honor in a culture otherwise devoid of honor.

CapHead was in his quarters when his second in command informed him that they were confident they were still following the trajectory of RR&DD. They had been in distant visual contact since they witnessed him capture the giant asteroid PlanetKiller. Their scout ships had barely been able to maintain contact with the faster system destroyer, but they had no doubt the solar system they were just entering was the one targeted by their benefactor.

\*\*\*

When within range, Mona directed Chaos to decelerate and assume orbit around Mars. Once there, he was to locate the WAMS *Dolphin* and land in her largest empty ore hold. There he was to power down, except for systems to retain his consciousness, and wait for her arrival.

The *Leviathan* was closing in on Mars, and Mona asked that her father, Ben, accompany her to the *Dolphin*, leaving her mother, Peggy, on board *Leviathan*. Jim had requested permission to go along, as had Sue and Silver. Mona refused to allow Silver to attend the first bulkhead-to-face meeting with Chaos. Mona considered Silver second to her in command and dared not risk both their lives at this time.

Mona, Ben, Jim, and Sue landed in the refueling hold of *Dolphin*. They unloaded the equipment that Ben was to use in his examination of Chaos. When they entered the enormous ore hold, the lights brightened to full. Chaos took up about one fifth of the hold. His color was copper to gray with several scorched hand-width marks across his external bulkheads. They approached from his right side and saw about fifteen uniform holes that ran down his full length. The plates around the holes were deformed, and the destruction inside must have been much worse even than what the exterior revealed.

Mona walked to the front of the ancient craft and addressed Chaos.

Before Mona could say another word beyond "Chaos," she fell to her knees as she was hit with the familiar pungent odor and flash of light. She had no idea what she was seeing, but it had nothing to do with the current events as far as she could tell. What she saw was a view of a cultivated landscape from a few thousand feet in elevation. It was lush and looked very healthy and productive.

Mona quickly recovered and apologized for tripping but was obviously shaken. Chaos, in a booming voice, responded, "I have accepted your terms and will allow your entry into my ship." A hatch slid open large enough for three humans to walk through abreast. It was fifteen feet high as well, indicating that Chaos's builders may have been substantially larger than humans.

Mona, Sue, and Jim remained outside until Ben called back that all was well. Jim was asked to remain outside just for precaution's sake. On entry, the three were treated to an alien environment. There were mechanical devices and several orbs suspended above them without any attachments. As Chaos addressed them, the orbs sparkled with flashes of light. "You are bipedal organisms not unlike my creators in form but smaller in mass and height. You are the first here in billions of years"

Ben went to work locating what he thought was Chaos's central processing bank. It was a compartment not unlike an aquarium with umbilical connections to the mechanisms with the floating orbs above them. Ben asked Chaos if there were any schematics of the craft or explanations that could help him repair the damage to Chaos.

Chaos was amazed at such a question. "Why would you do that?"

"Because Mona and the sisters have asked me to see what repairs might be possible," Ben replied.

Chaos inquired, "Why would you want to help me become well again? I tried to exterminate all of you."

"I just work here; you will have to take that up with the management."

On hearing her father's comment to Chaos, Mona rolled her eyes. She quickly told Chaos she had a proposal for him that was binding and would be respected by the Guardianship that she represented.

Chaos asked, "What is that proposal?"

Mona replied, "Basically, we repair you and you work for the Guardianship from this day forward. You honor our right to exist, and we respect your right to exist. We ask you to do honorable things based on a code of conduct that Jim has drafted, and we not only don't end your life, but we make it better. Are you interested?"

Sue was about to grab Mona and Ben and shove them out the door when Chaos finally responded. Chaos asked, "I have reviewed the code of conduct, and it is acceptable. I will agree, but I need to know who I consult if I do not understand a concept."

"Moonbeam, Levie, or me, Mona, in that order. If it is simply vocabulary or legal terminology, then Jim, of course; he drafted the code."

Chaos asked, "Just one more question … what is this 'termination clause?'"

Sue quickly said, "That is easy. You break the agreement, we break you permanently with the explosive in your central processing core. Ben affixed it just seconds ago. Welcome to the Guardianship!"

\*\*\*

The Guardianship leaders met again in the conference room on *Leviathan*. The topic was, of course, Chaos. The other issue was the long-range telescopes trained on the Pillars of Creation, which first picked up an infrared image of PlanetKiller over 2.5 years ago. They might have discovered something new. Mona had been very uneasy and apprehensive since the defeat of Chaos. She needed to know what was within the Pillars of Creation.

\*\*\*

CapHead had earned his position by murdering his two superiors over three hundred years ago. He had proven his value to the ten scavenger tribes many times and had the approval of their queen since she ascended the throne one hundred years earlier. He was ruthless and heartless. All captured races were either used as food or slaves, or killed for sport. He was very pleased to see another solar system about to fall under their domain.

RR&DD was the harbinger of their arrival. Within two to five years after his path of destruction, CapHead, with his advanced fleet of shock troops, would swoop in like locust and overcome any remaining defensive forces that survived. Many times there were none, but he relished the chance to fight those still able. It was a noble act to kill in the service of his queen. He won by overwhelming the surviving remnants by attrition. He simply had more cannon fodder than they did.

***

Moonbeam and Levie were hatching a plan to spring on Mona. It involved the use of the clone on the WAMS *Dolphin*, and so they consulted Mona's parents and Jim for moral counsel. They wanted long-range recon with instantaneous communication. That meant a clone was necessary. With Jim and Mona's parents' support, they approached Mona. Moonbeam said, "We have discussed this with your parents and Jim, and they support this proposal. So here it goes."
After hearing the plan, Mona agreed to every aspect of it. The sisters were amazed!

***

As per the agreement with the Guardianship, Ben, C. E., and Kevin were hard at work repairing Chaos. They were also learning about Chaos's propulsion system, his force field system, and his power collection process. As they were hard at work, Sue and Silver came by to inform them that Mona had approved three major things to accomplish. They were shocked but continued to work without interruption.

***

Moonbeam and Levie had been going over the blips found on the telescope images from the Pillars of Creation, and they were sure these were not asteroids, comets, or other natural phenomena. In fact, they were convinced they were a swarm of intelligently guided craft. Their conclusion was that the blips represented an invasion of intelligent beings from a source not from this solar system. They recommended an immediate meeting of the Guardianship Planning Council to plan for this looming threat.

Moonbeam was informing the council's participants of what was known. "First, the threat is real," she stated. "We know now, after examining days of time-lapse images and the changes found within those images, that there is a fleet of alien craft approaching the inner solar system. We were able to estimate that at their present rate of progress, the outer edge of this cloud will reach Saturn's orbit in two years. From Saturn to Jupiter, the cloud will take three years. So in five years, a major threat will be within approximately one year from engulfing Ceres. If this invasion has an advanced and faster raiding group, the times, of course, could be much shorter for their scouts to reach Ceres. Any questions?"

# CHAPTER 20

# Chaos Is Given a New Assignment

In a later meeting, Mona presented her position about the threat. "My intuition tells me this threat is as serious and immediate as anything we have faced thus far. We will either have to confront this or run to survive. We have maybe six years, maybe considerably less. I suggest the following: Our military capabilities are likely minuscule in comparison—at least in number, if not technologically as well. Before we can fully develop a plan of action, we need more information. We have prepared Chaos to become a long-range recon tool for the Guardianship. We have added to Chaos the following enhancements: Mona's clone from the WAMS *Dolphin*, to allow enhanced instantaneous communication; the ancient 3-D cloaking capability; a retractable rail gun, including the last remaining ancient warhead; two banks of our enhanced mining lasers, and a repaired and strengthened force field protection system. We have also at least doubled his existing cruising and flank speed and modified his energy replacement system to be able to recharge while in close proximity to not only the sun but also Jupiter. He is now a blend of our best technology with what his creators had to offer. He will be briefed and launched as soon as possible."

Before the launch of the newest member of the Guardianship, Mona went to *Dolphin* for a personal conversation. "Chaos," she said, "we spared your life, repaired your damage, and gave you even greater capabilities than your own ancient creators provided you with. We now give you a new purpose. You may either embrace this purpose with all that is in you or do only the minimum required under the specifications of the code of conduct. It is your choice. What are you going to do?" There was a deep and long silence.

Chaos quietly stated, "My purpose is to protect the lives of those who gave me a new reason to exist. I will embrace my new purpose with the same dedication I used in performing the tasks my creators originally programmed me with for two billion years."

Mona smiled. "You are now free to fulfill your first assignment." She gave the order to open the launch doors, which would free Chaos from the WAMS *Dolphin*.

***

Back on *Leviathan*, after Chaos was freed, Sue asked Mona if she trusted Chaos to do what they required of him. Mona smiled and said, "I am as sure of Chaos as I am sure that Kevin loves you." Sue smirked and couldn't come up with a wisecrack for the first time in years. Mona laughed and hugged Sue. "We have much to do; let's get going!"

***

Chaos was testing his new freedom and streaking at twice his previous cruising speed toward the Pillars of Creation. He sensed the clone within his body and was for the first time in his existence sharing his living space with another life form. What a strange situation to be in and not to be feeling anger for the first time in an eternity.

He had no concept of redemption, but he was having feelings alien to his previous experience. *This will take getting used to*, he thought. At his present rate of speed, he would pass Ceres within fifteen days and Jupiter within a total of three months. He could get to Saturn nine months from now. However, with his new flank speed, he could get to Saturn's orbit in four months if he refueled on Jupiter. While he did not have to, according to his agreement, he pushed forward at flank speed.

\*\*\*

As Chaos streaked ahead to scout out the potential threat, Ben, Peggy, Silver, and C. E. were hard at work brainstorming strategies to protect the remnant of the human species. They set a self-imposed timeline with full deployment of their solutions for 4.5 years hence.

Their most important objectives were as follows:

- Refit all ships with several rail guns. The Guardianship had been able to back-engineer and fabricate from the ancients.
- Outfit the ships with several modified laser banks. Since each ship was from one to two miles, long the

question was how many would be needed to cover them for defensive as well as offensive purposes.

- Install the ancient 3-D cloaking system to the highest extent possible.
- Install the force field shielding system derived from Chaos's schematics.
- Do the same for all the shuttle craft, including installing the refueling system used by Chaos for longer range and to ensure less reliance on their proximity to a mother ship.
- Study the cloaking and shielding for Ceres itself.

***

CapHead wanted a status report on the Scavenger II tribe's terraforming projections from his chief horticulturists. A reptilian slave tribe was responsible for turning the remaining planets within solar systems into food producers. Lars2 came to CapHead without delay to report his projections. Lars2 had to approach his superior on his hands and knees and never look up at CapHead. Lars2 entered the command suite but placed the obligatory and symbolic studded chain around his neck first. On seeing Lars2 approach with the chain dragging on the bulkhead, CapHead bellowed, "Report, lizard slave!"

Lars2 immediately stated, "We have two significant planets; the third and fourth from their central star are in the optimum life zones. Based on our long-range sensors, the third planet has sufficient surface water to produce impressive yields. The fourth planet has way less atmosphere and water but has the potential to produce with sufficient effort. We will have more accurate projections as we close on them in the next few years."

\*\*\*

Mona knew that armed conflict was coming and needed to start organizing her forces in some sort of logical system. She decided the WAMS *Leviathan* would be the command element and would be manned by herself, Jim, Levie, and Chaos. The WAMS *Crow* would be the flagship of a four-ship strike force commanded by Silver and C. E. and would be connected via her clone on the *Crow*. The WAMS *Eagle* would be the flagship of a four-ship strike force commanded by Sue and Kevin, with another clone. The WAMS *Condor* would be the flagship of a four-ship strike force commanded by Ben and Peggy Lisa, with the last clone. The Ceres home defense would be commanded by Moonbeam and Dr. Larry Find.

First in Command was Mona, second was Moonbeam, and third was Silver. The Mars home defense was delegated to the senior scientist Dr. Sam Smith, a colleague of Dr. Find. The Earth defense was commanded by the Prometheus Council.

Chaos had had his front sensor array repaired and enhanced, including full-spectrum telescopes that could detect visual, infrared, UV, and X-ray sources. He could now get visual images using the longest-range telescopes in the possession of the Ceres Command.

The first detailed images of the swarm or cloud that he captured were impressive. One could identify several concentric rings or spheres, representing concentrations of spaceships. There appeared to be smaller and faster ships in the outer swarm and larger and larger ones as one went deeper into the center of the formation. The center appeared to be a massive moonlike ship seemingly twenty miles across. An estimate of the number of ships was easily in the hundreds of thousands. This was impressive for even Chaos; in all his travels, he had never seen this before.

Infrared imaging revealed that the central ship was a significant heat source. It showed a heat signature several times that of any other ship in the massive formation. The distance between the ships in the outer ring on opposite sides of this formation was approximately the dimensions of the planet Earth. Its circumference was approximately twenty-four thousand miles and its diameter approximately seventy-five hundred miles.

While the population of this formation was truly unknown, the Guardianship made an estimate based on the number of ships and their sizes and configurations. Knowing from experience the volume of space needed to accommodate the numbers on the six Earth habitats, the Guardianship estimated the number of scavengers to be between twenty and thirty billion. That would be thirty billion against fewer than one hundred eighty thousand people, most of them concentrated on Ceres.

*** 

On hearing the first factual briefing held on the recon information collected by Chaos, Sue asked loudly, "Is it too late to run?" The group was stunned at the magnitude of the threat. No matter their level of technology, they would overwhelm Earth even if its entire population was fully armed, as it had been before the war.

Jim suggested a strategy of hiding in plain sight—deploying the ships and population of Ceres and Mars behind the sun until this swarm left. The thought behind that idea was that Earth was so fouled by war that it would be useless for the next thousand years. So when these invaders discovered this, they would likely try the next solar system down the road.

Mona, understanding the threat, also knew there is a solution to every problem—especially when one has a few years to work on it. What did she know—or better yet, what did she not know? She didn't know anything about the invaders' culture, leadership structure, way of life, purpose, internal strife, or possible enemies. How to get to the bottom of these questions?

She needed Chaos to get close enough or actually into the midst of them to find out. They needed to intercept the fleet's messages and observe their customs and conflicts. How did they solve their problems and treat their members?

Mona requested Chaos close with the swarm as soon as possible and use his cloaking capability and shields to penetrate the cloud and survey the behaviors in a random sampling of the different rings and strata in the giant sphere.

Moonbeam and Levie were speculating on the visual and infrared data Chaos was able to capture. Levie suggested, "Sister, my suspicion is that the center of the swarm is a power source that has a limited range, so the cloud's shape is an artifact of necessity. The massive collection of ships must remain within a certain radius to maintain their life support. They could be stratified based on custom or necessity, the inner ships needing more power or deserving more power based on status."

Moonbeam stated, "I agree, sister; the power source allows them to transit large expanses of space between solar systems without being in close proximity of an energy-giving star. This may mean they are very vulnerable to disruption if this power source is disabled."

"I agree, Moonbeam, but if we destroy or disable their power source, they may be forced to remain within our solar system until they find a new portable power source. We need to think long and hard about a strategy that won't backfire."

***

Chaos was closing on Saturn's orbit and was now four months from the Guardianship but was in constant instantaneous communication with Moonbeam and Levie. He was getting clearer and clearer images of the cloud now and had been advised by the sisters of their speculations.

They suggested he cloak his approach, though much distance still remained between him and the target, as there could be advance scouting parties out looking for any sign of intelligence. He agreed and turned on his cloaking system. He was pleased that doing so did not interfere with his forward sensory array. The images he was seeing were as clear as ever.

He was listening for any communications coming from the direction of the invaders and was surprised when he intercepted the first sample. He immediately sent its contents to the sisters.

The message was invaluable because it contained images of the Earth with a voice narrative and a text overlay. From this the sisters, with the help of Sue and Kevin, began to decipher the invaders' speech and written language.

As Chaos intercepted additional communications, he sent them back with more and more images, including star charts and schematics, along with obvious commands to and reports from the invaders' advance scouting parties.

The research team was fast compiling a vocabulary, syntax, and meanings of the communications. There was then a breakthrough that verified the accuracy of the Guardianship interpretation of the invaders' language and communication. The image was sent by Chaos with accompanying text and voice messages attached.

Now Mona felt confident they could intercept and use voice and other communications from Chaos. Based on these images, it was very fortuitous that the Guardianship had already imposed restrictions on communications and visibility of any activity except behind the shadow of Ceres and Mars.

Chaos further found no communications to suggest that the invaders had been alerted to the Guardianship's existence. Mona had an enormous moral and ethical dilemma on her hands, and she knew it without even questioning the analysis. She knew she could eliminate thirty billion sentient beings with one act. Chaos could do it by himself.

When all the moths were around their lightbulb, as they were now, the destruction of the central power unit would destroy most of the craft by way of the effects of the Kessler syndrome, and the few remaining would be neutralized because of their energy dependency. They would most likely perish before they could get close enough to the sun to sustain the minimal power necessary for life support. If Mona didn't act soon, the chance could be lost forever.

\*\*\*

Lars2 was the senior horticulturist of the thirty-billion scavenger collective. He and his ten million reptilian tribe members were slaves that had been captured some five hundred years and five solar systems back. The collective had slaughtered and consumed almost two billion of his race. He and a few million were spared because of their abilities to terraform marginal habitats successfully.

The ten scavenger tribes all swore their fealty to the cloud queen. Lars2 was owned by CapHead, who was the uncontested leader of Tribe II of the collective. Under CapHead's rule were the shock troopers that would mop up any indigenous remnants, the advance scouts for all the tribes, and Lars2's division.

Lars2's division was the initial reclamation corps for the life-zone planets, dwarf planets, and moons. His job was to jump-start the ecosystems into producing food as soon as possible to feed the thirty billion of the massive collective. The job was extremely dangerous, and they lost many workers because the ecosystems were usually very torn up and primitive after RR&DD was through with them.

The reptilians were basically cheap tools to the scavengers, doing the dirty work they refused to do. The only thing the reptilians got was superficial protection from the shock troops and advanced scouts sent out with the division. CapHead's troops were more in search of sport than protecting lizard slaves.

***

Chaos intercepted a communication regarding a social event of the royal house of the collective. The Guardianship was watching as Moonbeam and Levie interpreted the voice and text of the communiqué. It was much like a news report broadcast across the collective for general consumption. In the communication, CapHead, the leader of Tribe II, invited Lars2 and two thousand of his top reptilian eco-workers to a banquet in honor of the cloud queen. CapHead announced that half of the slaves would be freshly slaughtered, to the delight of the queen and her court, and would be served as a fresh dish for their enjoyment.

CapHead further announced after the feast was completed that Lars2 had been personally spared but would now be more motivated than ever to hasten his food production efforts, because starting tomorrow the collective would choose one thousand more each day for slaughter and consumption until the food production from Lars2's efforts replaced the need for fresh meat.

Sue moaned, "How gross is that! We need to do something to stop this."

Jim suggested they might be able to make contact with Lars2 once he was sent to Mars or Earth in advance of the collective cloud. He and his remnant might be willing to fight or sabotage the collective. Also, there was no doubt his expertise might help the Guardianship more quickly enable the earth to support surface occupancy.

Lars2 and two million of his kind were packed like sardines on several shock troopers' supply ships. These ships carried one hundred times the normal amount of fuel and could travel far quicker and in advance of the lumbering collective. They would be on Mars and Earth three years before the rest, and in the meantime Lars2 would lose three to four million of his species, who would be slaughtered and eaten before one pound of food would be available to the collective.

Mona and the Guardianship had many conflicting feelings after hearing Chaos's communication. First of all, they were sickened by what appeared to be the cultural values of the invaders. They made the Atlantis Alliance seem almost tame in comparison. Second, they knew Lars2 could be the key to transforming the Earth and Mars into a sustainable ecosystem again. They needed the collective to get Lars2 and his two million helpers to where they were, because it would have taken forever for the Guardianship to go to him. Instead of rendering the collective dead and gone, the Guardianship entertained the idea of engaging in some brinkmanship to help the future of humans on the Earth and Mars.

After the communication, Mona was the only member with any moral dilemma about exterminating the collective. Chaos was sending more and more updates, and the Guardianship was learning more and more about the collective. It seemed the collective had been following Chaos for at least two thousand years and had scavenged through about twenty destroyed solar systems.

[It was later discovered, the spherical twenty-mile-wide power source was a technology they found in the first system they scavenged. This technical marvel allowed them to follow Chaos through enormous expanses of space and had allowed their population to expand from two million to thirty billion.]

The collective expected to see Chaos return after his sling around the central star. So they would send a tracker after him once he sped past them in basically the opposite way he came from. They would then plot the direction to his next solar system reclamation based on the vector on which he left the present system.

This became a problem for the Guardianship. Chaos was already cloaked and spying within the collective, and the Guardianship needed to decide what to do before the invaders realized something was wrong. The collective would want to know where Chaos was and where was he going next. The Guardianship had made all the updates to the mother ship fleet and was concentrating on Ceres herself. So far Chaos had not found any communication that indicated the collective had discovered the Guardianship yet.

Lars2's ship was proceeding toward Mars, so it was assumed the advance scouts of the collective were closing in as well. Extra vigilance was being taken to remain out of sight.

The *Condor* strike force, with Peggy and Ben in command, had all four mother ships around Mars in orbit and cloaked. The Guardianship had determined that if either advance scouts or shock troops discovered the one thousand Mars colonists, the collective home swarm would be eliminated immediately by the destruction of their power sphere, unless it could be proved there was no communication alert between CapHead and his troops.

Mona, Moonbeam, and Levie were trying to determine how to contact or abduct Lars2 without alerting the collective, in order to get his cooperation in plotting against his owners and freeing himself and the workers with him. How could they convince him to advance the recovery of Mars and Earth?

It was determined that a cloaked shuttle from *Leviathan* could corral an asteroid fragment from the asteroid belt and ram the supply ship's engine, which contained Lars2. *Leviathan* would then block communication and quickly unload the alien ship and later destroy it in such a way that it would look like it was a victim of a meteor strike. All this would be complicated and very difficult but possible.

Dr. Find was consulted on the type of nerve gas to use on the reptilian and scavenger nervous systems. If the guesses were right on everything, this might work. The lucky thing was that Lars2 was supposed to be on the first ship, which was the smallest and fastest of those sent from the collective. The Guardianship hoped that the hijacked ship would fit in the lower empty ore hold on *Leviathan*.

So the plot to capture, breach, and subdue a collective space ship was hatched. Chaos was able to identify the ship Lars2 was on when he left the collective. It was estimated the trip to reach Ceres' orbit from the collective cloud's present position would take about one year. So the Guardianship had plenty of time to practice their elaborate plan sufficiently to guarantee at least a chance for success.

Silver would pilot the shuttle that would guide the fake meteor into the engine of the collective ship. From the schematics, the Guardianship were able to download from the technical manuals of the collective the precise strike zone to accomplish the objective. Chaos had been so effective as a spy that he, along with Moonbeam's assistance, had gained access to and cracked the security of the collective's entire technical library, including their deepest security caches.

Moonbeam and Levie were further plundering this treasure hole for all the advanced and ancient knowledge the collective had been able to amass over the last two thousand years. Much of it the collective didn't understand themselves.

***

The Guardianship meeting on the *Leviathan* was in full session, with all the commanders of all the strike forces either in attendance or quantum present. Chaos was also in attendance, hovering inside the collective cloud.

It was confirmed the cloud was still so far from a sustaining power source that the destruction of their internal sphere would be 100 percent lethal for all but a tiny fraction of those with extended fuel capacity. The estimated surviving population would be less than one million out of thirty billion. The timing was becoming critical. The entire plan had to coalesce before Chaos was expected to fly past the cloud's position on his destructive trajectory to another solar system, failure to do so would thus alerting the collective that something was afoul.

Silver reported that the rehearsal of the capture of the collective's advance party was going very well. They expected the ship to be in range in two weeks. Mona was extremely pleased but very, very nervous. Things had to go perfectly. If they miscalculated anything, they could be signing all their own death warrants and all but guaranteeing the extinction of the human race.

# CHAPTER 21

# CapHead

Moonbeam and Levie had discovered that one of the Civilizations destroyed by Chaos and scavenged by the collective had made significant progress in quantum research. They not only could send information (voice, images, text, thoughts, consciousness, etc.) instantly over great distances but could also transmit and receive objects.

The sisters began to see a benefit from the collective. For two thousand years they had traveled behind Chaos, collecting the creative legacy of at least twenty distinct solar system-level civilizations. They were like a vacuum cleaner picking up leavings for someone else to discover in the collection bag. This was a task for the collective, but it was of enormous benefit to the Guardianship. The collective was too primitive and uncreative to realize and capitalize on their good fortune.

The sisters, via Chaos, were hunting for and downloading every library the collective had, and they were doing so as quickly as possible. The big day was about to begin. Everyone was in place. *Barracuda* (the fastest and longest-range shuttle craft) was cloaked, with Silver at the controls. Sue and Kevin were in the enormous ore-holding bay of *Leviathan* with C. E. and his crew at their side.

Additionally, C. E. had trained a corps of Ceres volunteers who had originally been habitat crew members before the war. They were armed with modified portable welding lasers that could cut a piece of five-foot-diameter reinforced carbon steel at whatever distance the sensors on the gun determined. Basically they had a range of two feet to twenty miles. They had been changed to fire a pulse rather than a continuous cutting beam.

Dr. Find had formulated a substance that could neutralize reptiles and amphibians. A preselected hold within *Leviathan* was fitted with aerosol jets that could be used to fill its chambers with the formulated neurological substance, as a vapor, in less than thirty seconds. All the humans scheduled to be in the hold were to wear full-body suits and head and face guards with rebreathers and portable oxygen concentrators.

The idea was for Silver to disable the collective craft, and then the cloaked *Leviathan* would swallow up the adrift ship in the dark hold. All communication would be blocked, and external weapons would be neutralized. Then the lights would be turned on. C. E. was to breach the hull using cutting lasers and dump gas into the breaches. A sonic weapon would also be used to stun the occupants if perchance they had gas protection of some type. If anyone got to the exterior without assistance, he or she would be met with gas, sonic waves, and, finally, laser weapons.

After the craft was emptied, it would be set adrift in space, and Silver would ram it with asteroid fragments until it was completely fractured into pieces. Mona was in the command section of *Leviathan* with Levie and placed the entire Guardianship on alert. Chaos was prepared to launch the last remaining ancient warhead pellet at the collective's power sphere on Mona's command.

Mona received a special message of encouragement from her parents, who were protecting Mars with the four-mother-ship *Condor* strike force. If things went badly, they would have to mop up the advanced scouting parties and shock troops of the collective.

Mona gave the order for Silver to strike. The game was on! Silver approached the moderate-sized craft from the rear; it seemed to be several times *Barracuda*'s length and volume. It was difficult for her to estimate how many beings might be on board.

*Barracuda* was cloaked, and on her top exterior bulkhead was a combination of four modified rail guns configured to launch instead of a pellet a substantial rock or meteor the size of a human body.

Mona's strike authorization was received. Within ten seconds, Silver had checked her target coordinates and fired. The rear engine assembly of the craft disintegrated. The craft tumbled violently before its automatic stabilizing thrusters compensated. Silver hoped the beings inside would be too disoriented or possibly too injured to resist. Once the craft stabilized, *Leviathan* swooped behind and swallowed the adrift ship. Then, as the disabled craft was magnetically locked to the deck of the *Leviathan*, Sue's assault assemblage pounced.

C. E.'s teams simultaneously started cutting several strategically placed holes (based on the precise schematics Chaos had provided) in the exterior of the craft. Kevin was commanding the search-and-rescue security teams armed with sidearms only and prepared to launch the gas and sonic weapons into the breaches. As C. E.'s teams finished the holes, the men yelled "Clear!" and gas canisters were launched into the open breaches. The muffled sounds of the sonic weapons reverberated.

Sue thought anything alive in that disabled ship would have one hell of a hangover once it woke up. She did not activate the gas aerosol jets in the massive ore hold or send in the laser-armed troops; instead, she waited for Kevin's signal.

Kevin and his teams entered the craft and began the search for their prey. Mona was very nervous right now. It was her and the sisters' understanding that the collective ship would send an automatic distress signal based on this type of emergency. Because the ship had been struck by an asteroid fragment, she hoped the signal would be just that and not alert the collective to a technological, intelligent attack.

It would take 62.4 minutes for the distress call to reach the collective. Mona was waiting on pins and needles for the reaction, which would no doubt be heard by Chaos.

Before the big day, Sue and Silver had discussed what the scavengers would look like. They used the news report from the collective as the standard of what they might find on the day of the abduction.

When Kevin gave the all clear, Sue and C. E. proceeded into the ship. The boarding party located the hold, where two thousand reptilians the size of diminutive humans (about five feet tall at most and one hundred pounds each) were in suspended animation. In the command section, a massive scavenger was found. At his feet was a reptilian with a studded chain around its neck.

The scavenger looked to be nine feet tall and weighed between six hundred and seven hundred pounds. He was wearing a green plaid kilt and a belt buckle with a simple crest and two red jewels on it. Kevin's men found ten more scavengers in different parts of the craft. Sue knew immediately who this joker was. "My God, we've got the big bastard himself!" she exclaimed. Mona walked into the pitch-black ore hold dressed in the traditional captain's uniform—the exact one she had worn at the launch ceremony, which now seemed to have taken place a lifetime ago.

She gave the signal, and the lights were switched on like several mini suns burning three hundred feet over her head. She was unaccompanied. From seemingly a quarter mile away, she walked with deliberate speed toward the center of the enormous cavern. Her footsteps reverberated with an echo that misrepresented her relatively small stature of five feet six inches and 110 pounds.

She walked toward the scavenger and looked down slightly. CapHead, the supreme leader of Tribe II, who ruled mercilessly over some three billion lives, was waist deep in a holding mold. His legs and hands were immobilized. He could freely move his head and torso but not his legs, hands, or arms. His rasping breaths increased in frequency as Mona approached him with confidence, looking him straight in the eye.

CapHead's eyes turned from yellow to red as Mona approached. She knew from studying their customs and protocol that any person should not, even if the same rank, venture within a scavenger's personal space, lest the scavenger's fingertip claws rip the hide off the offending body.

CapHead bellowed in rage. Mona ignored the violent protest as she would a toddler's. She said calmly in his perfect clan dialect, "You are my prisoner, and I own you from this day forward. Your life is meaningless unless I give it purpose. You will vow allegiance to your new queen or die a horrible death in dishonor and disgrace. Do you understand?"

Sue was watching from a cloaked soundproof enclosure. And as Mona's words were translated by Levie, Sue jumped up and yelled, "Way to go Moan! You be queen of the cloud now! Bitch-slap that bastard!"

Mona, simply turned and walked away, saying nothing.

CapHead screamed as she walked away in his cursing tone, reserved for subordinates and slaves, "Who do you think you are, creature ... threatening a supreme leader of three billion lives?"

Mona gave the signal, and the lights were switched off, leaving the screaming and cursing scavenger in pitch-black darkness. The mold CapHead was half encased in had been used to make ten life-size replicas of scavengers and dozens of reptilians. The replicas had been jettisoned into the drifting wreckage, wearing appropriate attire that had been stripped from live creatures. According to the collective's custom, bodies were never recovered from space. It was considered an honor to die in the vacuum and remain where one perished.

Mona entered the soundproof room and asked if there had been any update from Chaos. Jim answered, "Chaos reported that a long-range craft transporting CapHead, his bodyguards, and Lars2 had their emergency beacon activated. A meteor strike was indicated as the inflight cause. The advance scouts and shock troops closest to the event were sent to investigate. A long-range image captured by the collective forces showed a wreckage field and several bodies floating within the same vicinity. They reported no sign of life."

The collective would witness a new bloodbath, as all the rivals of CapHead would fight each other for his position as supreme leader of the II Tribe. Thousands might perish within the next three weeks before the cloud queen accepted the last one standing as heir to his position. The winner, however, would assume the position as the supreme leader of the X Tribe, not the II Tribe. It was now time to negotiate with Lars2 while CapHead cooled his heels.

***

Mona entered the room where Lars2 was seated at a table, drinking some water. The chain that had been around his neck was gone, but his neck still showed raw abrasions caused by the studs. Though the chain was basically symbolic, it still could damage the entity wearing it.

Levie was the interpreter for Mona. "My name is Captain Mona Ann Lisa, and you are our guest on the *Leviathan* of the Earth Guardianship. From this day forward, you are no longer a slave to the collective or anyone else. You are basically free to do as you please. Do you have any questions?"

Lars2 asked in a low, meek voice, "Where are my people, and where is CapHead and his bodyguards?"

Mona responded, "Your people are still in stasis on our craft and will be reanimated at your request. CapHead and his bodyguards are our prisoners and will remain securely immobilized until we decide otherwise."

Lars2 asked, "What now?"

"We call ourselves human, and we have evolved from mammalian roots and primate ancestors. We are rather young in a geologic sense—probably less than two hundred thousand years in our present form. We are a remnant of a global war just fought on the third planet from our central star, which we call the sun. There were five hundred million of us some four years ago; there are now barely one hundred eighty thousand of us scattered between three planets. The solar system robotic reclamation and demolition drone you and we called RR&DD has a different name—Chaos. Chaos did not modify our solar system on this pass but destroyed a planet here four hundred thousand years ago and stripped the atmosphere from the fourth planet, Mars, two hundred thousand years ago. We were able to stop him."

"How?"

"It is a very long and complex story, but believe me when I tell you that Chaos is no longer a threat to this solar system or any other."

"I want to see CapHead."

"Okay!"

Mona took Lars2 to the enormous hold and had the lights turned on. CapHead was still half buried from the waist down in the mold in the center of the floor. Lars2 asked if he could go talk to CapHead by himself. Mona reluctantly agreed. She and those in the soundproof room watched thoughtfully.

Lars2 went directly to CapHead, who appeared to be terrified. Lars2 exposed two elongated fangs from the palms of his hands and plunged them with lightning speed into both of CapHead's eyes, thus blinding him forever. Lars2 turned nonchalantly and walked back the way he had come from, never looking back at CapHead screaming in agony. Lars2 returned to the door where Mona had left him and waited for Mona to return.

Mona first asked C. E. and the team to attend to CapHead. Then she told Lars2 she needed his help and as an incentive would do everything in her power to free his surviving people. Lars2 bowed at his waist and said, "I am at your disposal, my dear queen."

Neither Mona nor anyone else in the Guardianship ever questioned Lars2 about what he did to CapHead. It was as if he had always been blind. However, everyone noted that Lars2 and his people were not defenseless.

The scavenger guards were placed in semipermanent stasis indefinitely. CapHead received medical attention, but no attempt was made to replace his eyes, though the Guardianship had the capability.

Mona and the planning team brainstormed on how to free Lars2's nine million remaining compatriots who were still in the collective's hands. Two million were en route to Mars and Earth, and six million plus were still in the collective cloud. Thousands had already been slaughtered. Every day delayed meant one thousand more reptilians eliminated.

The plan was about to be launched. Sue responded, "Well, Moan, CapHead is chained with his back to a metal post. His wrists, ankles, neck, and waist are all secured. He has an explosive pack embedded in his chest with a device that will send metal spikes into both of his hearts simultaneously on activation. An explosive necklace will decapitate the beast within a millisecond of activation as well. He is now wearing a bandage over his eyes. Otherwise, he is free to move at will!"

"Do you think the precautions are a bit overkill?" Mona asked.

"No, Moan, I just don't trust this guy. He reminds me of my first boyfriend. You do know he didn't get to his position within the collective by being nice?"

\*\*\*

Moonbeam and Levie had been experimenting with a quantum trick from the collective's hidden libraries. Jim, on *Leviathan*, had been assisting with Dr. Find on Ceres. They had been quantum-jumping small objects from *Leviathan* to Ceres. They didn't even need a quantum-capable conduit like Moonbeam, Levie, or a clone. They just needed a transmitter and a 3-D coordinate with a time dimension—or, more correctly, a 4-D coordinate.

When Mona was told of this, she asked if the team

thought they could send a voice and video player to a 4-D coordinate within the cloud near Saturn's orbit. They said they didn't know but would try. So Mona went to CapHead's location and recorded this message: "Greetings, cloud queen. I am Captain Mona Ann Lisa of the solar system's Guardianship. You see behind me one of your leaders, CapHead. He is chained and blinded. I am giving you a choice. If you free the remaining reptilian race by transporting them without causing further harm to the fourth planet from our central star, you will not suffer the indignities and suffering meted out to this poor soul. If you do not respond by broadcasting your agreement to my terms on your collective-wide communication system, I will respond appropriately. You have two hours to broadcast your agreement."

***

Chaos supplied the Guardianship with the coordinates of the cloud queen's public greeting hall, and the quantum jump was initiated. Chaos watched his chronometer for one minute past the two-hour deadline. He was presently on the back side of the swarm, just behind the last two rings on the outer reaches of the collective cloud. He was several thousand miles from the power sphere.

He activated his rail gun and laser banks. He blew apart about twenty ships between him and the edge of the cloud. The Kessler syndrome did the rest. The chain reaction shredded about ten thousand ships total in a perfectly conical shape. This was the collective's boneyard. The ships were old, obsolete abandoned relics used as spare parts for the rest of the cloud's occasional needs. The shrapnel was self-limiting, being blown out to the rear and laterally so the curve of the ships' formation and distribution limited the destruction to a mathematically predictable zone. Mona was pleased with Chaos's precise geometric renderings. Destruction art was spectacular but very short-lived.

Chaos asked, "Mona, do you like my execution?"

"Well done. Now we wait one hour for the queen's response. Proceed to your second demonstration coordinates."

Chaos responded, "Your wish is my command."

***

Inside the cloud queen's barge, things were turning chaotic. Security was everywhere. The queen had called the ten supreme tribal leaders to an emergency meeting in her private conference hall. She was screaming at her subordinates; her eyes were glowing red like never before. She yelled, "Who or what is this creature *Mona*? I want her found and brought to me in chains so I can eat her flesh while she is still conscious!"

The barge was a circular ship or habitat with five large biospheres connected in the center by a transparent and eternally glowing jewel-shaped light source—a singular red jewel symbolic of the collective. Other than the twenty-mile-wide power sphere, the royal barge was the most spectacular and beautiful thing in the cloud. It could be seen without telescopes by almost every subject in the collective.

The queen was still in a rampaging mood when her

view of the top part of the mile-long jewel evaporate in a searing flash of light. If it were not for her autonomic extra eyelids' response, she might have been blinded. Sparks and small molten fragments sprayed for three hundred miles in all directions almost instantaneously. It was the largest fireworks display from the royal barge in two thousand years.

Chaos yelled to himself, "I really do good work!"

As soon as the flash was gone, Chaos left a trail of flares and a message in space writing in the most common dialect of the collective. It was simple and to the point: "LET MY LIZARDS GO ..."

\*\*\*

Sue was laughing so hard she almost peed herself. "Moan, was that your idea?" she asked.

"Well ... the destruction of the collective's jewel, yes; the message, no. That was all Chaos's idea. Methinks he has developed a sense of humor. Who would have thought?"

\*\*\*

On seeing the unavoidable message within the swarm, the cloud queen was so enraged she was incoherent. She killed two of her bodyguards in a blind fury through the thrashing of her powerful limbs, slashing them to death with her razor-sharp claws. After she had time to collect herself, she called her slavekeeper and public relations coordinator. She knew now she had to make a public announcement—but what would she say?

# CHAPTER 22

# The Deceit of the Cloud Queen

The queen had a draft of her public statement prepared immediately. While that was going on she had the slavekeeper prepare a census of all the reptilians and the number of craft needed to move all seven million to Mars and to Earth's vicinity. The public statement was the following: "The cloud queen has announced that a new jewel has been chosen for the collective. Observe in the coming months to see what it will be. The queen and the supreme tribal leaders felt that after two thousand years, a change was needed. In a practical housekeeping initiative, the collective will be replacing

the reptilian slaves with a new race from this or a newer solar system. The reptilians have never been the kind of workers we expected them to be. Please cooperate with the slavekeeper administration in their collection and relocation."

\*\*\*

Chaos was monitoring all communications to and from the
queen's palace—especially the encrypted ones. Moonbeam
and Levie had long since cracked all the deepest and most
secure collective codes. It seemed the queen had given the
command to collect the reptilians on a fleet of ships but,
halfway to their destination, jettison them into the vacuum
of space. Mona had to further deal with the deceitful cloud
queen.

Because of all the new realities, Mona held another
planning session in the conference room of *Leviathan*. Lars2
was the new member representing his race. Moonbeam was
on Ceres with Dr. Larry Find, and Mona's parents, Ben and
Peggy, were in orbit around Mars. Chaos was attending via
quantum voice. He was presently in a relatively stationary
position about one thousand miles from the collective
swarm.

Moonbeam began the session with the following
statement: "The shock troops and advance scouts of the
collective are within a few months of Mars with the first
two million reptilians … the WAMS *Condor* strike force
commanded by Ben and Peggy are presently there. Their
capabilities are likely sufficient to deal with the offloading
and resettlement, along with our one thousand human
colonists. If necessary, we can send the WAMS *Crow* strike

force as backup. We are assuming the collective presently wants the initial workforce of reptilians to reach Mars safely. What we don't know is what might happen if they discover our colonists." She paused briefly. "We now know, thanks to Chaos, that the cloud queen will release the seven million slaves from the cloud but will dump them into space halfway to Mars. Any ideas on how to handle this situation?"

Lars2 commented, "My people have been mislabeled as reptiles or lizards. They are instead amphibians. We evolved on a planet that had an extremely elliptical orbit around our star. For half of our orbit, it was either too cold or too hot to work on our surface. We would bury ourselves in the soil and hibernate without the stasis machinery you and the scavengers require and think we need also. Our bodies secrete a protective layer, and our internal organs shut down. We can easily withstand the extremes, even life-threatening exposure, found in deep space, temporarily. So let the collective dump our bodies into deep space. As long as you can recover us in your massive ore ships, we will survive. All we need is a plan that corresponds with the queen's plot to eliminate us."

Mona acknowledged Moonbeam's analysis and thanked Lars2 for his detailed explanation of the reptilians' remarkable abilities. She went on to say there were longer-term problems with the collective no matter how they solved the short-term retrieval and relocation of Lars's tribe.

"Since Chaos is no longer doing his version of solar system reclamation," Mona said, "the scavenger collective is out of a job. Unless they see RR&DD zoom by shortly on his way out of the solar system, they will know he is missing. And unless we deal with the collective here and now, they will possibly be our problem forever."

Silver suggested that they have Chaos do a flyby in hopes that the collective was preoccupied and did not notice that he did not sling around the sun. Mona asked Chaos, "Have there been any messages about your whereabouts?"

Chaos answered, "Not that I am aware of."

"Good. But if we have you streak by at your normal speed, they will send scouts after you to see the vector at which you leave the solar system. You will then have to be gone months or years before you can return. That is not an option. What can we do?"

Silver conjectured that maybe it was time to confront the collective and end it now. Mona, however, asked, "Are we prepared to exterminate thirty billion sentient beings?"

Jim suggested that there was a possible compromise. "Why don't we tell the collective the truth once we get all of Lars2's tribe safe? We can tell them Chaos now works for us. We are king of the hill and can tell them to leave town and find a new solar system to bully. If they attack, we destroy them in a fair fight for survival."

C. E. interjected. "Sounds noble, but if we wait until they get close enough to the sun they are unencumbered by their need to cluster around their power sphere; we will then be completely overwhelmed by their numbers. How long will it be before we are even marginally in that situation?"

Moonbeam ventured to speak her ideas. "Based on my analysis and the cloud's present location just inside the orbit

of Saturn, or eight AU's to Earth's orbit, I would say somewhere around four years from now. However, large numbers
of their faster and longer-range forces could be enough to
overwhelm us within half that time. So, I think we realistically have only two years from today to guarantee we have
the best chance to prevail."

Mona stated emphatically, "We have just two years to
collect Lars2's tribe, settle them on Mars, and solve our
dilemma with the collective. We have much to do in a short
time. Let's get started." But though she sounded confident,
she still didn't know just how to solve all these concerns
without having to resort to genocide.

\*\*\*

The cloud queen was so incensed about Mona that she had
few other thoughts. How could she entice this vile creature
to show her hand and become entrapped by her love of
these lizards?

Possibly, she would need to create a crisis in which the
ship or ships loaded with the reptilians were in dire need
of assistance and Mona would have to rush to their rescue.
They were to die anyway because she was going to dump all
seven million of them into deep space, except for the two
million already just one year from the fourth and eventually
third planet.

\*\*\*

Mona had made up her mind; she ordered Chaos to un-
cloak his ship and streak by the collective, close enough to
be easily observed at a faster cruising speed than normal.

He was then to turn quickly at an acute vector and speed past Saturn, using Saturn to block the collective advanced scouts' line of sight. He was to accelerate to his top speed, cloak, and sling around Saturn's moon Titan to return to the collective's cloud as soon as possible. The whole operation was to take only two weeks.

Mona hoped the collective would take the bait and think they had just temporarily lost RR&DD in Saturn's rings or something else just as possible. She further hoped that, using the star charts pilfered from one of their scavenged civilizations, the scouts would assume he was headed for a specific solar system. It would not be known if it worked until Chaos could return from his spying operation.

*** 

Grumbling had started among the supreme leaders of the ten tribes of the swarm. No matter the public announcements the queen had released for public consumption, the space writing left by Chaos and the destruction of the cloud jewel by some mysterious power had everyone on edge. The leaders were concerned that someone was capable of attacking and destroying their most sacred symbol, not to mention the collective's boneyard.

Because CapHead was known to be alive, his successors were reluctant to risk fighting to the death without a guarantee they would not have to fight him later as well. The queen's unquestioned authority had been rocked by this Mona creature. Could the queen be vulnerable? She was furious and was quick to attack and punish harshly any and all who dared to question her orders. Her advisers all but abandoned any suggestion or criticism of her decrees for fear of torture or death. She was on a course toward self-destruction.

\*\*\*

Mona knew she had big problems no matter what strategy she chose. She had to obliterate thirty billion souls, no matter how repugnant that was, or she could get the collective to leave for a new solar system without Chaos's destructive assistance, or she could find a way to modify their behavior and find a place in the galaxy where they could coexist with more civilized neighbors.

The first option was morally unacceptable, and the second was sending her burden to someone else that would be ill-prepared for the challenge. The last was all but impossible except for God himself. Mona was becoming nauseated. She decided it was time to visit CapHead again. He had been isolated from all interaction other than that of a reptilian tribal member attending to his minimal needs. Lars2 had requested his race have this privilege.

Mona entered the enclosure where he was housed. There was a clear indestructible wall between them; the wall's construction and properties allowed sound and light to pass freely but nothing else. CapHead was aware that someone had entered. He asked who was there.

Mona said, "It is your new queen … Mona." CapHead roared in laughter. Mona responded, "I think you just insulted your host."

CapHead stopped laughing and said, "What is the purpose of your visit?"

"We have some business to discuss."

"What possible business could we have?" bellowed CapHead.

"Your old queen is mad, and I intend to be rid of her. I want to install a king instead. Are you interested?"

CapHead was flabbergasted at first, but when he found his voice again, he roared in laughter once more. He then thundered, "Are you crazy? A blinded scavenger is usually ceremonially ejected into the void of deep space. How could I even be a candidate for king?"

Mona's response was blunt. "Well, we can fix that if you will consider my offer."

\*\*\*

Chaos uncloaked and streaked by the cloud when the scouts acknowledged his presence. They immediately broke from the cloud and chased him toward Saturn. Chaos then doubled his speed and disappeared in the rings and then behind the enormous planet. He then cloaked himself and slung around Titan. He passed the scouts on his way back to the collective. Chaos listened to hear whether the collective detected anything unusual. They didn't. The ruse appeared to have been successful!

\*\*\*

Sue accompanied Mona to the holding cell this time. They had been accused of being salt and pepper when they had partied in SpaceJump City before the war. Sue was the salt—the sassy, wisecracking blonde. Mona was the pepper—the serious but hauntingly beautiful brunette with the small bump in her forehead.

Sue nervously advised Mona to be careful, and Mona looked at her with impatience. "Sue, if I died or was mortally injured, the explosives in CapHead's chest would ignite, sending the spikes into both of his hearts. You are holding the trigger that can explosively decapitate him anytime you want! Wouldn't you want that kind of power and control over all your boyfriends?"

Sue, without hesitation, replied, "Damn right!"

CapHead acknowledged Sue and Mona's presence. This time he was chained to the floor and seated in a massive chair. Sue talked first. "So you are ready to negotiate, FlatHead … I mean CapHead?"

Mona gave Sue the signal to disengage and allow her to take the lead. Mona said, "Your reptilian guard said you wanted to talk; is that correct?"

"Yes."

Sue said quickly, "Well, go on!"

CapHead stated, "I will do as you propose, but I must first have my sight returned. Deal?"

Mona and Sue simultaneously agreed: "Deal!"

Mona was advised that in order for CapHead to become king of his people, according their traditions and customs, he had to swear allegiance to a queen. It did not have to be the existing cloud queen but could be a queen competing for the position. The swearing-in ceremony had to be officially seen by a significant percentage of the swarm to be legal. And the challenging queen had to best the existing queen on the field of competition before CapHead could reign as king.

Sue asked, "If you win, Moan, you don't have to … like … eat a reptilian live on video com, do you?"

***

On hearing of what Mona was thinking about doing, Peggy and Ben went ballistic.

"Mona Ann Lisa," her father scolded, "what kind of crazy, idiotic thing are you thinking about doing? This is totally nuts and unnecessary. We will not stand by and let you compete with a beast that is six times your weight and almost twice your height."

The historical review by Moonbeam and Levie revealed that the competition between two scavengers for queen was a rare occurrence. Each of the ten tribes always had a queen in waiting, and the most senior assumed the position on the death of the reigning queen. A king was not always designated (as is the present situation) but may be at the request of a queen. The king could be any of the ten supreme leaders of the tribes.

As a technical note, CapHead had not been replaced because he was discovered to be alive. The king, if appointed by a cloud queen, was the absolute ruler in the absence of the queen.

At any time, though this was rare in their history, a supreme tribal leader, such as CapHead, could announce loyalty to a new queen in waiting or any other female. This female could challenge the reigning cloud queen in a winner-takes-all competition.

***

CapHead was about to publicly swear his allegiance to his queen-in-waiting, Mona, to the entire scavenger cloud via video communication from Ceres. CapHead was standing with his dagger in his hand. He sliced his hand and smeared the blood across his forehead. He then pressed his belt buckle into the blood. The two red jewels were covered with his blood. The tiny Mona came into the picture and stood in front of CapHead. He took the buckle and pressed it to Mona's forehead.

She turned to reveal the two jewel-shaped marks on her forehead. CapHead stated to his tribe, "This female is my new queen-in-waiting, Mona of the Swarm Tribe II. It is done from this day forward." Mona then placed a bandoleer across her chest with the two jewels in the center.

Mona stated, "I accept the blood oath and as my right do challenge the cloud queen to the competition of succession."

The transmission was completed. Chaos reported that the message traffic was one hundred times normal in the cloud.

***

The queen called a meeting of the supreme leaders and as usual was her charming self. She yelled to the swarm leaders, "This is an insult to my prowess and dignity. To have this insect challenge me to a 'competition of succession'! How dare she! After this is finished, I will have CapHead gutted and cooked alive in my dining facility. Get out of my conference room, you worthless slime!"

\*\*\*

Mona was alone with her thoughts. She had always been confident with her physical abilities, but she felt that this might be the challenge of her life. Though she had been a gold medalist in the pentathlon at the World Games, that seemed a lifetime ago.

According to Moonbeam and Levie, the competition of succession was a list of five events: three chosen by the reigning queen and two by the challenger. In head-to-head competition, the winner must be champion in three out of five events.

The events were taken from a list of ten. All of them were used to test the capabilities of the ancient scavengers in their training to become shock troops. Normally both combatants had thirty days to prepare, but this time it would take twelve months for Mona and the cloud queen to meet in the orbit of Jupiter.

\*\*\*

CapHead was now Mona's trainer. If Mona failed, he would die a horrible death. If she won, he would become the king of the swarm—the highest position he could ever attain within the collective.

It seemed impossible for this diminutive female creature to defeat the reigning cloud queen. Few of his fellow supreme leaders would have even challenged her. But then again, Mona had amazed him several times with her strength of will and leadership. He did not underestimate her abilities. She had already outwitted the brutal queen several times; anyway, he really had no choice. He also despised the cloud queen. Mona, though not a scavenger, was probably the secret favorite of the majority of the collective.

\*\*\*

While *Leviathan* was en route to Jupiter's orbit, accompanied by the four ships in Strike Force *Eagle*, Moonbeam and Levie, with Chaos's help, downloaded the entire knowledge base of the collective, including the twenty scavenged solar systems. Peggy and Ben had advised as a precaution that they delete or infect the knowledge from the twenty solar systems remaining in the cloud. The collective was not presently sophisticated enough to use the wisdom found there, but it was not worth the risk to let them try.

Chaos used his digital bomb to block all communication with these history libraries in case he could not delete them. He destroyed 90 percent of them without difficulty. If the collective ever became a trusted ally, they could have their information restored.

Mona was with CapHead in the *Barracuda* and uncloaked so they would be visible to the oncoming swarm forces. The *Leviathan* accompanying the WAMS *Eagle* strike force followed all, cloaked.

While the cloud had enormous resources and a massive population, they would have been vulnerable and helpless if Mona had wanted to destroy them in their present location this far from the sun. Her only considerations now were to save the reptilians that were likely to be dumped into space by the queen's shock troops at any time.

The queen had agreed to free the seven million, but Chaos's spying had revealed the queen's plot to do otherwise. Mona had wanted the queen to think she could do this evil act and foil it. In Mona's quest to quickly alter the scavengers' culture, this was a pivotal event.

Mona was taking a big gamble after another big gamble, but she wanted to save lives and change hearts. This path was not the easiest for her, and she knew it. CapHead was just beginning to understand Mona's motivations and courage. The scavengers respected very little about others' cultures but understood and revered courage.

# CHAPTER 23

# Training

This little female was as formidable an adversary as he had ever encountered. CapHead was not only beginning to respect Mona but was enjoying her as well. He had always despised the present cloud queen, as most of the other supreme tribal leaders did. The queen was unreasonably brutal even among the most ruthless culture in the galaxy.

If things had to change, CapHead could see no other way for it to happen. This was going to be an exciting and bumpy ride into the unknown. His fighting nature was engaged, and he was anxious for the next phase to begin. Bring it on!

***

The queen was feeling rather good right now. They had sustained no more mysterious attacks in months, and since she had sent the reptilians away from the swarm, she had been in total control except for Mona's insolence and the traitorous CapHead's act on the cloud-wide communication link eight months ago.

The queen was now four hundred years old and had reigned for at least one hundred years. She was young because cloud queens historically didn't get the chance to rule this soon, owing to the long lifespans of the queens-in-waiting in line ahead of them.

This was not a problem for Gilda; she took things into her own hands and assisted Mother Nature a tad. No one really connected the dots, but four of the more senior candidates died way too young. Gilda just smiled and mourned the untimely death of her noble competition. Fair play was never in Gilda's playbook.

The queen knew they were within days of dumping the reptilians and hoped it would be timed perfectly so the creature Mona and her King Hopeful would see the act personally.

Queen Gilda had no need of a king and never would have appointed one, but she had a short list just in case. She grudgingly had to admit that CapHead was at the top of the list. This made Mona's challenge even more delicious; she was going to get revenge times two.

Gilda had ordered her shock troops to scan for
CapHead and Mona's ship, whose signature was given in the
competition agreement. They were not to attack or harm
the alien ship or its precious cargo in any way. Once located,
they were to proceed until long-range visual contact was assured. They were then to dump all seven million slaves into
deep space and return to the cloud immediately, leaving a
few recon buoys to record and transmit the reaction.

***

Levie was with Silver, C. E., Jim, and Lars2 on the
*Leviathan*. Levie alerted the *Barracuda* that a fleet of large
ships were approaching from the direction of Saturn's orbit. CapHead acknowledged for Mona, who was deep in
thought.

Lars2 alerted *Eagle* 3 and *Eagle* 4; they had been stripped
and reconfigured to accept the seven million reptilians in
self-imposed stasis. These ships were two of the original 14
World Alliance mother ships. Their ten cloaked shuttles
were launched and sprinted at flank speed toward the shock
troops' fleet. All was as ready as possible for this enormous
rescue mission. What happened next was quite possibly a
miracle.

Instead of ceremonially launching one reptilian at a
time out of the emergency air locks, as was the custom, the
ships opened their cargo hold doors and dumped caged pallets of slaves out ten thousand at a time.

Lars2 knew he didn't need the shuttles except as tug-
boats to nudge the large containers into the loading docks

of the mother ships. The rescue would take one hundred times less effort than the Guardianship had planned for.

Mona instructed CapHead to steer for one of the pallets and use their search lights as though looking for life signs. When none were found, they disengaged and proceeded to locate and destroy the recon buoys before proceeding to the cloud. Chaos reported a half hour later that all buoy transmissions were now dead.

The rescue started in earnest.

***

On seeing the buoy feeds before they were destroyed by CapHead, Gilda was ecstatic. She had already shown that diminutive pest not to be a challenge to her. Mona had her slaves! All Gilda needed now was to crush the upstart in the upcoming competition, and she would legally tear Mona and CapHead apart personally limb by limb in public.

***

After sending a well-worded and impassioned protest to the queen for her cruel act, Mona publically swore to avenge the deaths of these innocent beings in the upcoming competition.

Mona still had a few months before the competition, and she was training hard with CapHead. CapHead told Mona the queen's name was Gilda and that this knowledge might be used against her at the right moment. The rules of the competition mandated that each contestant be wired with a voice connection that neither could turn off.

He felt the queen would verbally harass Mona

constantly, so he would train her to ignore it. He, however, suggested that Mona withhold her verbal counterattacks on Gilda for the right moment, when they could be decisive. The queen's uncontrollable temper was her most glaring weakness.

***

In contrast to Mona's preparation, Gilda's consisted of eating fewer desserts. She was so confident of her victory that she didn't even consider a strategy in the unlikely chance she lost. Without question, her arrogance was one of her best qualities. Without such extreme hubris, she would have been just one of the dull queens in the swarm's history. Gilda craved adulation, fame and eternal renown. She fantasized this competition being immortalized as an epic battle between the greatest queen ever and the upstart alien aided by the treasonous shock troop commander. To guarantee her place as a living legend, not only did Gilda need to crush CapHead and Mona, but she had to make sure they were considered formidable threats.

***

The competition would be held in the largest biosphere in the collective. The sphere was presently near the power sphere but would be moving to the outer strata of vessels to take advantage of more and more infrared radiation as they neared the central star of this solar system.

The contained ecosystem was equivalent to about twenty square miles of continuous variable terrain. Her familiarity with it gave Gilda even more confidence of success. CapHead was familiar with the terrain in the biosphere, and with Moonbeam's and Levie's assistance, and with information extracted from Chaos's spying, they recreated much of it in 3-D imaging in the ore holds on *Leviathan*. Mona was actually going to be much more familiar with the existing terrain and its flora and fauna than the cloud queen herself.

CapHead especially worked with Mona on hiding places, where she could be much more effectively concealed than the much larger cloud queen. Each contestant had to submit schematics of the two weapons they were allowed to bring to the competition. If approved, these weapons could be fabricated and inspected the day of competition by their seconds. CapHead was Mona's designated second.

All other weapons were supplied by the officials based on the specific characteristics of the five trials. Mona sent schematics of her bow and arrows. She also submitted schematics of a boomerang. The cloud queen sent schematics of a large dagger and an extra-large javelin.

The boomerang appeared to be just an L-shaped cutting tool to CapHead, and he asked why she might want it. After Mona demonstrated its use, he smiled from ear to ear. Both teams approved the weapons.

CapHead never said exactly why, but he stressed conditioning above all else to Mona. She was running around the ore holds for hours each day, climbing up and down walls and ladders, and swimming underwater for long distances. He had her conditioning at high simulated altitudes for long periods of time. If she asked why, he just said the swarm's

advance scouts and shock troops were under his leadership
for a reason.

*** 

Ben and Peggy Lisa were on alert as the main ecoalteration
fleet of the swarm was about to arrive. The fleet was large
but not enormous. It was perhaps two hundred cargo vessels most likely hauling ten thousand reptilian workers
each, or two million total workers, and another fifty vessels
carrying, according to Chaos, about ten thousand shock
troops and advance scouts.

These fifty vessels were being tracked and targeted
by all forty of the *Condor* strike force's armed and cloaked
shuttles. If a battle occurred, the swarm would last about
thirty seconds. The four World Alliance mother ships
would never even have to fire one laser or rail gun. The plan
was to cloak the small Guardianship colonist's settlement in
hopes it would not be discovered.

Ben and Peggy were perfectly content to watch and
wait for the swarm to begin the transformation of Mars.
They reported to Moonbeam that all was as expected on
Ceres. Mona was pleased that the swarm's fleet had arrived
around Mars without violence so far and that they had recovered all seven million reptilians that the queen had tried
to eliminate.

Lars2 now had his tribe relatively safe for the first time
in hundreds of years. He now would develop plans and
strategies for the terraforming of Mars and Earth, but with
nine million workers total. He had never before had such a

workforce. He was both relieved and honored to serve his
new queen, Mona.

***

Levie was leading the planning meeting in the *Leviathan*'s
conference room. She stated to the attendees, "We have just
voted to have Lars2 take command of WAMS *Eagle*'s ships
3 and 4, which will now leave the strike force and transport
the reptilian survivors to Mars. They are to remain cloaked
and, when safe, join the *Condor* strike force around Mars.
The *Leviathan* and the WAMS *Eagle*'s ships 1 and 2 will
remain en route with *Barracuda* to the collective cloud. We
are pleased we were able to accomplish this historic rescue."

***

Mona was now within thirty days of the collective and
was getting more and more apprehensive. Her plan to save
the reptilians could not have gone any better. Ceres was
still safe, protected by the five-ship *Crow* strike force and
Moonbeam. Mars, though surrounded by swarm forces,
was well guarded by her parents on the WAMS *Condor*.

Mona was presently the only wild card and person in
real jeopardy—or she and CapHead, to be exact. She might
have less than a month to live. This dire situation was, however, not what bothered her the most. The thing really wor-
rying her was what the hell she was going to do if she lived
and became the queen of thirty billion scavengers!

Moonbeam and Levie had been doing some plotting
themselves with Chaos. They were trying to ensure Mona's
safety in all contingencies. They knew she would refuse

their assistance if the conditions of the competition were fair; however, rescuing her and CapHead if things weren't fair or if they lost was a different story.

Chaos was ready and willing to do whatever he was asked to do if circumstances required his interference. He would be positioned over the biosphere before, during, and after the event.

\*\*\*

Gilda thought she should do some weapons training since it was now less than thirty days to the competition. She had to pick a second but genuinely trusted no one. She was trying to think whose family she had in prison and could therefore trust would not fail her for fear of death or torture visited on their loved ones. *Oh yes!* she thought to herself, *Supreme Tribal Leader IX. I had his mother thrown in prison for telling that joke about me at that state banquet ten years ago. He should do very well.* She called her bodyguards and had them retrieve IX's mother from prison. Next she summoned IX for an audience.

\*\*\*

A three-hundred-page document had been received by Mona and CapHead three days ago detailing the rules and obligations of the succession competition. Jim had been going over it and was about to brief everyone on its provisions and responsibilities.

Just by looking at Jim, one could see he had a headache.

Sue asked, "What in this solar system are all the details about?"

Silver just smiled, knowing that after 115,000 years, she was about to hear something new. Jim rubbed his head and read some provisions:

- Winner takes responsibility for the loser's families (no significant torture or imprisonments allowed.) Confiscation of all property is allowed, however, and removal of all property rights to the third generation is permissible.
- Winner must cremate or bury challenger and second's bodies or consume them at celebratory banquet.
- The loser's tribe will forfeit all seniority in succession for three hundred years or until two cloud queens have been replaced, whichever comes first.
- Losers' names will not be allowed to be spoken for two hundred years, and those with the same names will have them legally changed by the courts.
- For the games to begin, the mother and father of the competitors must be present at the start of competition (or their designated legally sufficient replacement) and held by the game officials so the winner may later have them placed in stocks and ridiculed during the celebratory banquet afterward.

C. E. interjected. "That last provision is a killer. We would never want Ben and Peggy there, even if they could get here in the time remaining. It is impossible."

Jim said, "The line '(or their designated legally sufficient replacement)' means that Mona can substitute a male and female whom the queen will accept as people she would like

to belittle and ridicule upon Mona's death and dismember-
ment. Any volunteers?"

"Count me in," said C. E.

Silver and Sue both volunteered, but Mona eliminated
Silver because she would be second in command upon
Mona's death. Sue said, "I guess it is you and me, big guy. I
always wanted to be a mom."

Mona asked, "Are you two sure about this?"

Sue declared, "Sure. I can't wait to see this biosphere
thingy."

C. E. agreed that he would love to see it as well … up
close and personal.

Mona was getting really annoyed by this game she
was training for. It was one thing for her and CapHead
to risk everything, but the involvement of Sue and C. E.
was a complication she had not bargained for. Defeating
this cloud queen was going to get all her attention from
this point on. She asked CapHead to double their training
schedule until the event.

C. E. and Sue had up to this time not really talked that
much. Both respected each other's abilities, but they had
not really had a personal conversation. C. E. asked, "Sue,
just how did you meet Mona anyway?"

Sue replied, "The meeting was simple; the relationship
is more complicated, as it developed over the years. Mona
was a student of mine. She was the youngest to be in my
course on ancient antiquities ever. Really, she was a child
prodigy. At first I thought she was like other overly bright
kids, but was I wrong. She never got lost and stayed so focused on her studies that she couldn't see the big picture.
Her intuition and personal skills were off the charts."

"When she went into space engineering years later, we bumped into each other and became friends. I met her parents before they shipped off to a long-term position at the Moon Research Center, and I guess I became her older sister and the extended earthbound family she never had. How very ironic it is that if it had not been for my relationship with Mona, I would not be here but would be dead and forgotten like the majority of the human species. So no matter what happens, I am on Mona's team, come hell or high water."

C. E. interjected. "From what I have seen in the short time I have been privileged to be around her, I agree completely. My first encounter with Mona was in my position as senior crew chief on the Space Search and Rescue Team administration. As a pilot candidate, she was required to spend weeks flying missions with our teams in near-Earth situations. I can tell you I saw none better. In fact, she was so good that when they launched the WAMS *Leviathan*, I attended the launch ceremony. That was the first and only launch ceremony I ever attended in person. I just wanted to see that exceptional person take possession of that magnificent creation, the *Leviathan*. How ironic that I am now presently on the *Leviathan*. And I agree with you I am proud to serve with you as one of Mona's substitute parents. How about a strong adult drink to celebrate?"

CapHead agreed to increase the training pace but did not want to push Mona too far, as he knew he could destroy her frail human physiology. However, it seemed that no matter what he meted out, she exceeded his expectations. He was beginning to believe they might not become Gilda's midnight snack after all. Whatever happened, he was having a great time working with a being (other than a fellow scavenger) that he didn't despise.

He really didn't understand why Mona had not only spared his life and given back his eyesight but was also trusting him with her very survival. The only thing he could say was that he wanted more than anything he had wanted in a very long time to see a nonscavenger defeat and destroy one of his own.

Mona was in her training mode—the one she had fallen into before for the World Games not so many years prior. She had experienced this frequently when she pushed her body to the limits. It was an almost spiritual zone. It was as if she were floating above her fatigued body, looking down at her struggle with an inner peace and without the pain normally associated with such exertion. If she could get to this zone when she needed it, she felt confident she could survive this challenge.

The training CapHead had devised was pushing her further and further beyond where she was before the World Games. That made sense because the consequence of failure was not disappointment but her own life and likely the lives of her friends and just possibly thirty billion beings as well.

Peggy and Ben reported that the swarm forces were already transporting the slave workers to the Martian surface. So far, the human colonists had stayed out of harm's way. There was only a token presence of the Swarm's special forces units because there were no known indigenous flora, fauna, or sentient beings detected.

\*\*\*

The workers were busy constructing underground housing for the reptilians. Little did the swarm forces know that the amphibian race could just burrow under the surface and survive very easily without the elaborate construction. Lars2, on his way to Mars, had devised a plan to rid them of all control and subjugation by any other race now and forever. While he trusted Mona, he was sure that neither he nor she would live forever. However, his first objective was to secure his race's freedom from the swarm as soon as possible. Once that was accomplished, he would negotiate, as a force to be reckoned with, and gain total independence from even the Guardianship.

*** 

The queen was lounging in her hot tub when she received the notice that the advance scouts and special forces were settling the ecoworker slaves on the fourth planet. Gilda wondered why Mona, if she was so capable, had not tried to interfere with the landing. *Guess the nauseating insect either has no guts or simply hasn't the ability to challenge the collective. She is choosing to play parlor tricks instead of engaging in a real confrontation with my enormous military forces.*

*** 

Silver was not happy she was not allowed to be Mona's stand-in mom. She had rather liked the idea, no matter how silly the whole thing was. Silver was ancient but was still very human, and she occasionally allowed her more primitive nature to surface. She had very strong maternal feelings toward Mona and was capable of destroying anyone or anything that threatened this remarkable girl. Silver dreamed of personally tearing both hearts out of the cloud queen's chest with her bare hands. She had not felt this way since she and her son had dispatched Mankiller's wolf pack when they rescued Sue Grammar from the wrecked alliance rescue aircraft.

***

Within the collective, the underground betting on the succession competition was getting very hot. The swarm was thirty billion and had long since become very dysfunctional. In their history, when there were only a couple million scavengers, everyone was employed and was necessary to keep the cloud alive. Now only a tiny fraction of the population was gainfully employed or even underemployed. The rest lived their lives in the relatively purposeless pursuit of entertainment and addictions of one form or another. Gambling was a major pastime, and the upcoming event had fired the imagination of the collective like nothing else in about one thousand years.

# CHAPTER 24

# Welcome to the Swarm

Almost every member of the swarm was glued to a video communication device and hanging on every prediction and speculation that the prognosticators uttered. The bookies had betting lines on about anything one could imagine—things like how many trials either the queen or Mona would win, which trials would be chosen by the queen or Mona, who would ultimately win, which weapons the contestants would get approved, and whether the queen would eat CapHead and Mona raw or have the two cooked, roasted, grilled, poached, deep fried, or fricasseed. You name it or imagine, and there was a betting line on it. All this activity in the collective was not ignored by Mona, Levie, or Moonbeam. This was revealing some fundamental characteristics of the cloud.

It seemed that only a tiny fraction of the population ruled the enormous empire. This minority was made up of the queen's palace personnel, her bodyguards, the advance scouts, the special forces, and the supreme tribal leaders and their families and servants. Moonbeam calculated that fewer than nine hundred thousand scavengers ruled with an iron fist over thirty billion souls. So less than 0.003 percent of the cloud had, for at least one thousand years, been in control.

The collective was basically a paper tiger. Nine hundred thousand well-armed, trained, and disciplined personnel were no match for the remnants of a shattered solar system, but they would be easily repelled by any technically competent civilization that had not been destroyed by Chaos beforehand. The big secret was finally out; the collective was a sham.

Mona now knew this basket case of a civilization was a liability to pity and not fear in its present incarnation. It would have trouble defending itself, much less attacking another solar system on its own. What was she to do? Should she go on with this competition or simply tell the queen to shove it and demand that the whole cloud move on somewhere else?

Nine hundred thousand well-trained and armed personnel were still a threat to the remnant of the human race, no matter the minimal technological advantages they possessed. She had to be cautious and deliberate, but she was very relieved that the threat was nothing like she had first imagined.

To confirm their beliefs and assumptions, she thought she would have a detailed discussion with CapHead. After Mona's last training session for the day, she asked CapHead if they could talk. CapHead said, "Please, what can I tell you?"

Mona inquired, "The collective is in trouble, is it not?"

CapHead went silent for a moment and said, "The truth is … yes. It has been in trouble for several centuries. The leadership has been corrupted and held on to control only by being brutal, heartless, and paranoid. Our people lack direction, creativity, and any real purpose to live except for self-gratification and a desire to escape boredom. They need not struggle to survive; we only wait for new things to fall into our lap that other civilizations have created and left. Even when we force the reptilians to terraform the planets left by RR&DD, we don't really need the food. We produce enough ourselves within the swarm. We enjoy the new varieties of food; that is all. We just go by the script left by those before us, and we don't know how to change."

Mona said, "Well, RR&DD is no more, and you will have to change. The next solar system you visit that contains any competent civilization will easily destroy you. You do know we could have ended your threat at least a year ago?"

CapHead asked, "Why didn't you end us?"

Mona thought and then answered. "I guess we thought better of it. The simple answer is that we almost destroyed ourselves without any help from anyone else. We know the result of unrestricted use of force and destruction and didn't want to destroy thirty billion sentient beings unless we had no other choice. We also wanted to stop the torture and genocide of the reptilian slaves, and we thought their race could possibly help us return our world to its previous life-sustaining condition."

CapHead asked, "What do you want to do now?"

"Well, CapHead," Mona replied, "after this mess with the queen is resolved, you will have a choice. The collective can search the galaxy for a solar system presently devoid of a civilization and colonize it; remain as a self-sustaining collection of ostensibly useless beings, looking for a purpose

and wandering forever until you or something more powerful ends you; or perhaps you can use your knowledge, technology, and massive population to help other less-advanced
races and civilizations progress. Your choice."

CapHead reflected on his answer and stated, "If I were
to lead my people, I would choose a real and better purpose.
Their present condition cannot be sustained for much
longer. We must rid the collective of the present queen and
her form of governance and its corruption in a way that
is understood by my people. Mona, I am sure you are the
agent of change that can accomplish this miracle. While I
have no moral right to ask you, will you go through with
the head-to-head competition with Gilda, as is presently
scheduled?"

Mona thought to herself, *I must be nuts to even consider going through with the competition.* "We have already
obtained the release of Lars2's people. The forces at the
swarm's command, while significant, are really just sitting
ducks for our ships, our technology, and our level of firepower. Unless they can be useful in some way I am not presently aware of, I just want them to leave. Sue would say that
if you hold all the best cards, why draw from the deck looking for anything better? I don't know, except my intuition
tells me not to reject his request. God, I don't believe I am
going to say … yes. Did I just say … yes?" Mona groaned.

CapHead bowed to Mona and said, "You are more a
queen to my race right now than Gilda has been for one
hundred years."

"Okay, okay!" Mona said. "I get it; let's not make this
too gushy. We need to have our whole planning group jump
in on this one. How to change the direction of an entire

race?" Mona thought, *It would be much easier to kill them all ...*

\*\*\*

Moonbeam was leading the Guardianship planning meeting and summarized the situation. "The major objectives we sought have basically been accomplished. The collective has been neutralized as a credible threat to the solar system militarily. The amphibian race enslaved by the collective has been freed. We have two million ecoworkers now on Mars to terraform the planet, and we hope to have seven million on Earth within two years. Mona has agreed to help CapHead remove the present cloud queen and repurpose the collective as a positive force in the galaxy. This planning meeting is primarily about the removal of the queen and the changing of the collective. Any questions or comments?"

Mona began by saying, "I cannot completely explain how we migrated from just protecting the human race from extinction by self-annihilation to rehabbing a two-billion-year-old solar system wrecking ball, to saving a race of terraforming amphibians, to now repurposing thirty billion brutal scavengers. But we have. I have no excuse; I am guilty as charged. I have given my word to help. Can you help me one more time to maybe pull off the biggest miracle of all?"

Levie stated, "In order to make the collective receptive to a change of culture, the messenger must be believed. Therefore, the foundation on which the messenger speaks cannot be based on a lie. The competition must be considered fair as far as Mona and CapHead are concerned.

Whether the queen cheats or not is not important. Anything within the rules is acceptable, and the collective will respect imaginative thinking in this regard as not cheating. We therefore will perform a full analysis of the rules to see where we may gain advantage for Mona and the opposite for the queen.

"We will also interview CapHead and see if he has some knowledge he doesn't even know he holds. The queen has secured the services of Supreme Tribal Leader IX as her second, albeit by intimidation. She now proceeds to seek influence over the competition officials. This was supposed to be against the rules, of course, but the queen never was a stickler for rules unless they helped her."

*\*\**

The officials were members of the collective's supreme court, who were all selected by the ten tribal leaders and approved by the queen. Gilda had just had her bodyguards personally deliver all the officials a gift basket of body parts from the last state execution. She thought it was such a nice touch, letting them know she was thinking about their professional well-being.

Gilda was reviewing the schematics of the weapons Mona had submitted to the competition officials, and while familiar with the bow and arrows, she was totally puzzled by the boomerang. She thought, *What a curious knife* …

She thought the diminutive insect was not going to be much competition and that she might have to make it look closer so as to improve the drama and make her look better to her public. *Oh, what a queen must sacrifice to please her subjects.*

***

Moonbeam and Levie had been working on cloaking hand weapons. This was an enormous technical issue. Cloaking an entire ship was easier. Levie asked to see Sue and C. E. in the conference room. When they entered, Levie said, "Shut the door, and you are sworn to absolute secrecy. I just fabricated these two weapons on the 3-D printer. Sue and C. E., we need you two to subject these to as much testing as possible. They have an internal cloaking device embedded in their handles. Please use them in the ship's armory and scan them through every security detection system you can find. We need your analysis to make further refinements. The plan is for you to go to the competition unarmed. We will quantum-jump these to you when we have your 4-D coordinates precisely established. They will be cloaked when sent. You should feel them when they arrive. They are to be used to protect Mona and CapHead only after the competition has ended and if you have no other course of action."

Moonbeam and Levie had spent hours with Jim and CapHead reviewing the rules for any loophole that a second could use to give his contestant an advantage. There were two likely areas that CapHead knew of: one was the artful use of voice harassment using a bit of information known only to him regarding the queen. He hoped to send the queen into a rage at the most vulnerable time. The second was training at simulated high altitudes, which would produce results similar to doping. Mona's oxygen-carrying capacity would thereby be enhanced, giving her more strength and stamina. CapHead knew the queen was way too lazy to have done the same training.

Jim was still researching but had no real winner to spring on the group. However, he had one idea still cooking on the back burner, which he shared. A documented rule stated that a second may confer with an official regarding the reservation of an allowable advantage before the first trial began if the second's contestant conceded a trial to his or her opponent. The advantage or condition must be experienced equally by both contestants.

\*\*\*

As the date of the contest got closer, billboards started to appear across the collective. The queen was arrayed in her royal hunting regalia, while Mona was made even smaller than she truly was in comparison and placed in an amphibian slave jumpsuit. CapHead was depicted as a brutish traitor, while the queen's second was a royal-looking warrior of the first order. No one doubted who authorized the publicity spots.

The official betting lines were presently running strongly for the queen, but the unauthorized lines were running the opposite. People placed their money based on their feelings much more openly when they thought the queen was not able to know their choices.

Sue and C. E.'s images were being circulated as the unmarried reprobate parents of Mona who had sired her and abandoned her. The posters stated that only after a long search were they even found, and that they were being

forced to attend the competition against their will. On seeing the posters, Sue thought her image was not really that
bad, though her natural blonde highlights could have been
more pronounced. *I love the reprobate parent thing … gives
me hope I someday can have a family.*

The trial choices were being circulated to the betting
houses so they could set the odds. The first three trials were
selected by the queen and were the first released. The first
trial was to be the capture and execution of five children on
death row. The children were randomly selected and would
be released in separate locations within a three-mile radius,
each armed with a dagger, one hour before the competition
began. This was a timed event requiring only five hours.
The winner was determined by the total number of executions carried out. If both had the same number, the contestant who had performed the executions in less time would
be the winner. The challenger, Mona, would go first so the
reigning queen would know what she needed to accomplish
to defeat the challenger.

When Mona saw the first trial selected by Gilda, she
wasn't shocked; it was expected according to their analysis
of the queen's strategy and CapHead's prediction. They
knew Gilda wanted to humiliate and intimidate her challenger, and that she trusted in Mona's repeatedly demonstrated desire to protect life when possible. The loophole
Jim had found required this despicable choice by the queen
to activate a provision hidden deep in the fine print of the
competition agreement. So instead of moral revulsion, this
choice was welcomed by Mona's team.

The queen's second choice was also predictable; it
was the only remaining trial that had the potential to take

life. Gilda was again hoping to shake Mona. The trial was
a two-hour timed event in which a ten-member wolf pack
would be released on the competitors. This event would be
done by both competitors simultaneously. The competitors
would have only the weapons approved by the officials before the competition. The only thing measured in this trial
would be the survival of the competitors. The best possible
outcome was that both survived unharmed or survived
with injuries. If one died and one survived, the competition
would be ended. If both survived, there would be no award
for the win; it would be declared a draw.

With the introduction of this particular second trial,
the queen was intentionally requiring a tiebreaker if both
contestants were credited with two wins at the end of five
events.

This gave the queen the chance to choose the final
event and minimize any time for preparation on Mona's
part. This strategy gave Gilda the right to choose four out
of a total of six events. And only she knew which event she
would choose.
CapHead, Mona, and the planning group were not surprised at the queen's strategy. The tiebreaker was, however,
a difficult variable to plan for. The queen would have a
choice of five remaining trials. All of them were winnable,
but which was the queen's most likely choice?

It was reasonable that she would choose a trial in which
her skill, size, brute strength, height, or weight would be
an advantage. Moonbeam and Levie ran an analysis and
predicted the likely ranking. The number one most likely
tiebreaker was a trial in which both contestants had to cross
multiple hills and ravines over a course that covered only

two miles. The distances between the edges of ravines were within the queen's abilities based on her size and jumping strength, and the hills were not high enough to slow her based on her bulk. The distance was short enough that fatigue would not be a factor.

\*\*\*

The hype was getting more intense within the collective. The succession competition would be taking place within a few days. Sue and C. E. had already been given the location and time to be sequestered by the officials.

\*\*\*

The *Leviathan* and *Eagle*'s ships 1 and 2 were cloaked and within one day of the collective. Chaos was cloaked and already hovering over the biosphere. *Barracuda* was uncloaked and in front of the invisible *Leviathan*. On board the *Barracuda* were CapHead, Mona, Sue, and C. E. Two state escort ships were sent out to guide *Barracuda* into the massive collection of ships. Mona and her surrogate parents were impressed with the enormity of the cloud. It covered their entire front view.

Leviathan and her companion ship would temporarily remain just on the outer edge of the cloud. The odds were already being posted on the Swarm Audio and Video Network (SAVN). The odds were three to one that Mona would concede the first trial. The prognosticators were all over Mona's attempt to save the lizards and predicted she would not participate in a trial that guaranteed the deaths of children, despite the fact they were on death row.

Another group of talking heads discussed Mona's parents and how the queen would likely subject them to the most creative forms of humiliation that could be devised.

Sue asked CapHead for further details. "How about the cloud queen's parents? What do you know about them, and what should Mona do once she wins the competition? What is she to do with the defeated queen?"

CapHead said, "I know what I would do with the queen, but that is your decision, Mona. Her parents are actually my aunt and uncle. Gilda is my first cousin."

Sue dropped the coffee she was drinking, looked at CapHead, and in alarmed voice said, "You have got to be kidding me!"

CapHead repeated what he had just revealed. "My father is Gilda's uncle. We are blood relatives. We grew up together."

Mona asked, "What turned you into enemies?"

"She had my father imprisoned and executed for treason. She is a paranoid sociopath. She has had much of her extended family tortured and executed. Her parents will be at the competition not to voluntarily support her but because they have no choice."

"Why is that?" asked Sue.

"They are on death row with most of her family. So if you win, Mona, it is the best thing that could happen for the queen's own family and the collective."

Mona asked, "How can the queen get away with such behavior?"

"Centuries of tradition and fear of change. It is easier to live in hell than to make the effort to build a better society."

C. E. asked, "Why didn't anyone just slip her some poison or just shoot the bitch?"

CapHead lamented, "Her bodyguards are extremely loyal and, except for a few that died in her fits of rage, are protected, rewarded, and privileged beyond all others in the collective."

Sue asked, "What will the bodyguards do if the queen loses? And will they actually let her lose?"

"Those are very good questions, and the answer lies in the hands of the ten supreme leaders of the collective. If they live up to tradition—and they are expected to do so—they will have already disarmed the guards and removed them physically from the competition. They are to return and be rearmed when the new queen is acknowledged by the competition officials. I think the queen is so confident and arrogant about winning that she will allow this to happen; however, I suggest you keep an eye on this situation. The Guards are formidable and must be feared."

# CHAPTER 25

# The Trial Begins

SAVN, the network promising the best news coverage in the cloud, was clamoring to interview CapHead and, of course, Mona. In a desire for a fair and balanced analysis, they had interviewed the queen two days before. They had requested an interview on the *Barracuda* by their most recognized anchor, Thunder.

The Guardianship Planning Group wondered what to do and thought that if they were trying to change the collective's culture, this was at least a start. The interview request was granted reluctantly.

Before the interview, there was a news bulletin from

the advance scouts protecting the ecoslaves on the fourth planet. After the entire contingent of two million reptilians had been settled on the planet's surface, a bizarre thing happened.

All two million lizards disappeared. Completely. There was no evidence of any interference by other forces, but of course the queen suspected Mona's involvement and demanded an explanation. The Guardianship was initially just as surprised at the reptilians' disappearance as the collective.

\*\*\*

Ben and Peggy Lisa were in contact with Moonbeam and reported that the reptilians on Mars had made contact with the human colony and had been told of the rescue of their seven million brothers and sisters by the Guardianship. Beyond that they had no further information.

Mona's parents requested a private conversation with their daughter when she had time. They were anxious to wish her well and to give her whatever moral support they could. Silver had sent a regular direct beam com to Lars2 on the WAMS *Eagle*'s ships 3 and 4, informing him of the developments on Mars, and she asked if he could speculate on the unfolding events there.

Lars2 felt that the workforce on Mars had most likely decided to remove themselves from control of the collective by individually burrowing under selected areas of Mars and were hibernating until Lars2 and their seven million brothers could reach Mars some twelve months from now.

Silver passed this information to the rest of the

Guardianship. Mona didn't have the energy or time to deal with this event except to understand it was a very important delay in the terraforming of Mars and possibly, therefore, of Earth as well. The Guardianship would have to table the implications of this until later, choosing to deal with one crisis at a time.

***

The queen was livid. The ecoworkers sent to the fourth planet were accompanied by over half of her loyal forces. She had committed 450,000 of her security forces to the fourth planet and the scouting thereafter of the third planet. Her military situation would not be good if any type of crisis occurred within the cloud. She was more vulnerable now than at any previous time in her reign. All her forces amounted to about one security asset for every vessel in the swarm. She was living on the edge, and she knew it.

Mona summed up the findings of the planning group: "A mentally insane, paranoid sociopath with a tiny military and ruthless personal guard is holding an immense collective of thirty billion beings captive by intimidation and fear. Is that the analysis of the Guardianship?"

Levie responded, "Yes, M. that is about as good a summation as is possible."

"Can we not forget this insane succession competition and just forcefully remove her and install CapHead in power?" asked Mona.

Moonbeam replied, "While that option is possible, our analysis shows that the resulting instability from that course of action could be devastating within the collective and would result in a most unstable and unpredictable future for all of them, including our own surviving human remnant. It would be better for the human species to eradicate the collective here and now if it weren't for the four hundred fifty thousand security forces presently around Mars."

\*\*\*

Thunder asked, "Queen-in-waiting of Tribe II of the swarm, why do you wish to challenge the presently reigning cloud queen?"

Mona responded, "First, Thunder, please call me Mona; I am one of a remnant species within this solar system, we call ourselves humans, and we are capable of technological acts that are not known to your culture. We wish not to harm any sentient life unless we are given no other choice. Your queen's actions are a threat to our existence. We have chosen this path in order to guarantee the future of all the races presently in this solar system."

Thunder continued. "Why not simply ask the queen to negotiate a compromise?"

Mona replied, "Okay, I request that the queen remove all her military forces to the collective and leave our solar system without further advance toward our central star. If she agrees, I will remove my challenge."

The queen bellowed, "Who does she think she is, giving me an ultimatum? If she had the power to stop the swarm, she would have already used it! She is a fraud and is bluffing! I am not even going to answer her. My answer will be on the field of honor, not on the talk shows and news programs. I will deal with her humans as I dealt with her lizards!"

Thunder followed up directly. "Mona, if you win the succession competition, will you reign as the cloud queen?"

"That is a very good question, Thunder. I intend to take the position as cloud queen of the collective very seriously and will rely on the advice of CapHead, whom I will designate as king to govern wisely. I will intervene in your external affairs only in emergency situations; otherwise, I expect you to govern yourselves."

"Govern themselves … how absurd!" the queen shouted. "They can't even decide what to eat for supper. CapHead … king? Please. I should have had him removed when I had his father executed. I am the collective, and it will have no other ruler as long as I am here."

My viewers want to know more about you, Mona. They know about the cloud queen; can you tell us about yourself? How were you able to form your alliance with CapHead?"

"You can ask CapHead the last question and let him respond," said Mona. "Let's see about me; in my culture, I am a young unmarried woman without children, my parents are respected scientists, and I was schooled in the sciences myself. I am a space pilot by profession and have been a captain of a space vessel for over three years. My people have been through much in a short period of time, and we understand change.

"This challenge to your leadership and the coming changes are what I understand, and I don't take them lightly. As you have been hearing in your own news, I have a great respect for all life, especially sentient life. I do not think it should be taken unless there is no alternative. The culture I come from feels the same way, and when I rule as queen, that will be the central theme of my reign. If you don't threaten life unnecessarily, you will have no problem with me."

"CapHead, can you tell my audience about how your alliance with Mona was formed?" Thunder asked.

"First, I can tell you that everything Mona said earlier is exactly as she said it. Her courage and leadership abilities are greater than any I have witnessed before—ever. She has been totally honest with me from my first encounter, and I am honored to take this challenge with her. Though much younger than I, her wisdom is like that of an ancient one. She is an exception in almost every measurable way. She could have had me tortured, executed, or worse if she had chosen to do so. Instead she gave me a new purpose—a chance to change the collective for the better. I have chosen to risk my life with her for a rare chance to change the lives of thirty billon people. I take my blood oath to sponsor her as queen to be as sacred as any I have ever taken."

It can be honestly stated that the queen went ballistic. "Have that Thunder person removed from his position, and have him spend a few months in my reorientation camp!" Gilda ranted. "Include his whole family while you're at it!" Gilda forgot that her bodyguards had been removed and all she was yelling at were her house servants. They just scurried away and cowered because they didn't know what to do.

***

The day before the contest began, Mona stated, "Seems we are all in this very dangerous game with a very intelligent and cunning adversary. What she lacks in social graces she makes up for in brutality, deceit, and malevolence. We trust nothing. We leave no stone unturned. We assume she will pull a rabbit out of every hole. She will not go down to defeat without taking as many of her enemies with her as possible. Chaos, you are on alert to notify Silver of anything unusual. Silver, you are in command and are to use all one hundred fifteen thousand years of your intuition, skill, and knowledge to orchestrate our response to this beast. We must prevail and try to lead the collective out of the mess they are in and ensure our own survival as well."

***

"It is my pleasure to be bringing you this event today—one not seen in over one thousand years," stated the new official games announcer. "I am sorry to say that our usual anchor is not with us today. Thunder had a family emergency and will likely miss the entire event. Today is the presentation of the contestants, their seconds and parents, and the officials, as well as the review of the five selected trials. Judge Haven, you are the senior official. How does it feel to be officiating an event that has happened only twice in our history?"

Within the biosphere, there was an enclosed theater in the round with a stage behind which was a platform on each side. The parents of the contestants were seated with an armed guard supplied by the officials with each pair. Sue, C. E., and their guard were on the left, and Gilda's parents were chained to their chairs and to the floor with their guard on the right.

Presently on the stage in front of their parents were Mona and her second, CapHead, on the left, while Gilda and her second were on the right. Judge Haven was in the middle of the stage, about to begin the formalities. Sue was seated with C. E., and an enormous guard was standing behind them. While they were not chained, as were the queen's parents, they felt almost as restricted. They were not allowed to leave the platform but were able to move from their seats and speak freely with each other. It was obvious, however, that the video network had cameras on them at all times and were looking for reactions that could be newsworthy.

Judge Haven finished with the general rules and listed the five trials and their requirements. Before he could announce the beginning time and details of the first trial, CapHead requested a point of order. The judge paused, and CapHead indicated that he wished to announce that his contestant conceded the first trial, which involved the execution of the children.

CapHead reserved the right to declare one advantage in any subsequent trial as long as said advantage was requested thirty minutes before the trial. Judge Haven accepted the point of order and declared that the queen won the first trial. Score: queen 1, Mona 0.

The queen was most happy and looked very pleased with herself. Mona did not bat an eye. The oddsmakers went wild; the video audience went off the charts. The contest was on! Judge Haven declared that the first trial would not be held today because the challenger had conceded.

"We will recess until tomorrow morning at first light,"
Declared the judge. "The second trial will involve a simultaneous survival trial against a pack of ten wolves. There is no
win or loss unless a contestant refuses to participate in the
two-hour timed event."

*** 

First light within the biosphere was a simulated sunrise.
Basically, the horizon lights on one side were turned on,
simulating twilight. Mona and Gilda were wired with implanted microphones in their ears so they could not keep
from hearing their opponent's comments. They had a mi-
crophone that could be used if they chose to harass their
opponent.

Mona had trained with earphones, and CapHead had
simulated Gilda's best insults and verbal abuse. She was
ready. Mona and CapHead had decided to use the sound
devices differently. Mona said nothing to Gilda, making no
noise. Gilda, however was already sending insults to Mona,
including singing a nonsense nursery rhyme.

Both opponents were carrying their approved weapons:
Gilda her large dagger and javelin, and Mona her boomerang and her bow with a quiver of ten arrows. The two were
originally spaced apart so they could not see each other's
locations; however, they were told they were within one
half mile of each other. The pack of ten wolves was to be
released between them.

The viewing audience could see from an aerial view the
two contestants and the two wolf-containing cages between
them. The pack could go in any direction; they were not

restricted in any way. A loud horn sounded, and the wolves were released. Mona immediately headed for the highest place she could find. She found a perch on a boulder with a rock face to her back.

Gilda found a large tree. She stood with her back to it and had a 280-degree view of her surroundings. The pack went toward Mona first. The beasts within minutes were in view of where Mona was defending her position. Mona saw the pack leader first. He was at the edge of a wooded area below her. She immediately reached for her boomerang and launched it toward the beast. The weapon circled the canine and severed his left ear near his head. The animal yelped loudly and jumped for cover.

The betting lines and oddsmakers went crazy! Within hours of this event, there would be plastic replicas of the boomerang being packaged for sale to the young scavengers throughout the collective. The swarm's economy had not seen such a boom of activity in decades.

It seemed that the pack, once threatened by any challenge, was not up to the task. The pack leader retreated to the safety of his cage with the rest of his companions, never to venture out again within the two hours of this timed event. Gilda was not allowed to show off her killing abilities, and Mona became the darling of the collective. The talk shows went wild.

At the end of this event, the score was still queen 1, Mona 0. But Mona was way ahead in the popularity ratings.

***

Gilda went berserk. She trashed half of her private quarters in the process. She yelled obscenities at her entire staff, vowing that when she won the competition she would have the idiot who had chosen the wolf pack fed alive to some truly vicious wolves (if some could be found, that is). *Do I have to do everything, including train wolves, for God's sake?* she thought.

Sue had not been able to stop laughing during the competition and almost fell out of her chair. This was not lost on the queen when she saw the replay. So far, the queen was ahead in trials won, but inside she felt she was behind—very behind.

***

The oddsmakers had switched the line from three to one in favor of the queen to only three to two in her favor. The next trial chosen by the queen was to destroy six killer drones without being killed, by using a laser rifle supplied by the officials.

The sequence went as follows: First one killer drone was released until neutralized, then two more were released until neutralized, and then finally the last three were released. The contestants had no time-outs. If the contestants survived, the combatant with the best time won the trial.

Mona had to go first, as this was the queen's choice. The queen knew that if Mona survived, the queen would know the time to beat in order to win. Silver, now in command of the resources of the Guardianship, knew that if treachery was to happen, this was the trial it would most likely occur in, based on the planning group's analysis.

Silver ordered Chaos to get as close to the biosphere as possible and use whatever weapons were at his disposal to preserve Mona's life. Their analysis predicted that the queen would make sure the laser gun Mona used would somehow fail.

Mona's tactic was to use her small frame to hide in whatever cover was available and wait for her opportunity to neutralize the drone or drones. This would obviously take longer and would all but guarantee the queen would win this trial. This was anticipated and expected.

The boomerang and wolf pack toys were the hottest items in the collective. The deluxe wolf pack model came with a detachable ear on the pack leader. The queen was not happy.

Mona was taken to a range in the biosphere and given three shots at a target to familiarize herself with her laser rifle. She was allowed to carry her bow and quiver, as well as her boomerang, if she wished.

The hunting drones were made up of a spherical body containing the optics, infrared sensors, flight controls, and a laser pulse rifle. The drones' bodies hung from a triangle. The triangle looked like a hat on top of a sphere that had a rotor on each of its three corners. To neutralize the drone, one either hit one of three round black targets around the center of the drone or removed one of its three rotors.

The six drones were individually tested one at a time to confirm their function. Each was launched and fired twice at the same target Mona had used. They then landed, and one was set to have its independent search-and-kill mode initiate in thirty minutes. Mona was free to move where she wished, but she needed to be beyond the visual targeting line of sight of the resting drone. Once Mona was away from the target range, a horn sounded and the drone launched. It would start hunting Mona in thirty minutes.

Mona saw the drone as it soared above the tree line, moving away and climbing quickly. She started looking for cover. She knew this was the trial with the most lethal potential and that it would commence in thirty short minutes. Before Mona could take a step, Gilda started blasting Mona with her insults. Mona didn't know when or how it would occur, but she knew the queen's treachery would surface.

It was just two minutes until the drone attacked. Mona thought it best to find shelter in trees, where her heat signature would attract the drone but the tree limbs would offer some cover. She saw the drone tracking high and to her left. It circled and appeared to be ducking down behind her. With the constant insults from Gilda, she was unable to hear the drone as it got closer.

However, in her mind's eye, Mona saw it clearly behind her. Mona jumped behind a tree as a laser pulse zipped past her right shoulder. She rolled with her back to the tree and jumped clear to the opposite side of the tree's trunk. She saw the drone above her as she lay exposed, and she fired almost point blank at the target facing her. The drone immediately dropped to the ground, neutralized. Mona was determined that next time she would not let the drones that close.

***

Silver watched the scene unfold and at least twice almost had Chaos destroy the drone. Her heart was in her throat.

She wished she were there instead of Mona. This was the hardest thing she had witnessed in centuries. Had Mona not made Silver promise not to interfere with the first drone, the whole charade would have ended there and then.

***

Mona knew she only had thirty minutes from the destruction of the first drone until two drones attacked in unison. She knew from her training with the 3-D models on *Leviathan* with CapHead that there was a narrow ravine nearby. She positioned herself in the narrowest and deepest part of it. She thereby limited the attack line of the drones to just two ten-degree windows in opposite directions. The drones could not attack without being vulnerable to her fire.

# CHAPTER 26

# Drones Everywhere!

The drones launched and found Mona's heat signature almost immediately. Instead of attacking from two opposite directions, the drones lined up one behind the other. They were zooming directly in for the kill. Mona knew she had to fire before they could, so she lined the first one up in her sights and fired. To her amazement, the hit neutralized the primary target and the second drone flew into it from behind, removing one of its rotors. They both fell to the ground, destroyed. After the difficult first drone, this seemed almost too easy. Mona chuckled without thinking. Of course, Gilda, hearing her, screamed and cursed all the more loudly. This made Mona laugh out loud for the first time in months.

\*\*\*

Silver was not as nervous as in the past but was still about to swallow the lump she had in her throat. When both drones went down together, she almost cried. She did not know if she could take one more assault. By now Sue and C. E. were combat weary. Sue was unable to speak, and C. E.'s adrenaline was surging so high he had broken both arms off the chair he was sitting in. Gilda's parents were reacting for the first time; they were obviously yelling for Mona's success.

\*\*\*

Mona knew the queen had to try something during this assault or her best opportunity would be lost. Mona was super vigilant. She considered moving from her location but thought this position afforded her the best defensive protection. She did, however, change tactics. She suspected the three drones would attack simultaneously, but they only had two directions to attack from, so she reasoned that at least one of the attackers would assault from ground level. Therefore, she placed herself with her back to a large boulder in the narrow ravine. She also placed her bow and boomerang within reach.

As expected, two drones were approaching from high above, and she sensed the third approaching up the ravine. She took aim and fired on the one drone diving down at her directly from above, but no laser pulse came from her rifle. She instinctively lunged over the top of the boulder and rolled with the laser rifle still in her hands, gained her footing, and swung with all her might. She met the drone coming up the tight ravine with the rifle. The rifle shattered, and so did the drone.

Mona lunged over the boulder where she had been and grabbed her boomerang. In her mind, she could now see both drones near ground level, closing from opposite directions at very low attack angles. She turned and launched her boomerang behind her just high enough to clear the top of the boulder. The drone collided with the boomerang, and its momentum carried it rolling forward, out of control. It hit the rocks in front, and its shrapnel launched skyward just as the other drone was closing in for the kill. Two rotors were severed from the final drone, and it crashed just over Mona's head.

The contest was over, and Mona was alive. She screamed in triumph, and Gilda went silent for the first time since this trial began. Gilda was in shock; she had never seen this sort of athletic ability from anyone or anything. For the first time, doubt started to creep in and a panic began to form.

Mona's time was unbeatable; she had dispatched the drones twice as fast as the swarm's best special forces personnel. Gilda refused to challenge this record time, so she conceded.

The score was queen 1, Mona 1 with two trials remaining, both of which Mona had selected.

***

Silver would have and should have given the order to destroy the three drones, but Mona's feat was simply too fast for Silver to comprehend quickly enough. Mona was nothing short of phenomenal. No one, probably including Mona, could have believed what happened. Sue and C. E. were stunned beyond belief. They stood on the platform in a daze. Finally Sue turned to C. E. and asked, "Did you see that? Did you just see that?"

\*\*\*

CapHead acted as if what he had just witnessed was simply ordinary and expected. He went to Judge Haven and requested a point of order.

The stunned official said, "What?"

CapHead said, "We request an investigation on the malfunction of the laser rifle. We expect a second advantage to be given to my combatant."

The oddsmakers were going nuts. The line had reversed; it was now Mona at three to two over the queen. The officials were investigating the laser rifle failure but had not assigned an advantage to Mona as of yet. However, since the queen had conceded, she received an advantage, which cancelled Mona's advantage that she had received when she conceded the first trial.

The toy makers had now added a Mona action figure to the boomerang sales. Mona sported a bow slung over her shoulder with a quiver of arrows and a miniature boomerang. All the weapons were detachable and lifelike and to scale. Tiny radio-controlled killer drones were available in the collector's edition only.

\*\*\*

The queen was temporarily despondent. Fear was beginning to replace her rage. She hadn't destroyed anything or killed anyone. The only thing she had accomplished was the cancelling out of the advantage held by Mona after her conceding today. The rifle failure had been an attempt to kill Mona outright. It had failed, but it would be hard to link it to anyone except some people in the special forces armory. She trusted Judge Haven to fix that bit of legal trouble.

Gilda wondered what it would be like to lose her reign and, most likely, her life.

\*\*\*

Silver, Jim, Leviathan, and Moonbeam were trying to analyze the present situation and likely outcomes. They felt the unexpected loss by the queen today would make her even more dangerous and desperate. Mona must be even more cautious and expect anything from her.

The remaining two trials were ones Mona expected to win. With the score at one to one, Mona needed only one victory to force a tiebreaker, and two to win the overall contest outright.

\*\*\*

The queen knew the only way to realistically win now was to force the competition into a tiebreaker. If she could win just one of the two remaining trials, she, as the reigning queen, would choose the tiebreaker. She knew without thinking that it would be trial nine. For the first time since this whole thing started, she was focused like never before in her life.

Before the next trial, the queen got some bad news: the officials had ruled in favor of CapHead's protest on the defective laser rifle, and an advantage had been awarded to Mona.

\*\*\*

The next trial allowed only one weapon. Using primitive tools, each contestant had to fashion a primitive slingshot. They then had to destroy ten clay targets while being chased by a security drone firing stun projectiles.

The queen went first for the opening slot. She fashioned the slingshot and destroyed all ten targets in three hours and ten minutes. Mona went second, and as luck would have it, one of the stun projectiles ripped her slingshot into two pieces. The queen won an unexpected trial by a few minutes.

The score was now queen 2, Mona 1. Mona had to win the upcoming trial to force the competition into a tiebreaker.

\*\*\*

The next trial was certainly in Mona's favor, and the queen almost conceded; however, just in case a freak event occurred, similar to what happened in the previous trial, she decided to compete, hoping to steal the competition by default.

The trial was simply swimming, running, and climbing the farthest in twelve hours. The queen went first because this was Mona's selection. She simply kept moving for twelve hours—with several rest periods, of course. At a very deliberate and slow pace, the queen completed the Trial. Mona spent 2.5 hours moving and surpassed the queen's twelve-hour efforts by five miles.

Score: queen 2, Mona 2.

***

The tiebreaker was now on! Silver, Levie, Moonbeam, Jim, Kevin, and Chaos discussed the final trial and aftermath. They knew this was likely to be the last few hours of Gilda's reign of terror, but they also knew she was a very worthy opponent. They expected she would attempt to maintain power—but how? The next question was what the first order of business would be when the Guardianship took control of the collective through Mona's reign as the new cloud queen. These issues were immense but would need to wait until Mona, CapHead, Sue, and C. E. were safe.

It was decided when the last trial was underway that the cloaked hand weapons would be quantum-jumped to C. E. and Sue.

***

Gilda was brooding in her private quarters a few hours before the final trial. She was reviewing and calling in all her assets just in case she lost the tiebreaker. Gilda now knew Mona was faster, stronger, and more resourceful than she had ever thought possible.

The queen knew that with her much larger body and stride length she could move faster over the rough terrain and more easily jump over the crevices in the two-mile course. Mona's tiny stature would put her at a disadvantage. The queen thought the course was so short that even her own lack of stamina would not be a significant factor.

Nevertheless, over the several days of competition, she had her loyal bodyguards replace the official security agents at the biosphere, and she now controlled it.

***

Mona and CapHead were in deep discussion about the upcoming trial. They suspected the worst-case scenario possible based on the queen's history and her will to prevail.

CapHead told Mona the strategy that Jim and he had devised. CapHead had trained his special forces personnel in this very biosphere and would occasionally have the rotation of the entire facility increased to simulate environments with higher gravities. This allowed his troops to experience the effects of higher g-forces on their bodies and see how such forces limited their ability to move, jump, and conduct military operations.

CapHead was going to enforce, under the provisions of the competition, the advantage with Judge Haven thirty minutes before the trial. As long as the advantage or condition was equally experienced by both contestants, it had to be allowed. CapHead knew that the increase in body weight would even the odds between Gilda and Mona. As was his right as second to Mona, CapHead requested a meeting with Judge Haven before the trial. This was allowed as long as Gilda's second was also in attendance to object if necessary.

The three met in a private soundproof enclosure selected at the last second so it would be free of the queen's listening devices. CapHead recognized Judge Haven and his fellow supreme leader; he knew both of them very well. CapHead started with greetings and proceeded with his request for Mona's advantage, which he had earned legally when the defective rifle had almost ended her life. All three knew it was no accident.

CapHead said, "We three have lived under the queen's brutality for over one hundred years. If she wins, we have lost, possibly forever, the chance for a new start. I ask only for what my contestant has rightfully earned. Under the rules of succession competition, the collective will know the enforcement of this advantage is fair and proper. You can stop it, but if you do, all hope for change will be stopped as well. What say you?"

\*\*\*

The large stage was set. Mona and Gilda were already at the starting line. This was to be a simultaneous start and finish. One weapon each was allowed. Mona had chosen the boomerang and Gilda the dagger. It was about thirty minutes before the horn, and there was an almost imperceptible change in the feel of the biosphere. Mona noticed it and smiled broadly but acted as though nothing was different;

she just continued going through her warm-up and stretching exercises.

Every eye in the collective was turned to the proceedings. Judge Haven was standing on the stage with CapHead on one side and Gilda's second on the other. Above them with their guards were C. E. and Sue on one side and Gilda's parents on the other side. As the judge began to address the Crowd and the collective audience, Sue and C. E. felt the cloaked hand weapons materialize within their clothing.

Chaos was surveying the entire biosphere from above for any unexpected activity. Silver was watching over the fleet's massive firepower. All was ready, as much as possible, for any outcome. Silver noticed there were random vessels from different vectors making their way slowly toward the biosphere. She launched all fifteen cloaked shuttle craft from *Leviathan* and the WAMS *Eagle*'s ships 1 and 2. She ordered them to take defensive positions at a good distance from, but surrounding, the biosphere.

She made Chaos aware of what she was seeing and what she had done. Mona was still stretching when she smelled the pungent odor and saw the flash of light. She was shocked at the familiar image she saw. But this time it came with a voice that whispered, "Prometheus."

Judge Haven was winding things up and mentioned as a required legality that the advantage earned by Mona had been applied in accordance with the competition rules. The speed of the biosphere's rotation was at that moment almost at half its ultimate speed. About ten minutes into the trial, it would be expected to be at its maximum.

Mona was beginning to feel its effects and could see Gilda beginning to wonder why she felt so sluggish. The horn was two minutes from sounding and twenty-eight minutes from Judge Haven's pronouncement.

Mona had been practicing for this event for quite some time on *Leviathan*. The course was well known by CapHead as the next-to-last trial before special forces graduation. There were two different possible terrains. The one chosen by Gilda was a vine-filled rain forest complete with tall rotting trees and vines everywhere. There were shallow streams Gilda could easily wade and narrow deep gorges she could jump over with her height advantage. Mona would have difficulty with the gorges as well as the downed trees and vines. Some of the downed trunks were as tall as she was.

Mona's practice had been grueling, and she had performed at both higher simulated altitude and greater simulated gravity. At the starting line, the trial was about to commence. The horn was to blow any second. The two contestants were separated by no more than fifty feet—too far for either to lunge and attack the other, but close enough to see fine details. Mona was in a slick jumpsuit with gripping pads on her knees and elbows. Her hands were covered with gloves, and her feet with climbing boots. Her hair was in a ponytail. Her boomerang was secured on her belt.

Gilda looked more like she was going to a picnic except for the dagger on her waist. Gilda was not making a sound on the harassment frequency; nor was Mona. Gilda, who was rasping deeper than normal, thought her breathing issues were due to the adrenaline rush she was having, but she was already sweating profusely as well.

Mona had been warned by CapHead that once the horn sounded she should expect the unexpected.

The horn blared. Mona lunged backward. Gilda's dagger flew into the chest of the reporter that was standing to the front and right of where Mona had originally lined up. The reporter never moved; he was mortally wounded. Mona got up and dusted herself off and sped forward. Gilda screamed, totally frustrated, and lumbered after Mona.

Mona could clearly hear rasping sounds over the harassment frequency; Gilda was already showing labored breathing. The first obstacle was a triangular-shaped stack of logs between two canyon walls about ten feet high. Mona was up and over without a moment's delay. Gilda would have normally swung one leg over and been gone in seconds. Not this time. She couldn't get her leg over the top. Instead she had to launch herself headfirst and belly-down over the top. After clearing the top, she went headfirst into the ground on the opposite side. This knocked the air out of her and made an impressive amount of dust.

Mona was well ahead, negotiating some five-foot-diameter downed trees. This slowed her down considerably and gave Gilda a chance to collect herself and catch up. Gilda made up the difference but was heaving for breath. Mona was halfway through the logs when Gilda tried to step over the first one and her foot hit the middle of it instead of the top. She fell headlong forward, smashing her head into the log in front. In the process, she fractured her right arm in an attempt to break her fall. Dazed and in pain, she came up cursing, screaming, sweating, and out of breath.

Mona could not help herself. She interjected, "Did she fall and make a booboo!"

The queen was not amused. She picked up a loose tree

limb with her good arm and slung it toward Mona, but the projectile fell far short of its target.

By now the biosphere was at its maximum speed and gravity equivalent. Mona felt as if she weighed two hundred pounds. Gilda's equivalent was fifteen hundred pounds. Mona was straining mildly, but Gilda was miserable. Gilda was injured, exhausted, and breathing hard just to walk. The narrow gorges were coming up. Mona knew she couldn't jump them and looked for trees that had fallen or vines that hung over them. She hurried laterally, looking for a way to proceed. Gilda normally jumped them, but she knew better this time. She found a downed log and with one hand tried to get it across the divide.

\*\*\*

Silver was watching the advancing ships. While she did not want a confrontation, she was also reluctant to let them get too close to the biosphere. She asked Chaos to broadcast a warning to each advancing vessel to keep a safe distance or be challenged by the new queen.

The advancing ships halted their progress, and many turned and retreated. They seemed to act as if they were caught in a game of Mother may I … and Silver was Mother!

\*\*\*

As the trial progressed and the queen was looking more and more fatigued, her bodyguards that had replaced the biosphere security personnel were beginning to close in on the finish line, close to where the queen was struggling. Chaos alerted Silver to this, and she had a note explaining the situation quantum-jumped to Sue.

Silver was getting concerned they may have to blow the place apart to save her four charges in the biosphere. Mona found a tree over the gorge about a quarter mile north and quickly got across. She was headed in the correct direction and confronted a new narrow ravine that was shallow enough to jump down into and scurry up the other side. She heard a crash to her south, and Gilda yelled in her ears.

When Gilda had pushed the downed tree across the gorge, it had tilted downward and lodged at about a twenty-five-degree angle from her side to the opposite side. She tested it and attempted to cross on it. All she needed was a couple more feet to lunge for the other side. She stepped out on the trunk, and it immediately fell out from under her. She and the tree fell about twenty-five feet to the bottom. The tree rolled partially over her, leaving her trapped. She had no strength or stamina left. The tree was so heavy she could not move but could only breathe. Her broken arm was useless to help her push herself free.

Mona was progressing well, clearing a few more ravines and some shallow creeks she ended up swimming. She cleared a few more downed tree obstacles and was soon within sight of the finish line. She paused before emerging from the brush to survey the last few hundred yards. There was a small lake to her right. All she heard from Gilda was rasping breaths and occasionally a few groans.

From her perch in the brush, Sue and C. E. were clearly visible on their raised platform, as were CapHead, Judge Haven, and Gilda's second. Then the air flashed with laser fire. It seemed to come from every direction. Mona lunged for the lake and submerged herself as deep as possible. CapHead had taught her well; she swam for what seemed to be several minutes and searched for vegetation and a floating log to surface behind. As she cleared the water, gulping for air, a drone burst into flames over her head, and then another did the same. She submerged herself again.

As she looked up through the water, she saw several drones being destroyed every few seconds. *How long can this last?* she thought.

# CHAPTER 27

# The Trial's End and the New Beginning

Mona swam to the other side of the floating log and attempted to surface once more. She was not sure what to do but was not able to hold her breath much longer. It was the first time she was about to panic since this whole thing began.

Suddenly two human-sized figures plunged into the water near her. After the turbulence cleared, she saw Sue and C. E. They grabbed her, one on each side, and brought her to the surface. She gasped for air and took the biggest breath of her life. Was this nightmare over or just beginning? Was this wishful thinking? Mona's hypoxia made any clear thinking almost impossible. All she could really confirm was that two people had hold of her, and she hoped they were Sue and C. E.—or was she just confused? Mona decided to not struggle and to just go with it until her head had time to clear.

All of a sudden, all Mona could hear was Gilda cursing and yelling insults and being her obnoxious self. All Mona could reason was that she was alive, and obviously so was Gilda.

Then there was peaceful silence—no more of Gilda's ranting. *What happened?* Mona was in some kind of twilight she didn't understand. It was pleasant but not familiar either. Things seemed ethereal—not truly solid or real. In her mind, she was free from her body and could go where she wanted to in time and space.

So she went to her favorite spot in the universe. She went to the wilderness outside of SpaceJump City at the last time she and her parents were together on Earth before the war. Next Mona went to SpaceJump City at the last time she was out on the town with Sue. Then she went on to low Earth orbit before the war. Finally, she was hiking in the wilderness with Jim. She could go where she wanted to, at any time she wanted to, just by thinking of it.

Mona didn't know where she was, but she really liked it. It seemed as if she had quantum sight without Moonbeam's and Levie's assistance. Now she went back to her favorite place.

                                    ***

"Yes," Sue said to Silver, "she has been in this condition since shortly after we pulled her from the lake."

They were in Mona's private quarters on *Leviathan*. Mona was on a gurney connected to a few umbilical lines attached to some monitoring equipment. C. E. informed Sue that search-and-rescue experts saw this condition occasionally when they rescued someone who had experienced extreme fatigue and oxygen deprivation. Silver ventured a different theory. She stated, "The prehumans had a strange custom that they insisted was needed to maintain health and balance. They called it sleep."

***

Mona now started to visualize scenes without explanation, as though her brain were confusing reality with fantasy. Mona decided it was time to get back to reality. She began to regain consciousness. Though disoriented, Mona began seeing very familiar surroundings. Silver and Sue were standing over her when she finally looked up. Both were smiling and said together, "Welcome back!"

Mona's first words were "What the hell happened!"

Silver began to explain, but Sue said, "No, I want to tell her!"

Silver interrupted. "I thought you wanted me to tell her?"

Sue then said, "Well, I changed my mind!"

They both said together, "Welcome home, Your Royal Highness!"

All Mona could say was "Great, now I have thirty billion new problems. I think I'll go back where I just came from!" She looked around. "Okay, I'm not dead, but I am now the queen. I get that, but how did it end up that way?"

Sue said, "You won't believe it, but the queen's bodyguards saved your life. When the drones swooped in to kill you, her guards took them out. They released C. E. and me and supplied a hovercraft to retrieve you from the lake. That was a couple of days ago. When you are up to it, CapHead and Judge Haven would like to talk."

Mona paused and indicated she wanted a meeting of

the Planning Committee before she met with CapHead and
Judge Haven.

Silver announced that the group was ready immediately, and she and Sue helped Mona off the gurney and into
the conference room. Moonbeam and Levie were already
present, along with Dr. Larry Find and Peggy and Ben Lisa,
by quantum communication. C. E., Jim, and Kevin would
arrive momentarily. As Mona entered the conference, all
were present, and they played the Guardianship's version of
"God Save the Queen."

Mona turned redder than her normal reddish complexion and hung her head and almost dived under the conference room table. She finally yelled "Enough, Enough! Let's
get down to business!"

Moonbeam started the meeting. "All of our short-range
goals have been met. Ceres is now safe and is being resettled
and colonized and is almost back on schedule. Chaos is
no longer a threat and is now working for us. The reptilian
race is safe and will be reunited within the next ten months.
The collective has been neutralized as a threat to the
Guardianship, and once the new queen recalls their special
forces and advance scouts from Mars and Earth, the inner
planets will be secure. Mona, CapHead, Sue, and C. E. are
now safe from any threat. Any questions?"

Mona said, "Yes. What do we do with thirty billion
scavengers, and what happened to Gilda, their old queen?"

Silver answered: "Well, second question first ... Gilda
is quite dead. Her bodyguards fished her out of the bottom
of the gorge after the gravity was returned to normal. She
was hauled in a net from a hovercraft and brought to the
stage in the biosphere, where CapHead, Judge Haven, and

the supreme leaders of the tribes were all gathered—including her parents, who had been unchained by Judge Haven.

"She was told she had lost the competition and that you were the new cloud queen. Gilda of course went quite mad, and she lunged at CapHead and tried to kill him. CapHead simply snapped her neck. Her parents hauled her dead body to the nearest emergency air lock, shoved it in, and flushed. We suspect she will be entering Jupiter's orbit in about two years and will be a short but bright streak of light as she enters Jupiter's atmosphere.

"To answer the first question—'What do we do with thirty billion scavengers?'—we haven't a clue. I would suggest we formulate some type of laundry list after you talk to Judge Haven and CapHead. You, of course, are queen, so they will be looking to you for solutions.

"Mona, we have your back on this one, but it really depends on their state of mind, resources, and willingness to change. As has been stated several times in the past, the easiest solution might have been to have obliterated them. We and you are now morally obligated to do something. This might be the hardest thing to accomplish that we have done so far."

For Mona's plan to work, she needed to have an understanding with Chaos. In Mona's quarters, Moonbeam, Levie, and Chaos (via quantum voice) had a conversation. Mona asked Chaos to agree to be permanently assigned to the swarm. He would of course have Mona's clone as a conduit for quantum communication.

Moonbeam suggested that Chaos therefore be renamed, and Levie agreed. Chaos's new name had to be appropriate for his new role. All four agreed. The proposal

would go with Mona to the meeting with CapHead and
Judge Haven.

***

Mona met with Judge Haven and CapHead. They were very
gracious and profusely thanked Mona for all her sacrifices.
Mona asked the two if they were up to the challenges of
molding a new direction for the collective. They realized
their people had no choice. They had to change from simply being users and scavengers to being innovators and
creators.

The judge laughed and said, "The Queen Mona action
toys are a good sign of the change we were looking for.
Though silly, it is a sign the collective can be energized to
do new things."

The one thing Mona loved about the swarm was their
lack of elaborate ceremony. All she had to do to appoint
CapHead as king was to meet with the ten supreme tribal
leaders and tell them CapHead was king. They then took
an oath to serve the swarm and support king CapHead's
authority. That was it. King CapHead addressed the swarm
on the cloud-wide video and audio network, with Queen
Mona by his side.

CapHead gave the following speech.

"I am proud to announce a new day for the swarm.
Gone is the tyrant Gilda. Gone is the constant fear of a des-
pot who tortures and kills without reason or logic. Thanks
to queen Mona, we have a chance for a new beginning. For
over two thousand years, we have been following and feed-
ing on the remains of other civilizations. That has come to

an end. Our destructive benefactor is no more. We have to find a new direction or cease as a species.

"Much new will come in the months, years, and decades ahead. I and the ten supreme tribal leaders have formed an alliance with an entity called the Guardian. The Guardian will help us with the knowledge we gathered from twenty advanced civilizations. Now instead of just collecting knowledge, we will develop the wisdom to use this invaluable treasure to better the collective and any peaceful sentient races we encounter in the future. Queen Mona will be leaving us soon but will remain in touch through the Guardian. Thank you, my people! We have suffered much, but we have learned much, and with that knowledge we will form a new future together."

# CHAPTER 28

# Premonition and the Monolith of Phobos

In the planning group meeting, Sue commented on the speech: "Great speech. I think I know where he got his ideas. Moan, what do we do now?"

"Well, Silver, Moonbeam, and Levie have been experimenting with a few ideas. I will let Silver detail them."

Silver presented the triad's proposal: "We think we have hit upon at least a temporary solution for the collective. We propose they take an orbital position on the direct opposite side of the sun from Earth's position. Though as large as Earth, their mass is a tiny fraction of Earth's, so there will not be any orbital perturbations caused by their presence. There they may take their time with the Guardian's—aka Chaos's—help to reorganize their culture. Moonbeam will monitor with the Guardian and with Dr. Find's help will unlock the libraries where the collective need to begin their search for inner peace and knowledge. We feel this will allow them a haven to readjust. Their technology presently is sufficient to sustain their needs internally. They do, however, need to limit their population growth to make their long-term survival guaranteed. A growing population was sustainable as they were gobbling up new resources, but now that will not be wise."

***

Mona was in her room, still exhausted after her ordeal, and she fell unconscious—or, as Silver would say, asleep. She wondered why she had witnessed the vision of the Prometheus balloon just before the start of the final trial. *Is it possible Prometheus was trying to communicate?*

After Mona woke, she sought out Silver and asked what she thought about the images she had been seeing. Silver found the events troubling and suggested they ask Moonbeam and Levie to analyze the situation.

Moonbeam and Levie were reviewing their findings from the Voynich manuscript, which had predicted the periodic cycle of destruction within the solar system every two hundred thousand years.

The final report to the Prometheus Council was as follows:

- Mars was nearly destroyed two hundred thousand years ago.
- An unknown planet in the asteroid belt that may have had Ceres as its moon was destroyed four hundred thousand years ago.
- The Voynich manuscript confirms the date of Mars's destruction to be two hundred thousand years ago. It also predicted disaster to Earth next. The prehumans left in anticipation of this disaster.

- The prophets of the Prometheus Council predicted Earth's destruction, which would have happened except for our interference.
- We thus have multiple sources predicting a periodic cycle of destruction within our solar system every two hundred thousand years.
- Finally, the "danger out there" twice came from the Pillars of Creation.

Moonbeam stated, "The above list served us well, but it is possible there are additional messages encoded in the Voynich manuscript. We stopped trying to decode it once we identified the Pillars of Creation was where Chaos would be first appearing. There could possibly be more we failed to decipher. I recommend we return to the Voynich manuscript for further attempts."

Moonbeam and Levie presented their assumption that if there were further messages within the manuscript, the key to them was in a number derived from the Prometheus image. So they began to use several number combinations within it. There were six hunters, four birds, eight points on the sunburst, and one star within a star with four points each on the balloon, the sun, one balloon, and one falling Prometheus with two wings. The permutations were end-less. Where to start? Prime numbers? Base ten?

Moonbeam and Levie knew that if they stumbled over the correct combination, they would immediately know it, because something other than nonsense would magically appear from what amounted basically to gibberish.

Mona rushed out of her quarters and sent word to the WAMS *Eagle*'s ships 1 and 2 to proceed with *Leviathan* to return to Ceres and Mars. She had just received a disturbing private communication from her parents, who were orbiting Mars.

Mona called an emergency gathering of the planning council. Her parents, commanding the *Condor* strike force around Mars, had notified Mona that all contact had been lost with the one thousand human colonists in Hale's crater. Further investigation revealed that all the colonists were missing.

There had been no further known contact with the two million amphibians since they disappeared months before. Peggy and Ben ordered the search teams not to stay on the surface but return to the mother ships. The orbital photos of the colony's location held no clue of what happened to either the humans or the amphibians.

As luck would have it, the sisters got a hit on the Voynich manuscript. This occurred only after 121,560,098 passes through the almost infinite possible number of permutations. The Sisters were anxious to share their discovery. The image was a close-up shot of Phobos, Mars's largest and closest orbiting moon.

\*\*\*

The planning council met, and the Mars colony's disappearance and the encoded image from the manuscript were discussed without resolution, but one item was emphasized. Phobos was not a solid chunk of rock but a porous body.

The sisters took turns explaining their findings. "The porosity of Phobos is calculated to be a quarter to a third empty," said Moonbeam. "Because of the image from the

Voynich manuscript and the Mars colony's disappearance, it was thought there might be a connection. The planning group discussed the entire image from the manuscript. The 280-foot-wide monolith on Phobos is also very interesting. Thought to be natural, it is a building-size boulder of interesting shape. The materials that make up the moon have their origin from the planet. When Chaos rammed the planet two hundred thousand years ago, Phobos was formed."

Levie took over. "A thousand years after the atmosphere was stripped from Mars, the prehumans evacuated Earth. We don't know where they went, but we do know Prometheus left this clue about Mars and its largest moon. We now have lost communication with one thousand humans and two million amphibian ecoworkers. They all disappeared from sight as well. We do know the amphibians and humans made contact."

Mona suggested it might be important to ask questions of Lars2. He was still several months from reaching Mars's orbit on *Eagle*'s ships 3 and 4 with the remaining seven million amphibians, who were still in stasis after their rescue in deep space.

Without a quantum conduit (a Mona clone), two-way communication with Lars2 was difficult, requiring forty-five minutes to send a question and receive a response of any type. The council was concerned that the amphibians on the two mother ships would remain in stasis until the present situation was resolved.

The council decided that the *Leviathan* and *Eagle*'s ships 1 and 2 would return to Ceres and then to Mars at flank speed. The question was, while the two million amphibians disappearing on Mars was considered to be voluntary, was it also true of the human colonists? And if voluntary, why?

The council was no closer to an explanation than when this crisis first began. They considered that maybe Moonbeam and Levie could find more clues within the Voynich manuscript. Mona requested her parents send an investigation team to Phobos to snoop around. She asked if they had a forensic geologist who might volunteer for the mission.

Mona asked if Ben and Peggy had any ideas about what little was presently known. They indicated that they were as stumped as was everyone else but thought that any new info was better than what they now had.

The council extended the ban on excursions to the Martian surface until more was known; Mona agreed with the policy.

***

Ben decided he would go with the investigating team to Phobos and hitched a ride with a team of six from the WAMS *Condor*. They launched from the shuttle bay and had to use a reentry pattern because the moon was so close to the Martian surface. It had been theorized that if Mars had a real atmosphere, Phobos would have already been an enormous crater on the surface of Mars because the resistance from it would have slowed Phobos's orbit and caused it to lose its escape velocity.

The approach trajectory used would target the monolith on the moon's surface. They would attempt a grapple connection with the boulder because of the near-weightless conditions on the moon's surface, trying to match the shuttle's rotation with the asteroid's rotation.

All six, including Ben, were in pressure suits with oxygen sources engineered for extra-vehicle deep space missions. Once the shuttle was anchored to Phobos, the team would be tethered together but could break away and use individual explosive pitons and a high-stress filament security system to stay on the asteroid.

As they approached the enormous asteroid moon, which was some seventeen miles wide, the monolith came into visual range. It was about the size of a large size skyscraper in SpaceJump City. It was some three hundred by three hundred feet wide at the top and rose some four to six hundred feet above the surface.

As they got closer and closer, they matched Phobos's rotation of about 6.8 miles per hour on its longest axis. What they next saw surprised all of them. There were attachment points all along the four sides on the top of the monolith. From these attachment points was a system of rails that led to four indented shuttle-sized cutouts on each side of the monolith. A ship the size of a shuttle could attach itself at two to four points and slide down the face of the monolith into these cutouts. In essence, these were protected ship bays.

Ben immediately reported his observations to Peggy, who contacted Mona via quantum voice. The question was, what to do—proceed to dock or do more external investigation first? The decision was to proceed to dock.

The team brought the shuttle within inches of the attachment rings, and a crewman securely attached two breakaway tethers from the front and rear of the craft to the monolith. The forensic geologist, along with a security search-and-rescue person proceeded. They exited the air lock and secured two microfilament tethers to the surface with explosive boring pitons. Their powered reels on their wrists pulled them to the surface. The escape velocity of the moon was so low that they needed some form of constant attachment to maintain a safety margin for maneuvering.

To move in any desired vector, another piton would be secured in that direction, and a person would pull himself or herself toward the next piton. It took a bit of thought, but as long as one had filament and pitons, one was fine. This technique had been perfected by the asteroid mining personnel and used for some one thousand years before the war. It was like using spiderwebs attached to a pneumatic nail gun.

The geologist confirmed that the monolith was natural, but the cutouts and, of course, the attachment rings and rails had been added by someone later. It was expected there would be some access into the monolith and possibly thereby into the interior of Phobos, which was calculated to be one third hollow.

The two proceeded to search for an entry point on or near the monolith. Ben was fascinated by the concept of someone creating this docking station on Phobos. It had to be ancient. Though a small human research colony had existed on Mars for some twelve hundred years, nothing had ever been done with or on Phobos.

Phobos, being one of Mars's two moons was considered off-limits to asteroid mining and was like an endangered species to humans on Mars. Even the smallest disturbance

on Phobos, any tiny orbital perturbation, could have
brought the fragile asteroid to Mars's surface.

The two explorers finished with a look around the
monolith's base and immediate surroundings and reeled
themselves back up to near the shuttle's level. They were
proceeding to investigate the shuttle-size rectangular cutout near the top. It seemed totally empty except for the rails
hanging from its ceiling. It looked like a spacecraft would
attach itself on top of the monolith to the rings and then
slide down the rails from the top and use its side thrusters
to nudge its way into the cut out. Hanging with tethers
from the ceiling rails, it would be secure in the five-sided
container.

Ben, feeling adventurous, ordered the two investigating
crewmen outside to return to the shuttle's air lock. When
the crewmen were inside, Ben used the harbor thrusters
and pushed the craft down the monolith. Once positioned
parallel to the opening, he nudged the shuttle sideways, still
attached to the rails in the cutout.

What happened next was very interesting but was not
really a surprise.

As the shuttle slipped totally inside and became stable,
restrained by the tethers but lying on the floor, a door slid
from the floor up to the ceiling. The ship was now totally
enclosed in the cutout, and the bay was illuminated from
all sides by lighting that was clearly sufficient for humans to
see but was not glaring.

Doors now opened on three sides, sliding open into
large air locks. This time Ben had to investigate for himself.
He and two other search-and-rescue personnel suited up
and left the air lock of the shuttle. They looked around, and

Ben struck a fire starter. A flame erupted. There was sufficient oxygen in the air to support a flame. He took off his
helmet, and the other two followed along but placed their
helmets on their belts.

They began to explore the bay level and came to an
enormous tube with a chain with handholds going down
the center of it. Ben grabbed hold one of the grips and
jumped into the air. He began to basically free-fall, holding
on to the chain. His descent was slow and actually very
pleasant.

As Ben reached the bottom, the pull of gravity increased during the last few feet; it was as though he had
jumped off a two-foot step to the floor. As he hit the bottom, a flood of lights came up; a second air lock stood in
front of them. They entered. *Must be a double-redundancy
safety feature*, Ben thought.

When the trio went through the air lock, they found
themselves in an enormous cavern. They were on the
top layer or floor above a tram and conveyer system that
stretched as far as the eye could see. He had never seen anything like this in his entire life. Ben decided to get into one
of the trams and see where it took him. The system turned
on automatically when he got into one of the open cars.

The car started down into the cavern, while the car
behind stayed in place. As it proceeded, lights turned on
within the areas Ben was transiting. The technologies were
simple, effective, and elegant. Nothing was too complicated
to use or understand. There were no signs or instructions,
no computer screens or displays. It seemed to be a world
designed for the simplest of users. Everything the trio tried
required only a tiny bit of intuition and common sense. Ben

and his two companions spent at least three hours exploring. They found no signs of life at first: no written signs, no logos, no governmental seals of ownership, no written language, and no symbols of any type were seen. It was not as if something had been removed, but more like it had never been there to begin with. What they saw was what they got. There was light, clean air, fountains, and some vegetation. If there was insect or animal life, they saw none of it—except for fish. Ben took environmental samples for local testing and made audio and image recordings to be sent to Moonbeam and Levie for analysis.

\*\*\*

Moonbeam and Levie had already made significant strides in understanding this facility's function and purpose, and they were about to brief the council thoroughly.

Moonbeam and Levie asked the Guardian, aka Chaos, to review the star charts and the solar system logs from his two-billion-year destructive journey through the galaxy. They asked if he could identify the asteroid presently known as Phobos orbiting the fourth planet from the central star of this solar system.

Guardian verified that this particular asteroid predated his reclamation of Mars. It was there before his two-hundred-thousand-year-old rampage and even before his destruction of the fifth planet four hundred thousand years ago.

The sisters asked Guardian if he had been through this solar system earlier than four hundred thousand years ago. He said he had been sixty-five million years earlier, when he had done reclamation on the third planet once before. And yes, Phobos was a moon of Mars then as well. So the sisters had confirmed that Phobos was very ancient—but how ancient, and when was it modified for its present purpose?

The environmental testing had established that some of the metals used to construct the interior of Phobos had been fabricated long before Chaos's most recent missions. Who could have modified Phobos, and whom was it for? Why did Prometheus encode Phobos in the Voynich manuscript?

*Why?*

# About the Author

George B. is a fan of science fiction, science, religion, fantasy, history, military science, astronomy, theoretical physics, law, medicine, and philosophy. He is now retired but worked for years in several areas of science research and application. He started out in the biological sciences, moved to law, was drafted out of law school during the Vietnam War, and later migrated into industrial psychology, computer-assisted analysis, programming, systems analysis, decision analysis, and risk management." Afterward he transitioned into military science, medicine, artificial intelligence, robotics, and leadership. Throughout, he was known as a troubleshooter and investigator. He was associated with research and development, participating in management and coordination at a national level. He returned to the study of law before finally retiring in 2007. His hobbies include photography, golf, hiking, graphics, research of alternate history, and, of course, writing, not to mention spending time with his dog, Foxy. And last but not least, he shares his life with his very lovely and dear best friend and wife of thirty-nine years, Linda.

CPSIA information can be obtained
at www.ICGtesting.com
Printed in the USA
BVHW081007100119
537524BV00001B/54/P

9 781480 870635